MW01535152

M. I. Scarrott

The Pilgrimage

— A NOVEL —

Thy statutes have been my songs
in the house of my pilgrimage.
—Psalm 119:54

PRESS

ACW Press
Phoenix, Arizona 85013

Scripture quotations are taken from the King James Version of the Bible.

The Pilgrimage
Copyright ©2002 M.I. Scarrott
All rights reserved

Cover Design by
Interior design by Pine Hill Graphics

Packaged by ACW Press
5501 N. 7th Ave., #502
Phoenix, Arizona 85013
www.acwpress.com

The views expressed or implied in this work do not necessarily reflect those of ACW Press. Ultimate design, content, and editorial accuracy of this work is the responsibility of the author(s).

Library of Congress Cataloging-in-Publication Data

Scarrott, M. I.
    The pilgrimage : a novel / M.I. Scarrott -- 1st ed.

     p. cm.
     ISBN 1-892525-67-4

     1. Divorce--Fiction. 2. Christian fiction.
  I. Title.

PS3619.C3177P55 2002   813'.6
                  QBI33-270

All rights reserved. No part of this book may be reproduced, stored in a retrieval system, or transmitted in any form or by any means–electronic, mechanical, photocopying, recording, or otherwise–without prior permission in writing from the copyright holder except as provided by USA copyright law.

Printed in the United States of America.

Dedication

*O*ne of the greatest blessings we may experience in this life is that of good friends. The Lord has given me several trustworthy companions who have lifted me in prayer as I have labored on this work of fiction. To them I dedicate this novel.

- Marilyn Belcher
- Linda Bonette
- Ava Eskenasy
- Sheryl Eskenasy
- Amy Kaylor
- Eva Montgomery
- Mark Newman
- Bea Newman
- Karen Packard
- Violeta Valladares
- Steve and Joanne Wood

A very special thank you to my husband, Chuck, who is my dearest friend and soul mate; and to my daughter, Michelle Abbott, who conscientiously reads my manuscripts, offers suggestions and encourages as well as supports my efforts.

I offer an everlasting thank-you to Jesus Christ, my Lord and Savior, for giving me a new life and the desire to share it with others. To Him, I am eternally grateful!

Table of Contents

Chapter One

Beside the Still Waters

*I*t was a warm September afternoon and the ocean was quietly churning, its mighty waves rolling back and forth while the frothy bubbles blended into the glistening brown sand.

The briny salt air penetrated my clothes and filled my nostrils as I exercised Stardust in one of the paddocks below the stable, which was located on the lower portion of my grandparents' estate situated high above the Pacific Ocean. This was a daily chore I enjoyed immensely.

Stardust was a beautiful American saddle horse, a gift from Grandfather and Grandmother for my fifteenth birthday. He was a ruddy chestnut color, about fourteen hands high and weighing almost twelve hundred pounds. On his forehead was a dusty white marking, in the shape of a small star, the basis for his name.

"Rachel," Grandfather called my name from the stable yard above me and I turned and looked in his direction. Already mounted on Ebony, his favorite riding companion, he motioned for me to join him for our daily ride in the hills surrounding the estate.

I quickly maneuvered Stardust out the wide gate and we easily scurried up the low incline to the stable yard where Grandfather, whom I called Papa, was waiting.

Nutmeg, the golden retriever I had raised from a puppy, was already by my side, eager to be off on another scavenger hunt. We rode slowly together toward one of the back roads on the property, which led us through an orchard, up the hill, past the estate and into the mountains behind. Papa and I casually talked about the events of the day as we rode through the trees until we could reach open ground where we would be able to ride unhindered.

"How vas school today, Rachel?" Papa asked in the English that still carried a trace of an accent, his European ancestry evident when he spoke. Coming from a French-German area of Europe many decades earlier, Papa and Grandmother both were able to speak five different languages. I was able to understand a great deal of what they said, although I never completely mastered a second language myself.

"It was fine, Papa," I answered quietly. "My speech in history class went well even though I was very nervous. I'm not sure I will ever get used to public speaking. My palms sweat and my mouth gets dry and my heart pumps so fast I feel like it's going to burst." I laughed and Papa joined in. He understood me so well; it was hard to believe we were generations apart.

As we rode toward higher ground we were able to see the lovely rose gardens that were planted in a terraced area behind the back patio of the Gothic-style estate. Grandmother was visible as well as she left the rear of the house and headed in the direction of the chapel where she went daily to pray. The chapel was built on a small incline above the rose garden. When she looked our way she waved and I blew her a kiss as we galloped up the road and went off into the hills.

The September weather was still warm but each day the nights grew shorter and it became more obvious that winter was approaching. I wore dark brown corduroy pants and a cream-colored turtleneck sweater with a flannel shirt, knowing that as soon as the sun descended the air would become chilled. Papa wore blue jeans and a chambray shirt with a vest. He rarely got cold and loved being outdoors. His face was weathered and tan but always cheery and bright.

We rode for a while until we reached a stream that ran down through the hills. It was so peaceful and calm here, the quiet trickle of the running waters creating a safe haven. I loved this particular spot and we often stopped here to rest the horses and walk a little, absorbing the strength that came from the serenity of the surroundings. Papa dismounted with ease. He was a giant of a man and the hero of my young life. At six feet six inches tall and weighing nearly two hundred and fifty pounds, he towered over my five feet three inches. Nutmeg ran through the trees chasing whatever small critters he came upon. The brownish, bushy tailed California ground squirrel, which was prominent throughout most of the state, was a favorite although he often encountered pocket gophers or mice and the occasional brush rabbit. It always reminded me of a trip Papa and I had taken to visit some of his friends who owned a dairy farm just off the coast near Bodega Bay. As we drove down the small two-lane road we saw a black and white dairy cow chasing down a black-tailed jack rabbit. She was running and bucking at that tiny jack rabbit, who took off at speeds of probably thirty miles an hour, every once in a while leaping high into the air looking back at the cow chasing it. I laughed each time I thought of it.

"I love it, Papa," I said, "the trees, the streams of water and the beautiful ocean below—everything so fresh and clean. I don't think I could ever live anywhere else!" Papa only smiled.

"We have many blessings, yes." Papa agreed. "And one day, it will all belong to you, Rachel."

I remained quiet. I hated thinking about death. Living with my maternal grandparents hadn't been easy for me initially. The grief and pain I felt at the loss of my family was overwhelming at times. Thankfully, my grandparents had been patient and loving. They helped me through the long and difficult process of mourning, always responding appropriately to whatever I was going through. Never trying to force me to accept what I was as yet unable to accept. Weeping with me when I wept and in time when my ability to laugh and rejoice returned they rejoiced with me as well. Now, I couldn't bear the thought of losing either of them.

Nutmeg's barking in the distant brush caught our attention and after remounting our horses we rode in his direction. "Nutmeg," Grandfather called, "come here." Within a few minutes Nutmeg bounded out of the trees and rejoined us, trailing along at my grandfather's side. We rode pleasantly together up one hill and down another until it came time to head for home. Stardust and I were in the lead.

Nutmeg ran ahead to chase another squirrel and I followed behind him at a slow trot. It was dusky now and somewhat difficult to see. I rode around a clump of trees to see that Nutmeg had stopped a short distance ahead of me to bark at some object hidden under a shelter of rocks.

"Leave him alone, Nutmeg!" I said as we drew nearer. Suddenly, Stardust reared up. I held on tightly to the reins trying to keep my balance.

"Steady, Stardust!" I yelled as I tried to regain control of my mount, but fearfully he reared up again. Nutmeg continued with his unrelenting barking. Stardust was panicked. I never heard the noise of the rattler because of Nutmeg's barking but I saw him distinctly in the rocks. The brownish blotches down the spine were the distinct markings of a Western rattlesnake, fierce and venomous. Papa was somewhere close behind me. He tried to grab hold of Stardust's reins to steady him but Stardust only reared up again.

"Back up, Rachel," he yelled forcefully, but it was too late. Stardust reared up once more and this time, I wasn't able to hold on. I fell to the ground with a thud, landing on my side and hitting my head against a large stone. Stardust was in a flurry. Hovering over me, I felt his legs entangle with mine and heard something snap. I was stunned momentarily as stars appeared before my eyes. Within minutes my body was flooded with excruciating pain, particularly throughout my right leg. In fear and anguish I screamed out loudly for my grandfather—where was he?

Semiconscious, lying on the cold, damp ground, I began to shiver and cry. At the thundering sound of Papa's shotgun, fear took over.

"Papa!" I screamed. "Papa...Papa...where are you?" It was almost dark and my vision was further limited by my inability to move without suffering more pain. Everything began to move in and out of shadows, Nutmeg was silent. Stardust was gone.

"Papa!" I screamed again, in a voice full of terror as hot salty tears poured down my face.

"Rachel, I'm here sweetheart. Right here," Papa said, running to my side. He lifted my head and held me in his arms as I sobbed uncontrollably.

"There, there," he said in his soothingly calm voice. Don't cry, your Papa is here now." Papa tried to lift me in his arms but stopped when I screamed out in pain. He touched my leg and felt a warm sticky substance. Blood.

"Rachel, your leg is broken. Stardust must have stepped on you—the bone is protruding through the skin. I'll ride to the house and get help."

"No, Papa!" I screamed hysterically. "Don't leave me alone!" I shouted. "Please, Papa, please don't leave me alone!"

"Rachel, I must go to get some men and the jeep." Papa stood up and quickly mounted Ebony. "Nutmeg," he yelled, "stay here!" Nutmeg silently obeyed. "You will be safe, Rachel, I promise you will be safe. Trust me!"

Papa turned and frantically rode away down the hill in the direction of the estate.

"Papa," I yelled as he disappeared down the hill, "Papa, come back!" I pleaded once more but he was already gone. Sobbing uncontrollably I shouted toward the heavens, "Don't leave me all alone, Papa!"

Nutmeg lay down next to me and I clung desperately to his warm furry body. My leg was throbbing and I was quickly growing colder and colder. My head rested on the damp soil—the scent of brush filled my nostrils. Alarm crept into my soul as I pondered the reality of my situation; the estate was a good ten-minute ride down the hill and it would take Papa another ten minutes to get back with help. Twenty minutes. There was nothing I could do but pray.

Suddenly, Nutmeg's ears perked up and he began a low growl. Someone, or something, was near. I listened for the roar of the jeep but heard instead a series of yelps and barks followed by a long, low howl. Coyotes! I listened intently for the return, which came within minutes. Nutmeg sat up on his haunches and again began to growl and I silenced him, holding tightly to his collar so he could not get away. I listened as the howling and yelping grew closer and closer until suddenly, it stopped. The night was dark but there was a full moon and I could see my surroundings clearly, except that I could not move well. Papa's shotgun was by my side. Thankfully, he had the foresight to leave it. How long had he been gone? Time had slipped away quickly.

Suddenly, Nutmeg lurched forward and dragged me along with him. I yelled out in pain as the movement renewed the throbbing in my leg.

"Stop, Nutmeg!" I yelled. Then I saw him, less than fifty yards away in the wooded area just in front of me. He was light colored and long and slender with the typical pointed snout and bushy tail. He stood silently, watching. I feared he wasn't alone. I knew coyotes were around but they had never bothered us. They fed on rodents mostly—mice and gophers and even snakes, frogs or fruit. We often heard them at night, prowling the hills and valleys surrounding our home.

I continued to hold onto Nutmeg and carefully raised the shotgun, which carried one load of ammo. Papa had fired the other. I would never kill any animal…except if necessary. I prayed it would not become necessary.

The vibrations on the road from the jeep furiously racing up the hill could be felt on the ground where I lay before either the sound of the engines reached my hearing or the sight of its headlights appeared within my eyesight. The coyote turned and scampered away into the night; relieved, I lowered the gun beside me.

Papa was out of the jeep before Mr. Francis had stopped. Jody and his brothers came behind on horseback with flashlights and rode off into the dark in search of Stardust.

Papa had reached my side where I now lay silent—thankful to the God who watches over us all. Mr. Francis came up behind him carrying a long piece of wood for me to lie on. Papa gently lifted my body onto the wide board while Mr. Francis supported my leg. As quickly as possible, they loaded me into the back of the jeep and headed down the hill toward the main highway where they drove like the wind to get me to the hospital.

The doctors were busily setting my leg when Mary Francis arrived, bringing Grandmother and Isabelle, all nervous and frightened. With tears in their eyes, they kissed my sobbing face and comforted me. I survived.

In my room later that night, Papa sat by my bed holding my hand, stroking my cheek.

"Papa," I said, "I'm afraid…I'm afraid to be alone, Papa!"

"I know, Rachel. But you are not alone. I am here and Grandmother and Isabelle are here. People who love you surround you. And you know you are never really alone, Rachel because God is always here." Papa smiled.

I closed my eyes to sleep while Papa quietly prayed for me. Patiently he reassured me of the goodness of God. He was my hero, my source of inspiration, someone I wanted to emulate. Would my faith ever be as strong and powerful as his was?

"Lord, help me!" I prayed silently as I nodded off to sleep.

Years would pass, but I would never forget that fateful September day. It became a turning point in my life. My walk of true faith was only just beginning then. Today, the book of my life's history is packed with warm and wonderful memories. Its pages cover almost fifty years.

Papa's trustworthy God had become my God and I too had learned to trust Him. His word had become the roadmap for my earthly journey. Wherever He led, I followed. And I still enjoy our travels together beside the still waters!

⌒ Chapter Two ⌒

The Lion and the Lamb

*T*he wind beat furiously against the glass in the tower window where I stood watching the sun begin to slowly slip beneath the ocean below. The brilliant yellow orange colors cast its reflection upon the dark blue waters until it grew smaller and smaller and then finally disappeared into darkness.

I walked away from the long paned window surrounded by yards of beautiful chintz draperies and retreated to the solitude of my room. Everything in the house was quiet. I returned to the correspondence on my desk. My mind, however, was unable to focus on the letters I had been reading. The sound of a car driving up the long winding road to the estate caught my attention. A horn sounded from the circular drive below. I walked back to the window and opening the balcony door I stepped out into the cool night air.

"Rachel," the voice of my best friend, Marie Marshal, called out to me. "Sorry I'm late," she continued as she walked toward the front door. I waved to her from my fairytale loft and then hurried out of my room and down the long staircase to the foyer below to greet her.

"Hi," I said enthusiastically, "I'm so glad you're here." Marie's face was shining brightly as she came through the front door and I gave her a warm hug of welcome.

"Oh, I've been looking forward to this week for some time now. I think I am almost as excited as you are!" Marie said spontaneously.

"Sometimes I feel like I need to be pinched just to make sure I'm not living in a dream." I said. "It will be so much fun having you here all week. I hope Thomas knows how much I appreciate his taking over the shop so you could come."

"Are you kidding?" Marie laughed, as we walked into the parlor to sit down. "He and the boys couldn't get me out of the house *fast* enough. I'm not sure what the place will look like when I return. I may be afraid to go back. They were ordering pizza as I walked out the door and they probably won't eat a single healthy meal while I'm gone, but…that's okay too."

"When will they be joining us?" I asked.

"The day before the wedding, I guess," she responded. "Thomas' brother is working full time for us now that we are expanding the business and should be able to handle things in our absence. We also have several part-time employees that are trained and he can use them as he needs to."

Patrick came in through the front door with Marie's baggage and carried it to the second-floor suite of rooms I had set aside for her and Thomas and their two boys, Adam and Timothy. Her room had a queen-sized bed with a massive hand-carved mahogany four-poster bedstead without a canopy. There was also an old mahogany dressing table and a matching dresser and a huge wardrobe for her to hang her clothing in. Her sitting room had two big armchairs and a small sofa, all nicely decorated in heavy tanzanite blue brocade and covered with lace doilies. All of the bathrooms at the estate had been renovated with antique looking fixtures but had all the latest modern conveniences. The large bathroom they would share with their sons stood between their two bedrooms. The smaller one for the boys had two twin beds and was decorated in a similar style. My rooms were close by.

Returning to my childhood home almost two years earlier had been a blessing. Paul Todd, my husband of almost three decades had left me for a younger woman, a brilliant and gorgeous colleague. My three daughters, Victoria, Devon and Charlotte were grown women with lives of their own, which left me for the first time in many years, basically alone. Humbled by the divorce, my pride shattered, divine inspiration led me to return to the one place where I could find the inner healing I needed to go on and begin again.

My spacious living quarters had at one time belonged to my maternal grandparents. The rooms I now called my own covered most of the front area of the north wing of their estate, which was now almost sixty years old. The large stone building had been designed by my grandfather to reflect the Victorian period and its architecture was a mixture of Romanesque Revival and Queen Anne styles. I adored the stateliness and beauty of this massive edifice, which was graced with an assortment of tower windows and balconies. Living here once again brought back wonderful memories of the happier days of my childhood. Running through the hallways, climbing in the windows and playing hide and seek with Papa, my beloved grandfather, and the motherly love and affection I received from my grandmother and Isabelle were the healing balm I needed then to see me through the difficult days of mourning for my lost family.

Papa and Grandmother had been gone for some years now but their loving presence was always within the happy walls of this peaceful domicile I once again called home.

Marie and I enjoyed warming ourselves in front of the blazing fire we kept burning in the large stone fireplace that graced the parlor. One of my favorite rooms because of its coziness, I entertained most of my friends here. It wasn't long before Patricia, our chief domestic in charge of the daily affairs of the estate and Patrick's wife, arrived with a serving cart of refreshments.

Martha, who had returned to my palatial home with me when my marriage ended, had been nanny and cook to my children for almost thirty years. She now ruled the kitchen as queen supreme and happily spent her days cooking, baking and taking care of the nutritional aspects of our small family. She delighted in preparing for company and had spent the morning baking some of Marie's favorite desserts. The serving cart carried a pot of cinnamon spiced tea and fresh apple walnut scones, which were dripping with a delightfully sticky caramel sauce. They were mouthwatering, calorie laden and sinfully delicious!

I was just about to take a sip of the fragrantly stimulating brew when I saw Baby, my tiny toy poodle, approaching and I braced myself. My little ball of white fur loved to charge into a room and create havoc. Today, she jumped onto the big comfy couches Marie and I were relaxing on and plopped down in the middle of my lap.

"Baby! You're going to get hot tea all over you," I scolded, with my most disciplinary voice but she just licked my face and paid me no regard.

"My goodness," Marie said, "how does that little sausage get up onto the couch. She has no legs, just a little fat belly." She poked at her in fun and we both laughed.

"Now don't hurt her feelings," I said, "Baby doesn't like to be referred to as a sausage, even if she does look like one." My tiny toy poodle 'Baby' was a little over a year old and although she had been born with black tipped ears she was now a pure champagne white. Charlotte, my youngest daughter, had given me this tiny bundle of pleasure as a gift to ease my loneliness. She brought tremendous joy to my heart and ultimately she helped heal my troubled soul. Animals love so unconditionally. I often wondered why we couldn't be more like them.

"Well, what's on the agenda for the week?" Marie asked, licking some of the caramel sauce off her fingers.

"Tomorrow, we are going to the dressmakers for the final fitting on our gowns. They should be finished and they'll be delivered after they are pressed. The girls and their families will be arriving throughout the week. Victoria, Allen and my little grandson Michael will be here on the weekend. I am so excited…I haven't seen them for a while and Michael is growing up so quickly. Victoria is very good about sending me videos and pictures but it will be nice to have them at home—even if only for a short visit."

"She'll probably enjoy the California sun after being in Eng-land."

"Oh, to be sure," I agreed. "They're staying here for a few weeks and then flying north to San Francisco to visit their friends. By the time they return Christopher and I should be back from our hon-eymoon and we'll all be able to spend some time together with them before they head back to London."

"How is Allen's mother doing?" Marie asked. Allen's widowed mother, Audra, had been in very poor health for years. It wasn't until she was in serious physical decline that Allen and Victoria decided they needed to move to London to be with her. It saddened me to see them leave California only a few short months after Michael's birth and as much as I hated to accept it, I realized it must be God's will. It was a sacrifice for all: Victoria was leaving her family, Allen was taking a year off from teaching, his true passion, I was foregoing the delight of seeing my grandchild grow up close to home.

Allen was fortunate that the university he taught at outside the city of San Francisco granted him a sabbatical leave; a year away from teaching would give him the opportunity he needed to finish the book he had been working on.

It all happened too quickly. When the school term ended the preceding summer, they moved to London.

"Audra is *much* better," I replied. "Having Allen and Victoria there has been good for her. She has a renewed vitality, they say. Young people have a great deal of energy—it's inspiring. According to Victoria, Allen has almost finished his book and…well…she told me they have been talking about staying another year. I know Allen really wants to return to his teaching post but, ultimately, they will do what is best for his mother. What else can they do? They're both very loyal people."

"When are Devon and Joseph arriving? And Chris's daughter Chloe, where is she? And for that matter, how about the groom, when does he return?" The questions were endless but I answered them all in turn.

"Devon and Joseph are arriving on Wednesday, the wedding rehearsal dinner will be Thursday, and of the course the wedding is

Friday evening, Valentine's Day. Chloe is still in school at Stanford and so she will fly down on Thursday morning. Charlotte and Edgar will drive up on Thursday as well. Christopher, my traveling groom, has been in England at his apartment near London for the better part of a month. He had some business to take care of there and decided to stay and travel with his parents to California. They are arriving on Tuesday. We are going to have a house full of people." I smiled happily. "I can't wait!"

"How many people will the chapel hold?" Marie asked.

"About fifty or sixty," I replied. "Come with me, and I'll show you how lovely it is now that the wood has been restored and the pews reupholstered."

The small chapel was located off the rear of the north wing of the house across from the patio gardens. It was chilly outside as we left the warmth of the house and walked through the yard toward the chapel. The bells in the small tower above the structure tinkled lightly when the wind blew.

Marie and I walked quietly through the heavy oak double doors of the octagonal building. Its eight walls were tall, at least ten feet high. Four of the walls were oak paneled, the other four held long panes of hexagonal beveled glass. The center of each was beautifully decorated with a different stained glass picture. A four-inch strip of green glass bordered each picture, which tied them all together in a unifying theme.

The white marble altar stood opposite the two front doors in front of one of the oak-paneled walls. The stained glass window to the left of the altar was my favorite. An old wooden cross, carrying a swath of deep purple cloth stood in the center. Beneath it, lying down together among a field of white lilies was a majestic lion and a playful lamb. Rays of bright light emanated from the cross onto the pale blue background.

The floor was covered with white marble. There were eight pews in the chapel, four on each side facing the altar. There was a wide aisle down the center and a narrower one that encircled the entire building. The renovation was almost complete and the lovely little chapel was more wonderful than ever. The pews had been removed so they could be sanded and varnished and then reupholstered in dark green velvet. Deep purple carpet runners decorated with a pattern of medium green ivy lined the aisle ways, and one long strip of carpet ran behind the altar. Eight elegant crystal lamps hung from the ceiling above, one over each pew. White satin and lace now decorated the long marble altar and on it stood two silver candelabras.

"Rachel!" Marie exclaimed, "It's absolutely beautiful." We sat down together in one of the front pews. "It's a shame it was closed up for so long."

"Yes," I replied, my mind drifting back in time, "my grandparents loved this place. But, when I moved away with Paul and after they both died, it wasn't practical to keep it open. It always was a little drafty and took some time to heat, but I've had that fixed. Since I've come home for good, I decided I wanted to refurbish it and keep it open. The pews look great since they've been restored and a few of the panes in the stained glass needed to be repaired. You know Luther Calvin, my gardener, he's bringing an assortment of potted plants and greenery to go beneath each windowpane and I've ordered two large ceramic angels to be placed just outside the front doors. On the day of the wedding, there will be fresh flowers on the altar also."

"Is Pastor Edwards performing the ceremony?" Marie asked.

"Yes, and Hannah Moore, Miriam's daughter, will be my flower girl. Enid, my new dressmaker, has made her a charming gown. Wait until you see her."

It's so peaceful and quiet in here," Marie said.

"And comforting," I responded, "Papa and I came here often after my parents died. Always searching for answers, I felt drawn to this one place, in front of this stained glass. The mighty lion and the meek lamb lying together seemed so sweet when I was young, I guess because everything seems possible. As we grow and become more cynical our beliefs change. By the time I was in my teens, I just couldn't accept it…I guess I didn't want to. For me, it was very personal. The possibility of the fierce lion co-existing with the gentle lamb just didn't seem plausible."

"Well, in one sense you are right, you know. It is impossible for the lion and the lamb to live together in harmony. The one is fierce and carnivorous and the other is gentle and herbivorous. But this is really a picture of the world to come, isn't it? Don't we believe that one day, in the new creation, all the members of the animal kingdom will be tame and as harmless as God originally created them to be, before man sinned?"

"Well, yes, you're right, that's true. But I didn't have a problem understanding that. The difficulty I had was more in the underlying teaching of the *natures* of the two creatures. The lamb is known for its meekness, the lion for its fierceness. Could one person embody both natures? I didn't think so.

"One year, while in high school, I was working on an art project that led me to an important discovery. The class assignment was for each of us to create a collage that expressed who we were both internally and externally. Our teacher suggested we begin by looking up the meanings of our names. I'll never forget Caleb, a boy in our class who moaned when he found out his name means "dog." We all laughed at him when he playfully began woofing and howling. When I finally looked up my names, I too was shocked. But for a different reason. Can you imagine my surprise when I found out that the name Rachel is Hebrew for "ewe" which is a sheep and that Arielle is the French form or Ariel which is also Hebrew and means "lion of God?"

"Well, I couldn't wait to get home and share my discovery with Papa. Of course, he already knew. He told me the story behind my parents' name choice for me. He said, 'Your Mama prayed before you were born that the Lord would direct her as she chose a good name for you. She chose Rachel because it represents the lamb, which is harmless and gentle. She wanted you to be a woman who would have a meek and quiet spirit in all of your relationships and she wanted this to be your dominant nature. She chose Arielle because it represents the lion, which is fierce and courageous. She prayed that you would grow to become a woman of silent strength and fortitude that you might be able to withstand any storm and always be an overcomer.' It was then that I realized that it was *possible* for the lion and the lamb to live together in peace. Knowing that changed my out-look on life but especially it changed how I viewed myself. I have always tried to live up to that image."

"Rachel, do you think God chooses our names for us and then speaks to our parents?" Marie asked, inquisitively.

"Well, based on what the prophet Jeremiah wrote, I guess I do. He said that God has a destiny for all of us. Even the Psalmist wrote that God numbered all of our days before we were born. So, yes, I guess I do believe God influences parents in naming their children."

Marie snickered, "What about poor Caleb?"

I laughed out loud again, "Our teacher graciously pointed out all the good characteristics inherent in dogs. They are loyal, faithful and loving. He really didn't mind anyway. He told me he knew his parents had named him for the biblical Caleb, son of Jephunneh, a man who had unfaltering courage. A man who with Joshua believed that with God all things were possible, even subduing the Promised Land."

"And what did he grow up to become? Do you know?" Marie asked.

"Actually, I know he went to West Point and had a military career but I never heard much about him once my grandparents passed away."

"Perhaps, he did fulfill his destiny then. Just as you have, Rachel. You truly have become the woman God ordained for you to be."

"Thanks, Marie. You're always so sweet." I smiled and gave her a quick hug.

"It's going to be a wonderful week," Marie said as we stepped outside the chapel doors. We walked toward the estate and before entering I turned to look back at the lovely old house of prayer—the chapel bells situated on top of the building chimed slightly with the breeze; soon, I knew they would be chiming for me. Quietly, we went back into the house so Marie could unpack.

⌐⌐⌐ *Chapter Three* *⌐⌐⌐*

Joy Comes in the Morning

Marie went to her room alone and I returned to my own where I finished my correspondence. I then turned to review the final details of the new specialty catalog of gourmet coffees and teas that Noah and I were working on for my business, but my mind kept drifting away. Finally, I gave up for the evening and pushed everything aside.

Instead of working, I opened a tiny cabinet located on the top right hand side of my desk and removed the contents. On top was Grandfather's Bible; the black leather was faded and frayed in places. Underneath it was his photo album; it contained most of the pictures of my family that still existed. Old faded black and white photos of my mother, father and little brother, Riley. Of course, I still had a few letters and things of my mother's packed away in my treasure room upstairs. But the photo album I kept in my desk near to my heart. I flipped open the well-worn pages; each picture brought to mind fond memories from the past. They would be eternally young to me for that is how I remembered them all. I smiled as I always did, and even cried a bit when I came to my favorite photo of Riley dressed in a miniature blue and white sailor suit with a matching tiny cap. He had been charming and sweet like my dad, and I often wondered what type of man he would have become, had he survived the plane crash that took his young life. He was only five years old when he died. Dear, dear, Riley!

I replaced the photo album into its slot and picked up the old leather Bible and held it lovingly in my hands. Closing my eyes, I could almost see my grandfather sitting in his big oak chair early in the morning, reading the Holy Scriptures with reverence and passion.

"Rachel, come and sit on my lap and I will read to you," he would say in his deep melodious voice.

The village inhabitants referred to the mansion on the hill as the Winthrope Estate, after my grandparents who had built it when they moved to California from New York. Riley and I had called it "The Castle," because of its immense size and tall towers. After the deaths of my parents and only brother, it became my home. My maternal grandparents became my guardians; how fortunate I was to have been left in the custody of such fine people. My mother had been their only daughter and when she died, they were all that I had left to call family.

"Winthrope is an English name." Papa told me one day. I was always inquisitive about my family's roots, and he never tired of answering my incessant questions. "My father, your great-grand-papa, traveled to France when he was a young man. He met my mother and married her and they settled down in her tiny village to begin their new life. I was born there. I had two older brothers," he said, "but they both died in the war." And then he would tell me stories of his life growing up in a rural area of France. His brothers were bigger than he was, he boasted so often that I began to think of them as giants.

Papa often brought out his old photo album, which was filled with a multitude of pictures of family members I would never know. He even had pictures of his "fine brothers" as he called them, in their military uniforms. My favorite photographs were the few they had taken on their trip from Europe to America. Papa loved to reminisce and often shared about the pride he felt when he saw the Statue of Liberty for the first time. He and Grandmother came through the gates of Ellis Island, like so many before them.

"God was blessing my business, Rachel," he said time and again, always quick to give God the glory for every good thing, "and we believed He was guiding us to come to America to begin a new life." It all became true.

My grandfather's small furniture business had flourished and grown into a tiny empire, which over a period of time consisted not only of his own line of household furnishings but later was expanded to include a large import and export business dealing in a variety of costly European antiques. They realized many years later, when the Second World War began, just how fortunate they were! Destiny—and divine Providence—had guided them to their new country.

They took great pride in their adopted homeland and studied to become naturalized citizens. My mother was born in New York, the first true American citizen of our small family. Several years after her birth the family moved to California for its warmer environment and my mother's health

Here, on this small hill above the Pacific Ocean, my grandfather eventually built his palatial estate. A place of mystery and intrigue to many, it is filled with an abundance of secrets that I came to know about only after years of being one of its principal residents. "The Castle" was still a captivating place for visitors who were easily mesmerized by its fairytale fascination and charm; but very few were *truly* aware just how thrilling a place the old edifice really was!

The pangs of guilt that plagued my youth were now gone but not forgotten. Providence had spared my life and I easily recalled the days of grieving for the loss of my family and the times of almost overwhelming despair. Why was I spared? Why was I kept at home that fateful day? Only God had the answers to the questions that I so desperately wanted to hear. But for some reason, He remained silent. My greatest source of comfort in those days was not in God; I was too young to understand faith. And now, looking back, I could see how God was working in my tiny shattered life. He gave me two completely selfless angels to watch over me. My grandparents spent endless hours helping me to overcome my grief, my fears and my loneliness.

"Rachel," Papa would say while I rested lovingly in his lap, "what would you like me to read to you today?"

"Read me something joyful, Papa," I would say, and Papa would read to me from the Psalms. He would tell me of God's promises and he assured me they would never fail.

"But my heart still hurts, Papa!" I remembered crying to him so very often.

"Yes, little one, I know, it will hurt for some time. But the Lord promises that our weeping lasts only for a short time, like the darkness of the night, and then the dawn breaks through and with it joy arises."

"But I don't understand, Papa," I sobbed.

"I know you don't darling, but trust me, and one day soon, you will."

He would then rock me in his arms and sing sweetly to me and my fears would be calmed and my aching heart would hurt a little less. In time, I learned to understand many things about sorrow and suffering. I learned that suffering is painful but often only temporary and that when it ends, joy does break through the clouds of tears and then singing once again finds its place in our hearts.

"Rachel…" a voice called softly. "Am I intruding?" Marie spoke from the doorway, her voice barely above a whisper.

"No, come in," I said, still holding Grandfather's Bible.

"I'm sorry if I interrupted you," Marie said as she sat down in the chair next to my desk.

"Don't be silly," I said, "I was simply lost in old memories." I closed the Bible and placed it back on the top of my desk and closed the tiny door.

"Thinking about your family?" Marie asked, knowing me so well.

"Yes," I replied. "I was thinking of my grandparents, my grandfather in particular, and how he helped me get through those difficult years after I lost my family. There's just so much you don't understand when you are only ten years old. For that matter, there are a great many things we will never understand, regardless of how old we grow." I sighed.

"I often wonder why God allows some people to suffer so much, while others seem to glide through life unscathed?" Marie said thoughtfully. "And then, there's the age-old question of why good people suffer while the evil seem to prosper."

"Ummm, just think of the story of Job," I answered. "He can be a true source of comfort when you're going through trials and tribulations. Or Joseph even!"

"Oh, yeah, he's my favorite I think. His story is so inspiring. Don't you agree?" Marie asked with an expression of awe and respect shining in her eyes.

"Definitely!" I replied. "Grandfather taught me so much about life just by reading and reviewing the Bible and the lives of the characters within its pages. If we as a nation would return to biblical values, I believe we would find ourselves a more contented people, and society would perhaps be happier in general. In spite of the obstacles we face from time to time one thing is sure, *God sends both the sunshine and the rain for both are needed for flowers to bloom and grow.*"

⁓ Chapter Four ⁓

My Fair Lady

*T*he next morning Marie and I were up early for breakfast and a brisk walk in the old rose gardens behind the estate before we showered and headed into Santa Barbara. We chatted excitedly about the forthcoming wedding and I was surprised that I felt more like a schoolgirl than a middle-aged woman. Life was truly wonderful!

Christopher Elliott, my fiancé, and I had both been married before. I had known his wife Juliet through her charity work in raising funds for research, predominantly for cancer. I never knew she was suffering from the disease herself until I heard the dreadful news that she had succumbed to its fatal clutches.

I met Christopher casually one evening at a dinner party given by mutual friends. His celebrity status was well known—after all, he had won an Academy Award and was as handsome as he was charming. But our paths had never crossed until that fateful night. I was still married to my husband Paul at the time, and I was desperately clinging to the tattered remnants of a once happy marriage.

Even after it unraveled and he filed for divorce, I hoped and prayed he would return. He didn't.

Christopher grieved over the loss of his wife for some years until he was able to reach the point of acceptance. Once sufficiently recovered, he took up her banner and following in her footsteps he joined the army of people engaged in fighting the war against cancer and other devastating diseases. With a desire to help raise funds to combat the enemy that had robbed him of his beloved wife, he sought me out.

Although I wasn't a celebrity of the same genre as he, I was well known for my work in philanthropic circles. My husband Paul and I both hailed from wealthy, prodigious families whose vast fortunes garnered a great deal of notoriety. I had begun my charity work at an early age, helping my grandparents in whatever capacity I was able. One of my oldest childhood memories was that of learning the meaning of one of Papa's favorite phrases, "Noblesse Oblige," which literally translated means, "Nobility Obligates."

"People who have been blessed by God with position or rank have also been given by God the responsibility and obligation of using that position or rank in an honorable, compassionate and generous manner." Papa had explained it so often that the maxim became indelibly inscribed upon my mind.

Over the course of many years I found that the theory behind this maxim was not only true, but also wise, for wisdom itself teaches the need for restraint; and wealth unbridled frequently leads to corruption and destruction.

How often I saw the fruits of this theory evidenced in society. Overpaid sports heroes, pampered movie stars, along with the excessively extravagant rich and famous, and unfortunately their children, were all too frequently subjects of the evening news. Here they were, riding the highway that leads to ruin, wasting their time and resources, burying their talents and destroying their lives by overindulging their impulses and passions until they eventually became wholly unprofitable members of a degenerating society. It always grieved my heart.

Chris was so different from most of the movie stars I knew. He was levelheaded and down to earth. He didn't take his celebrity lightly and always behaved like the well-mannered, decent man that he was. The relationship that developed between us came about slowly; we became colleagues of a sort first and then we became friends. Love materialized in time. More than two years had passed since our first meeting, which we believed had been arranged by Providence Himself.

After the death of his wife, Chris determined to spend more time with his daughter Chloe, their only child. She had applied to and been accepted as a college freshman at Stanford University, located in Palo Alto, California, north of the estate where I lived. He obtained an apartment for her in the city near the university and also maintained his own residence in Los Angeles as well as one in London. He spoke with his agent who agreed, for a time, to find him work that would enable him to remain in the Pacific Southwest. This would keep him close to Chloe and, when otherwise unoccupied, able to work at a variety of fundraisers.

We didn't mean to fall in love. When we first met, I was in the midst of a battle to save my marriage, and Chris had adjusted to his life as a widower. Destiny intervened. Now, we were in the midst of joining our two lives together.

My own three daughters, Victoria, Devon and Charlotte, had readily accepted the new additions to our growing family. Charlotte's wedding the previous year had ended the child-rearing phase of my life. They were all married now and scattered about the world living out their own life's dreams. The relationship we shared had shifted and changed, as is the case once children grow and leave home, but I recognized the time had come to let go and I welcomed my new role as one of their loving advisors.

Planning a wedding, even a small one, can be an ordeal and given the set of circumstances Chris and I were now operating under, we realized there would be numerous difficulties to overcome. The largest obstacle was Christopher's celebrity status; he was a public figure and in much demand. My own celebrity was derived in part from my former husband, Paul, whose family was very wealthy and influential, and in part from my own family and the large estate I had inherited from them. More recently, I was making a name for myself as a successful businesswoman. All of these reasons combined were cause for concern. We wanted our wedding day to be special—not a public spectacle.

Great planning went into keeping the event as quiet as possible, one reason for having family members arrive so close to the wedding date. Only our dearest and most trustworthy friends had been invited. Christopher's press agent spread the word that we were hosting a Valentine's party for our friends and he even invited a few select journalists to cover the event. Fortunately, everything appeared to be working as planned.

Christopher and I were having a great deal of fun making our wedding arrangements. Even though it was going to be small, we wanted it to be romantic and elegant, just like a page out of our favorite fairy tale. After all, adults enjoy fantasy too.

One of the most beautiful ball gowns ever designed, in my opinion, was the one that Cecil Beaton created for Audrey Hepburn to wear in *My Fair Lady*. So I decided to use that as a starting point for my wedding gown—a model of sorts—having it altered to suit my body type, style and personal preferences. Chris spoke to a dear old friend from the theater about designing the gown for me. Enid was both an imaginative artist and a carefree romantic. Her creations were more than just beautiful bits of fabric and thread; they were the embodiment of our dreams.

Marie and I sat in a large private dressing room at the rear of Enid's dress shop waiting for her to bring in our gowns. Enid brought my gown in first and hung it on a high hook to keep the train from touching the floor. It sparkled from beneath its clear protective covering and Marie and I both gasped at its shimmering beauty. I couldn't wait to try it on.

I tied my long auburn hair into a ponytail and then twisted it in a knot on the top of my head. Enid gently lifted the delicate gown over my head and slid it down my body. The satin felt cool against my skin. I slid my arms into the long lace sleeves; one of Enid's alterations, which I believed made the gown a little more dramatic and mature. The dress fit my bodice snugly and hugged my breasts. Enid notched the pearl buttons in the back and, after stepping into a pair of satin shoes, I looked at my reflection in the mirror. Heavenly!

The gown was made of the palest soft pink satin, and it was covered with delicate lace and beaded with pearls. My hair was going to be braided with long strands of pearls and then wrapped around the top of my head. Enid, for the time being, arranged the small pearl tiara I had chosen on top of my floppy bun. It was covered with a tuft of pink netting that hung down the back almost to the floor. I was already wearing the beautiful teardrop pearl earrings Devon had given me as a wedding gift.

Just a few adjustments needed to be made before I removed the gown and placed it back on the hook and then helped Marie into her gown. It was made of soft pearl gray satin. It was very simple. It had a bateau neckline and short sleeves joined to the bodice, which was fitted at the waist. The long skirt fell softly to the floor and the slit in the back made it easy for her walk. Her jacket was made of a sheer gray silk and ornamented with small crystals.

"Marie, it looks lovely," I said as my friend admired her figure in the mirror.

"I love it!" she replied. "Gray has always been a good color for me, I'm glad you chose it."

"Wait till you see Christopher in his tuxedo!" I exclaimed. "He's so handsome he'll probably outshine both of us," I said and we laughed together out loud.

"Just one of the things you'll have to live with, being married to such a gorgeous guy!" Marie responded sarcastically. "What does his tux look like?"

"Traditional black with a silver-gray brocade waistcoat, a black ascot and diamond studs."

"What about Hannah? What will she be wearing?" Marie asked as she undressed and changed back into her street clothes.

Hannah Moore was now almost twelve. She had grown taller this year and while she still possessed the gangly legs of a young girl, her body was beginning to show signs of maturing.

Miriam Moore, her mother, had been hired to manage the bed and breakfast I determined to open after returning home to Winthrope's. The estate had been empty and idle for too many years. The community was in need of jobs and I was in search of a new life. With the help of an exceptional architect, I renovated the beautiful old horse stables at the bottom of the hill below the estate and turned them into a charming restaurant. The horse trainer's old residence was a stately Victorian situated nearby, it soon became a very profitable bed and breakfast. Miriam, recommended highly by my pastor's wife, Sarah Edwards, became her proprietress.

Miriam and Hannah were both extraordinary people. Hannah was enthused with vitality unequal to most youngsters her age, which was especially noteworthy because of her background. Her parents were alcoholics and her father had been physically abusive. Miriam endured a great deal but finally found the courage to leave her husband when he began to direct his abuse toward Hannah. They were both living in a women's shelter when I met them, where they had been in counseling for more than a year…almost two.

Sarah Edwards had asked me to interview Miriam for the manager position at the bed and breakfast, which included housing. The resume she presented was filled with stellar recommendations, as Miriam had been a very excellent cook at a large hotel in San Francisco. My real concern was that she was also a recovering alcoholic. Could she be trusted? My decision to hire her wasn't based on her resume or Sarah's recommendation, although both helped. I'm not sure why I hired her but reflecting back I guess I simply thought she needed a chance to start over…just like me. After meeting Hannah, I knew I had made the right decision. They had gained a new life but I had garnered more—the pleasure of their enduring friendship.

"Hannah's dress is two-tones," I began, my mind returning to the conversation at hand. "The skirt is gray and the bodice is the palest pink to bring out the coloring of her long blonde hair. She's going to carry a basket of rose petals to drop on the floor as she walks up the aisle of the chapel. She's terribly excited about being in the wedding and promised she wouldn't tell a soul until the evening was over. Her eyes twinkle when we talk about it and I told her she could share all the details with her friends once the wedding is over. I'm going to have the photographer make her a special album of her own and ask all the guests to sign it."

We continued to talk about the wedding after leaving the shop.

Chapter Five

Winthrope's Cozy Tea Cottage

The city of Santa Barbara rests between the Santa Ynez Mountains and the Pacific coast. It is one of Southern California's most beautiful vacation resorts. I drove into the city often to shop and always enjoyed meeting Charlotte for lunch when she was at the university. Today Marie and I went shopping at the stores along State Street and then stopped in a quiet little restaurant for lunch.

"How is your expansion on the coffee shop going?" I asked as we devoured our delicious Cobb salads. Marie and her husband, Thomas, had operated a small but prosperous gourmet coffee and tea shop for years. Having outgrown their present accommodations, they decided to expand their business by moving into the vacant suite next door.

"The structural work is done and now we are in the process of painting and decorating. I can't believe how many things I want to put into the new space we've acquired that I won't have room for. But, we expanded the cappuccino bar and have put in a few brass ice cream tables and chairs. We enlarged the area for gift baskets and increased our inventory there. We are creating baskets for every occasion—your suggestion in that area has about doubled our business. You creative people have the edge over those of us who lack imagination." She snickered.

"I don't think you lack imagination, Marie. I think there are times when we all benefit from the creative stimulus of others. Even after I decided to turn the horse stables into a restaurant, Mr. Lloyd, my architect, came up with wonderful ideas to enhance my plans—things I never would have imagined myself. You know the old adage, "Two heads are better than one.""

"Did you ever for a minute believe you would be as successful as you are, Rachel?"

"Hmmm," I murmured, devouring a bite of avocado, "I don't know really. To tell you the truth, I believed wholeheartedly in the project from the moment of its conception but I wasn't sure it would be successful. I hoped it would! I've hated seeing the estate unoccupied all these years but Paul never wanted to live there. It really is too big for me, but I could never bring myself to sell it, especially as long as Isabelle is alive. Why, she's lived most of her life under that roof. Eventually I'll be gone, and I doubt that any of the children will want to live there. Perhaps they will convert it into a hotel. At any rate, I'm happy to see the Tea Cottage and the Victorian thriving with people. The business as a whole has been a blessing to a number of people and I pray that it will continue to be," I replied.

"When will you start building the new kitchens?" Marie asked.

"Depends a little on the weather, and the designs aren't complete yet. I guess it may be a few months. Fortunately, Noah is handling everything with precision and expertise, as always."

Noah Adams was a bright, energetic young man in his mid-thirties whom I had hired to manage my businesses. He had a wonderfully organized mind and creative genius too. His sanguine charm made him a delight to be around and his blonde curly locks and big blue eyes complimented his cherubic face. Since moving to the coast his skin had become more tanned and his hair was now streaked with platinum from the sun. He and Miriam had begun to date after the death of her husband and while I had not heard them speak of marriage, I believed it would only be a matter of time. Fortunately, Hannah adored him. He would be the good father she never had.

"Why don't we stop by the Tea Cottage and the Victorian on the way up to the estate and I'll show you what's new?" I said to Marie as I finished my salad.

"Good idea," she replied, "it may inspire me further."

"Better not inspire you too much," I laughed, "or Thomas will find himself adding on to his new addition!" Marie only grinned.

Marie Marshall was ten years my junior but age had never been a problem between us. We enjoyed each other's company and while the worlds we lived in were very different our hearts were closely knit together. She was the sister I never had.

The drive to Winthropes was always enjoyable. Traveling up or down Highway 101 along the Pacific Coast overlooking the ocean was peaceful and relaxing, even when the waves were churning. Today, the briny waters lapped the seashore with a calm even pitch, and the sun sparkled atop creating little floating gems of tranquil beauty.

I pulled the car into the driveway and headed toward the back of the Victorian. There was a garage for patrons and a small parking lot for staff members built beside the property. We left the car and entered the Victorian through the back kitchen door. We looked for Miriam and Hannah but they were out shopping. The fragrant smells emanating from within were delectable and I could tell from the aroma that the soup du jour was vegetable beef barley, which was always served with immense chunks of hearty barley bread.

Marie and I walked down the gravel road toward the renovated stable, now our lovely Tea Cottage, which was doing a brisk afternoon business. The title of the establishment was Winthrope's Cozy Tea Cottage, named for my grandparents who had built the estate. Our sign hung majestically from a large brass stallion that stood at the highway entrance. The two front doors of the cottage were still guarded by a pair of friendly ceramic canines we secretly referred to as Jonathan and David. The old stable doors slid open from side to side and we walked into the foyer, which at one time had been the main aisle for the horses that paraded in and out of the immense stone building.

The horse stalls that ran alongside the north and south walls were now small cozy rooms decorated comfortably in the Victorian style. The waiters and waitresses wore period dress; they were busy serving customers, coming and going, in and out of the two rooms at either end of the building that served as food stations. These had previously been feed, tack and storage rooms. The storage rooms were still used for that purpose, and upstairs, the old hayloft had been converted to a reading room and boutique. More recently, Noah and I had built a cappuccino bar at one end and increased the boutique area to display a selection of our gourmet gift baskets, soon to be offered by catalog. A variety of art objects, creations of local artisans—many from the university—were for sale throughout the loft.

The wood floor was covered with large throw rugs and there was an assortment of small couches and comfy chairs for people to relax in. Bookshelves surrounded the walls, which were sloped due to the peaked roof, and our patrons were welcome to sit and browse before buying. The room was often as quiet as a library with only the occasional sounds of small laughter emitting from the people sitting together drinking coffee and munching on biscotti, bagels or muffins. Soft music played in the background; the composition of the moment was something from Rachmaninoff, a favorite of mine.

I heard someone heavily ascending the wooden staircase and turned to see Noah's curly topped head pop up.

"Hello," he said warmly, "I was busy with a patron when you came in." He sweetly apologized.

"Oh, that's okay, Noah," I said, "we just came up so Marie could see the new additions to the loft."

"How do you like it, Marie?" Noah asked.

"It's great! I feel inspired already," she replied, holding one of the gift baskets to see what was inside.

Noah escorted us around the room giving Marie all the minute details of the behind-the-scenes activities. He spoke of new distributors he had found and asked her if she would like to see the rough draft of the catalog we had been working on together for the next facet of the business. Eager to learn more of our latest enterprise, she followed Noah to his office, just under the stairs at one end of the stable. It was small and somewhat cramped but well organized. Fortunately, the plans for the new industrial-sized kitchens and catalog center that we hoped to build in the spring included office space for Noah and his staff.

I left the car for Marie and, after excusing myself, walked up the hill to my home.

Patricia greeted me at the door and took my coat while I went into the parlor to greet Isabelle, who was sitting by the fire.

"Hello," I said as I greeted her with a kiss.

"Hello, my dear," she said softly. "Is it cold outside?"

"Oh, it's chilly," I replied, rubbing my hands together to warm them, "but nice! You know how much I love the brisk air, Isabelle." I plopped down in front of the fireplace and let the heat settle into my bones.

"Just like your dear Mama," she said, reminiscing. I loved to hear her speak of my mother. She was my only remaining tie to the past.

Isabelle came to the estate with her mother when she was only a child. She grew up along side of my mother and therefore knew her well. When I came to live at the estate, she became my nanny, a second mother. She never married and instead happily devoted herself in service to the people she loved most.

In her younger days Isabelle had ruled the domestic scene at the estate with strength, efficiency and kindness. She was retired now and spent her days leisurely enjoying life's simple pleasures. She held a place of love and honor in my heart and I thanked God daily for her unselfish life.

"And your dress fitting," Isabelle asked, "how was it?"

"Isabelle, the dress is beautiful," I said, still basking in the glow of the moment. Eyes sparkling, I told her every detail. It reminded me of the day I bought my first party frock, went on my first date, dressed for the senior prom…Isabelle had been there.

"And I am sure you will look lovely in it," she said tenderly. "I am so happy for you, Rachel."

"Enid is coming tomorrow with your dress," I said, facing her while she rocked in her chair. "All of the alterations are finished. She just wants to see the dress on you to make sure that everything is comfortable for you."

"I should have gone with you, Rachel, instead of making her drive all the way out here," she said, feeling badly that someone was being troubled because of her.

"Nonsense," I replied, "You don't need to go out in this damp weather. You don't want to get pneumonia again. Enid's bringing all of our dresses with her so it isn't an extra trip and she will be recompensed for her travels so don't you worry." Isabelle only smiled. She had chosen a rich shade of jade green velvet for her gown, which flattered her ivory skin and beautiful silver gray hair.

We were still talking when we heard Marie come in the front door.

"I left the car in the driveway like you wanted, Rae," she said, as she entered the parlor. She greeted Isabelle and settled down on the couch in front of the fire. "Where's the Tiny Terrorist?" she asked, looking around the room. "She's usually lying in front of the fire this time of the day. Unless she's up to some mischief elsewhere."

"Now don't go picking on Baby," I said, with a smile. "She's probably under one of the chairs waiting to pounce on some unsuspecting target. Be careful or it just may be you!" Marie just laughed.

"I'll ask Patricia to bring us in some hot coffee or tea," I said, as I rose from the hearth. "And I'll snitch some goodies out of Martha's kitchen. What would you girls like?"

"I'd love one of her delicious chocolate raspberry brownies, if you're brave enough to get them," Marie snickered.

"I think I would like a pot of hot blackberry tea and honey," Isabelle said, "and maybe a cinnamon roll."

"Okay girls, I'll be back in a jiffy. If you hear any cacophonous sounds coming from the direction of the kitchen, you will know I got Martha's Irish temper up. But don't worry, her bark is always worse than her bite." I laughed as I walked off toward the kitchen, knowing Martha really didn't mind our intruding in her domain, but that she would put up a fuss anyway.

~ *Chapter Six* ~

A Double Blessing

*E*nid brought all the gowns for the wedding the next day, which created a flurry of fun and excitement amongst the household. Isabelle tried on her gown and modeled it for us. She said it fit perfectly and thanked Enid numerous times for bringing it in person. She loved the touch of the smooth velvet and said it was warm and soft. There was even a special jacket made of quilted satin that Enid had designed to go with it.

Anticipation began to mount with the delivery of the gowns and I sensed a happy anxiety growing within as the day of my wedding approached. Marie and I used our short time alone together in restful pursuits. We went for long walks in the green hills above the estate and enjoyed reminiscing about the past while sharing our dreams for the future. Her boys were growing up too quickly she feared and realized they would soon be heading off for college just as my girls had done years before. It was inevitable; life refused to stand still.

Peace and quiet didn't last long and we fully expected a modicum of chaos and frenzy to appear when all the members of our families arrived. When the weekend materialized, the days of our solitude ended. We drove to Santa Barbara together to greet the first of my children at the airport. Victoria's face was the first I recognized amidst a sea of others. With a kiss hello she explained that Michael was with his father.

"There they are!" I said, seeing my tall son-in-law exit the plane. Michael was held tightly in his arms.

"He's so BIG!" Marie exclaimed and she was right. Michael had grown considerably since my visit to London the previous year. Christopher flew there for a brief business matter in the fall before filming began in Arizona. I flew over ahead and met him and his parents and then stayed a bit with Victoria and her family. On the way home, I flew to Georgia to spend some time with Devon and Joseph. The warm weather was lovely but a little more humid than I was used to. Devon was a delightful hostess, taking me out to see the sights and introducing me to their small family of friends. I returned home blissfully aware that my girls were content and doing well. I then settled down to make preparations for my wedding day and my new life to follow.

Christopher, whom I had begun to refer to as "my traveling groom," arrived on Tuesday with his parents, Morgan and Clare Elliott. Morgan was a giant of a man; he and Christopher were alike in so many ways that it was obvious that Christopher had inherited his father's genetic makeup. Well into his seventies, Morgan was the picture of health and vitality. His laugh was jovial, his nature robust and he was extremely good-looking! Clare was lovely but very different. A small gentlewoman, she was serenely quiet and discreet. She spoke beautifully in soft melodious tones. During our first meeting in London, I also realized how much Chloe favored her grandmother; they had the same lovely eyes, winsome smile and genteel mannerisms.

Nothing amazed me more, however, than Devon's arrival on Wednesday. This trip to the airport Christopher and I made together. We waited somewhat impatiently at the terminal and were disappointed and a bit anxious when their flight was delayed. Finding a coffee bar, we purchased some warm drinks, bought a few magazines and found a quiet place in a corner of the building where we could wait virtually undisturbed.

Chris often wore a baseball cap and dark glasses when in public to keep from being recognized and most of the time he was successful. Occasionally he was recognized, and then he would graciously give an autograph. Most people, he told me, were rather kind. But every now and again, he would run into someone who was a little too pushy and sometimes even frightening. People were becoming overly obsessive and some fans went completely overboard in their behavior. Chris had learned to be cautious and wanted me to be watchful as well.

Finally the airplane arrived and, once the doors were opened, the passengers eagerly disembarked. Devon and Joseph emerged almost immediately. He carried a young boy in his arms; she walked with a young girl, hand tightly clenched to her own. Chris and I stared in amazement! Whose children were these?

Devon smiled as I gave her a hug and a kiss first, and then Joseph. The children were silent but keenly alert—timid but not frightened.

"Mom," Devon began the introductions, "I want you and Christopher to meet Alexandra and Pyotr, Joseph's niece and nephew visiting us from the Republic of Georgia. Alexandra prefers to be called 'Sasha' and we call Pyotr 'Petey.'"

I greeted each of the children with a warm hello and then we headed toward the baggage claim to collect their luggage. Chris didn't want to remain in the airport any longer than necessary.

"Is anyone hungry?" I asked before leaving the terminal.

"We ate on the first leg of our flight, Mom," Devon replied. "Sorry the plane was delayed; they put us on board and then had a mechanical problem so we had to wait while they fixed it."

Christopher and Joseph collected the luggage from the baggage return and after loading everyone into the Suburban we headed toward home. Christopher and Joseph rode in the front seat while Devon and I sat in the middle and the children were all the way in the rear. Captivated, I listened as Devon explained the appearance of her unusual traveling companions.

"Sasha and Petey arrived rather unexpectedly," she began. Joseph's younger sister, Natalie is ill. Her husband died a few years ago and she has been raising their children by herself. Unfortunately, her health deteriorated drastically and her illness lingered on, so she asked if we could take care of the children for a while, at least until she recovers. She also thought it would be a good opportunity for them to see America and improve their English. So, even though it will be somewhat inconvenient, we agreed. I knew you wouldn't care if we brought them and I thought it would be fun to surprise you. With all the changes going on in our small family, we thought we would extend our visit a little also, if you don't mind, so we can spend some time with Victoria while she's here from England. Is that okay with you, Mom?"

"Of course it is," I said gaily, "you girls know you are always welcome. I'm just sorry we won't be here during most of your stay. We are leaving on Saturday for our honeymoon. But hopefully Chris and I will be able to visit you and Joseph later in the year."

"Oh, that would be wonderful, Mom," Devon said, smiling, and we chatted about the two youngsters and how sweet they both were.

How different Devon seemed, so lighthearted and gay. She was much more relaxed these days. I guess we had both grown a great deal since my divorce from Paul. It had caused a painful separation between Devon and me, which time and prayer had finally healed. We were more comfortable with each other now, more patient and tolerant of the differences between us. We loved each other, and that was all that really mattered. Devon was still my most sensitive child but she too was maturing in new ways. She was learning not to take life so seriously and to enjoy herself a little more. Marriage had agreed with her and now…parenthood, of a sort, seemed to be changing her too, a double blessing.

The children had no problem adjusting to the busy life at "The Castle." Even with their limited English they seemed to enjoy using the old familial term. The older children fascinated Michael, who had just started to walk.

Petey was four and Sasha had just turned six. They both had light complexions and the same strawberry blonde hair, although

Sasha's was a little darker. Their short curly locks made them adorably cute. They were attached to Joseph by a common bond beyond family—language. But I knew they would learn English quickly. Children always seem to have fewer barriers to learning new things.

The noise in the house rose considerably with all the new inhabitants. The children enjoyed running through the long hallways upstairs being chased by the Tiny Terrorist and were constantly amazed by her speed and agility for fitting into small spaces. Peace and quiet only arrived at naptime and then, with all the angels asleep, the adults were able to carry on more meaningful conversations.

Chris and I drove to Santa Barbara again Thursday morning to pick up Chloe, and when Charlotte and Edgar drove up the hill to the estate that evening just before dinner our family was finally complete. Marie's husband and boys had joined us earlier in the day.

Pastor Edwards, his wife Sarah and their small son J.J., along with Miriam, Hannah and Noah were all invited for dinner, which we decided to have prior to the wedding rehearsal for the sake of the children. The large dining room was filled with happy faces and laughter, and the dissonant sounds of multiple conversations filled the air.

When dinner was finished and the children had eaten their dessert, they were put to bed. The wedding party and the family left the dining room and walked out to the chapel behind the estate. The staff had decorated it beautifully and only the fresh flowers were missing from the altar and the aisle ways. Noah arranged for their delivery to the restaurant on the afternoon of the wedding. All the bouquets, corsages and boutonnieres would be included. Weddings had become a normal part of our business at the Tea Cottage so it wasn't unusual for us to order fresh flowers for these occasions. This would keep down any undue speculation about the true nature of the activities taking place at the mansion on the hill.

Pastor Edwards stood at the front of the chapel with Christopher and his best friend, James Hamilton, at his side. Marie, Hannah and I were in the back, behind a tall portable partition that had been constructed just for this occasion. It was made of oak and had panels of dark purple glass so that we could see through it but opaquely. It would sufficiently hide the bride from the groom while we waited at the back entrance in front of the two oak double doors. It wrapped around the entire rear portion of the chapel behind the last row of pews. When all the guests were seated the wedding music would begin and then the center panels of the partition would open wide for the wedding party to walk through.

Charlotte and Edgar and their ensemble were at the front of the chapel in a section reserved for the musicians. She was at the piano; he was seated nearby with his fellow musicians. The music began on cue and when the doors opened the wedding party walked through.

The rehearsal went well with only a few minor gaffes, which gave us cause to laugh and record delightful memories for the future. When it was over, we returned to the main house for coffee and dessert, excitement permeated the room and laughter abounded. Chris and I stood together, hands interlocked as we fellowshipped with our friends. James was busily sharing humorous stories of his film career both in front of and behind the camera with the younger portion of our guests. Like so many directors, James had begun his career in the film industry as an actor. Eventually his desire to control more of the finished product led him to focus his attention on directing. There, he truly excelled. He and Chris had been friends for many years and worked together often. James was also a widower, whose passion now was for his craft and the traveling that went along with it. He wasn't shallow or egotistical. He was a sweet and fun-loving man and a good friend to many, especially to Chris. They talked about doing a new movie together and agreed they would look for an interesting script. I suggested they search for a nice romantic love story, or even a comedy, instead of another action film! They only smiled.

After all of our guests returned to their homes and lodgings, and our family had retired for the evening, Christopher and I sat alone in the parlor before the fire, which had all but died out. He had his arm around my shoulder and I reclined my head against his chest. Tomorrow we would become man and wife. It seemed like a dream.

When the last ember on the hearth burned out, we went to our separate rooms for the last time. Little Baby, exhausted from a day of revelry, was already asleep in her basket near my bed when I closed the door and put out the lights.

I turned on the stereo; a Chopin nocturne began. I walked over to one of the balcony windows and looked out into the night. The moon was high in the sky reflecting its brilliant beams of light on the dark ocean below. All was quiet. I stood silently before the Lord of creation and prayed. My journey continued on—taking me to new places. Inside, my heart sang a new song. I had followed my God through the storm and now the clouds had broken through and a new day was dawning. His word was ever true. If you live by his law you will find the grace needed to sing songs in the days of sorrow and rejoicing does come with joy in the morning when the dawn breaks through.

"Thank you, Lord!" was all I could say. Nothing more was needed.

~~ *Chapter Seven* ~~

A Gathering of Friends

*O*ur wedding day had arrived. When I awoke I sensed the presence of light shining brightly upon me, as though the morning sun had kissed my face and left some of its sparkling radiance upon my blushing cheek. My night had been peaceful and having slept well I felt rested. One look out the tower window told me the day would be stunningly clear.

The children were up as early as ever and their joyful sounds of play were heard resounding through the hallways. Little Baby, never one to miss an opportunity for mischief, disappeared through her small passageway in the bedroom door and could be heard barking in the corridors. No one would be sleeping late today.

I dressed casually in a pair of burnt umber corduroy jeans and a tan lightweight flannel shirt and joined my family for breakfast in the dining room. Martha and Patricia were in high spirits. The long mahogany buffet table was covered with an immense amount of food. There were fresh herbed eggs and bacon, sausages and pancakes and cinnamon roll French toast, a variety of fresh fruits and juices, cold cereals and hot Irish oatmeal. The scones with clotted cream and lemon curd looked delicious as well as the spinach quiche and of course, Martha was busily preparing omelets on demand. Our entire kitchen staff would be busy for some time to come.

Christopher was waiting for me at the table, drinking coffee and chatting with Allen and Victoria who were in the process of feeding little Michael. He greeted me with a cheerful good morning and a kiss, and poured me a cup of coffee while I filled our breakfast plates with delicious foods. He loved pancakes and sausages and had a bowl of fruit besides. I opted for the spinach quiche, a fresh brioche and fruit juice.

Isabelle, Morgan and Clare all strolled into the dining room together. They had been out early walking in the stark winter gardens and came in to enjoy a hearty bowl of Irish oatmeal. Isabelle and Clare both ate theirs with honey and milk. Morgan opted for cinnamon and sugar and had bacon and eggs besides.

We were enjoying our food and conversation when Devon arrived with Sasha and Petey who simply couldn't decide what to eat. There were so many things he wanted to try but Devon, knowing he would love the French toast, made him a plate and sat him next to me. Sasha was much more reserved and quiet. She hovered near her new aunt and decided on scrambled eggs and sausages and toast covered with strawberry jam.

The children were well behaved and quietly polite. Devon doted on them like a little mother and they responded to her with trust and affection. She was diligently working on their English and as we sat around the table, she would point to things and give the word in English for it. She too was learning a little Russian. Joseph joined us shortly and enjoyed a glass of orange juice while Martha prepared a vegetarian omelet for him.

Marie and her family and our other friends joined our happy company and the dining room was filled with a great sea of people coming and going, eating and talking. Everyone was in high spirits.

Edgar, Charlotte and Chloe were the last to join us at the table. They had gone out for a morning jog on the beach, being unhindered by little ones, and were filling up on juice and fruit while Martha prepared fresh waffles. Charlotte and Chloe had theirs covered with bananas and walnuts and smothered with hot maple syrup. Edgar ate his plain with syrup alone. I looked around the table at all the happy smiling faces. Never in all my years growing up on the estate had I experienced such a feeling of family and fellowship as I did today amidst this gathering of friends. There were disadvantages to being an only child; for me, loneliness had been the greatest.

But I had been blessed in many ways too and I grew up learning to be thankful to God for the good gifts I had in my life. My grandparents sat with me at every meal. We normally ate in one of the smaller dining rooms, and afterwards, Grandfather always read from the Bible. In the morning after breakfast, it was from the Proverbs. If I was at home for lunch, he read from the Psalms and at night, after dinner, it was part of the texts. We fed on earthly food and then on the divine. The Scriptures were such a part of our lives; I learned to quote many of the passages easily from memory.

Today, my heart lingered, as it often did, on the Psalms. One in particular struck me as I watched my children and their families. Psalm 128 declared that those who fear the Lord would be blessed and that their children would be like olive plants, seated around their table. Here were my olive plants. Oh, what a blessing. God's Word was always true!

"Rachel," Christopher whispered in my ear, "what are you dreaming about, dearest?"

"Sorry, got lost in old memories," I replied and he kissed me on the forehead.

"Do we have time for a walk?" he asked, his clear gray eyes sparkling like diamonds.

"Of course," I said. "I just need to go to the kitchen to talk to Martha about a few things. I'll only be a minute."

I excused myself from the table and headed down the hallway toward the kitchen, which was filled with numerous people, many who normally worked in the Tea Cottage down below. Martha had, with Noah's help, recruited some of their trusted staff to help out with all the wedding guests. She was busy talking with Sophie—one of our more industrious employees—and I waited patiently until they finished their conversation.

From a short distance I stood and observed the two women. Martha, my long time servant and friend, was graciously instructing her new and younger colleague. Sophie was forceful and somewhat enigmatical. Organized, efficient and hard working, with a passion for perfection, she was driven by some power within, her intense desire always to please. Yes, Sophie Anastasia, as we knew her, was truly unique.

"Martha, I need to speak with you alone for a moment," I whispered, once she had finished her conversation and Sophie had flown off to carry out her assignment.

We walked together toward one of the large storage pantries in the back of the kitchen. It was quiet here and we were alone.

"Is everything packed and ready for our trip?" I asked quietly.

"Of course, Mum!" she said with emphasis. "I personally took care of your things. I know exactly how you like your bags packed and what to take. I've been taking care of you and the girls for the past thirty years, haven't I?"

I kissed Martha on the cheek, "Yes, and doing a fine job besides!" I replied.

"My sister, Mary, will take care of everything here in the kitchen while we're gone, Mum. You won't need to worry about a thing. She'll take good care of our girls and their families." She beamed with pride when she spoke of her sister Mary and the children as well.

"I know, Martha. I know," I said smiling and, after giving her a little hug, I headed back to the dining room.

"Ready?" I asked Chris, who rose from his seat to meet me.

"Absolutely," he replied with assurance. And bidding our family good-bye, we left the estate through the back doors and headed up into the hills.

We walked quietly for almost an hour, just enjoying the day and our precious time together. We came to a large old tree with a low limb we could lean against while we talked. Christopher stood close to me, caressing my hair, which was still hanging loosely down my back. He kissed my lips.

"I love you, Rachel!" He whispered. "Very much!"

"I love you, too, Chris!" I responded softly.

We stood quietly together for a while, just taking in the beauty of the orchards and then began our short walk home. We took the trail that led to the rear of the southeast corner of the estate. The dirt path turned into gravel and eventually into concrete steps, which cascaded down onto a large circular balcony. Surrounded by bushes and trees the balcony was virtually concealed from the road below the mansion. We entered the estate through an open door.

The bright lights of the Waterford crystal chandeliers hanging inside the ballroom radiated warmth and illumination throughout the immense room. People walked in and out making things ready for the dinner reception, which would immediately follow the wedding ceremony. An assortment of round tables were placed around two sides of the large room and the long rectangular wedding table was situated in front of the fireplace. Silver gray linen cloths covered each table. The centerpieces were artistic creations of tall silver candles surrounded by white roses and clusters of misty blue.

The ballroom was by far the most magnificent room in the estate. The Gothic floor-to-ceiling windows running along one entire wall were exquisite. The long white marble fireplace that was in the middle of an interior wall was decorated with Gothic motifs. The room was painted a brilliant white and trimmed in a cool shade of gray-blue. The Gothic doors, which opened out onto the garden patio, were painted white as well.

Christopher and I looked around. Everything was perfect. We walked through one of the smaller hallways at the back of the estate used predominantly by the servants until we reached the kitchen. We stopped for a glass of juice and a snack and then we went our separate ways. I needed some time alone to pray before getting ready for the wedding and I wanted to take a relaxing bath before the hairdresser and manicurist arrived with their staff.

The house was relatively quiet—and when I looked at the clock, I realized why; it was the children's naptime. I went to my room alone. I closed the sitting room door and knelt down beside my bed. There, peacefully, I entered into prayer.

~ *Chapter Eight* ~

And They Shall Become One Flesh

*T*he hallways outside my bedroom and throughout the second floor of the estate burst forth with the music of laughter and joy once the beauty consultants and their entourage arrived. My luxurious bath had left me feeling warm and sensuous. Now, sitting in my robe, I was amazed at the skillful fingers creatively working on my long, thick auburn locks. Two women standing side by side were creatively braiding and coiling the hair with tiny chains of luminescent pearls. When finished they artfully placed my small pearl tiara on top. The netting still hung neatly by my gown and would be added just before the ceremony began.

A professional did my makeup after my hair and then I was able to sit quietly and enjoy my manicure and watch as the rest of the bridal party went through their preparations. Patricia brought a cart of refreshments to my sitting room where most of us were gathered. We sipped hot tea and munched on cookies while we admired one another's hairstyles. The manicurists busily painted one set of nails after another; I chose a lacy pink color, which I thought blended nicely with my gown.

Miriam had her long blonde hair woven into a French roll, which was very becoming. The weight she had gained over the past year had diminished all signs of the gaunt woman she once was, and last summer's tan was still evident in her now glowing complexion. The lavender taffeta gown she had chosen would look lovely on her.

Marie's hair was nicely coifed in a loose curly style while Isabelle also choose to have her long silver gray locks braided and wrapped around the nape of her neck in a tight bun.

Hannah quietly smiled while one of the cosmetologists tightly curled her long blonde hair in ringlets. A pink silk bow held her shiny curls in one place on the top of her head so that they fell down softly around her face. Once her angel pink nail polish was dry, she put on her beautiful new gown. She twirled around in front of the floor-length mirror admiring her reflection. She looked enchanting. Miriam beamed with pride and I watched as she pushed aside the tears that suddenly appeared on her cheeks. How happy we all were.

Martha and Patricia were included in the wedding party festivities and also had their hair and nails done. They had never been just servants or employees; they were long-time friends, and on this night in particular they were truly considered to be a part of my family.

The younger ladies all basically decided to wear their hair long and loose, some straight and some with a slight curl. We talked for hours about clothing and color and we enjoyed such a wonderful time of fellowship—it was beautiful. I looked around the room at the happy smiling faces of the women I had grown to love, young and old, and I knew in my heart the moment would linger on in my memory for many years to come.

"Rachel," Marie began, shaking me from my quiet reverie, "didn't you say that you and Christopher were planning to remodel these rooms?"

"Actually, we've already started," I replied. "I had a decorator in awhile ago to choose new colors and fabrics and they are going to start the work while we are gone. It will be more convenient for us and less hassle. We won't have to move into other rooms and they promised to have everything finished by the time we return!"

"What are you changing, Mom?" Charlotte asked. "Are you getting new furniture?"

"Oh, no! Never!" I replied. "Papa's furniture could never be replaced. Fortunately, Chris loves it as much as I do. No, we just decided to have new paint, new curtains and bed linens and some new chairs added and the old ones recovered. We wanted to blend our tastes into something we both could enjoy. You'll see it come together while we are gone."

It was dark outside by the time the beauticians had finished and departed. Everyone left my room and returned to their own in order to dress for the wedding. The final hour was quickly drawing near and I felt happy butterflies looming within.

Martha changed into her evening dress, fashionable plum satin brocade, and then returned to my room to help me into my gown. The dress slid easily over my body; the lace draped perfectly over the satin and just touched the top of my shoes. Martha's eyes sparkled with tears of happiness as she did up the tiny buttons on the back of my gown. When she finished, I sat down in front of my dressing table while she secured the netting to my pearl tiara. The pearl drop earrings from Devon graced my ears. Cool pink lipstick shined from my full lips and I used just a dab of rose perfume for fragrance.

"Ya look radiant, Mum!" Martha said proudly in her strong Irish brogue.

"Thank you, Martha," I replied. "Tonight, I actually feel a little like Cinderella—going to the ball to meet her handsome prince!" I laughed and Martha gave me a hug and a small kiss on my cheek.

"May God richly bless ya both!" she said and hurried from the room, hand tightly clutched to a tissue.

I stood alone, holding my train in my right hand, staring at my reflection in the mirror; I twirled around in delight. The satin and lace swished together merrily. I thought of Solomon's words, "To every thing there is a season, and a time to every purpose under the heaven."[1] Passing through a season of pain had been difficult but it was over now, and I was about to enter a new season filled with the expectation of gladness and joy.

Moments later, I heard the chapel bells ringing, beckoning my guests to its borders. My flowers were still in the florist's box on the table. This heavenly bouquet of cascading pink and white roses colored with sprigs of misty blue was stunning. I picked them up and walked to the door. My bridal party anxiously greeted me as I left my room and happily we gathered together to wait for our cue.

Charlotte and Edgar had arranged for their ensemble to play at the wedding, and they arranged for a small orchestra to play at the dinner. They also helped us choose the musical pieces that would be played during the ceremony.

The introductory music began with Cesar Franck's "Panis Angelicus." While the guests were being seated several pieces such as Bach's "Bist du bei mir" and "Sheep May Safely Graze" would entertain them. If time permitted they would play Beethoven's Theme from "Ode to Joy" (Ninth Symphony, movement 4). When the chapel bells sounded a second time, we knew that all our guests had been seated and that it was time for us to make our appearance.

Christopher's parents and Isabelle were waiting for us as we entered the chapel through the two large doors. Our entrance was shielded by the ornate oak partition; the light shining through the regal panes of purple glass cast a warm glow on the chapel. When the partition doors opened, Charlotte and Edgar and their ensemble began the processional music chosen for the entrance of Isabelle and Chris's parents; Bach's Cantata no. 140 "Wachet auf" (Sleepers Awake). Once they were seated, the processional for the Bridesmaid and Matron of Honor began: Handel's Largo, "Ombra mai fu."

Hannah slowly walked down the carpeted aisle tossing fragrant rose petals from her white wicker basket as she went until she reached the front of the chapel and took her place in the first pew. Marie followed after her, looking lovely in her gray satin gown, carrying a bouquet of pink roses and baby's breath. When she arrived at the altar, the processional ended and the music for the bride began. We had chosen something uniquely different for my entrance: Holst's "Jupiter" from *The Planets*.

I was nervous but smiling joyfully as I moved out from behind the shadows of the partition and into the center of the aisle way. The light fixtures overhead glowed softly on the small room full of guests and my dress shimmered brightly. Tall silver candelabras standing on either side of the altar gave the room a romantic air. Everyone stood as I began my journey toward my groom. Step by step I drew closer to the man I loved. He reached for my hand as I approached and I gave it to him gladly. We turned together to face Pastor Edwards and he began the ceremony that would finally make us one.

"Dear friends," he commenced, "we are gathered together, this evening, in the sight of God Almighty, to join this man and this woman together, in the state of Holy Matrimony. The institution of marriage is indeed holy; conceived of by God it was designed to be the fountainhead of each home and family. The Scriptures declare that a man is to leave his father and mother and cleave to his wife. And forever after the two shall be as one flesh united to each other for all time.

"But marriage is not without duty and responsibility. A man must promise to love, honor and cherish his wife above all others, serving and leading her gently, being willing to sacrifice his life for hers. A woman must promise to be helpful, reverent and gracious to her husband, and to serve him with a gentle and quiet spirit.

"Christopher Jonathan Elliott," he began, "are you willing to bind yourself to Rachel, keeping yourself solely for her, serving her in love, treating her with respect and honoring her above all others?"

"I will!" Chris replied, his eyes fixed upon me.

"Rachel Arielle Todd," he continued, "are you willing to bind yourself to Christopher, keeping yourself solely for him, serving him in love, treating him with reverence and honoring him above all others?"

"I will!" I replied, as tears of joy filled my eyes.

Marie and James, both standing off to the side of us, then stepped forward. She took my bouquet and handed me Chris's ring. James then handed Christopher the ring he held for me.

Standing face to face, the lights from the surrounding candles glowing softly in the background, we beheld each other silently. Christopher took my left hand and while placing the ring he had chosen for me on my finger he said, " Today, I marry my best friend, Rachel, my Beloved."

Tears of joy streamed down my face. "Entreat me not to leave you, Beloved, or to return from following after you; for wherever you go, I will go too!" I said in love.

Then, I took his left hand, and while placing the ring I had chosen for him on his finger, I said, "Today, I marry my best friend, Christopher, my Beloved."

Christopher smiled and replied, "Wherever you lodge, I will lodge: your people and my people will be one people, and together we will serve God and nothing but death shall ever separate us." And then he kissed me.

"By the power vested in me by the State of California, I pronounce that you are now husband and wife," Pastor Edwards declared.

"Ladies and Gentlemen," he said, "I would like to introduce you to the new Mr. and Mrs. Christopher Jonathan Elliott."

Our friends clapped their hands in joy as my new husband kissed me once again. It felt delightful.

I received my bouquet from Marie and together Christopher and I greeted our family and friends while Handel's "Allegro maestoso" from *Water Music* played in the background.

We spent a short period of time taking pictures with the bridal party before heading off for dinner in the ballroom. We graciously posed for photographs for the few newspaper and magazine reporters who had been prudently invited to attend the ceremony. They were completely caught unaware but grateful beyond belief for the exclusive coverage they received, an unanticipated privilege.

~~ *Chapter Nine* ~~

The Dance of the Swan

*T*he ballroom lights were blazing when we finally appeared at its doors that opened onto the garden patio. Applause filled the room when we entered and waiters and waitresses stopped serving the hors d'oeuvres temporarily while our guests welcomed us. The orchestra located in one corner of the room had begun to play while we cheerfully went throughout the grand ballroom greeting our friends and receiving their congratulations.

When dinner was ready to be served, Pastor Edwards said a beautiful blessing. We then settled down to enjoy a delicious meal of succulent fresh lobster and petit filet mignon served with tender spears of asparagus and oven-roasted potatoes. Hot flaky croissants and whipped butter came fresh from our kitchen. A light dessert of juicy red strawberries dipped in semisweet chocolate was also served. Christopher and I were both too excited to eat. We sat hand in hand, filled with the joy that we were now united before God and family. Our new life together had finally begun.

Once dinner was concluded, the lights in the ballroom were dimmed and Christopher and I arose from the bridal table for the first dance. The musicians played the "Anniversary Waltz" at our request. Magically, my groom's strong hands twirled me around the dance floor. Gently he guided me step after step always in time to the rhythm of the music. It was heavenly. And I remembered our first meeting, more than two years earlier and our first dance together. I had felt warm and secure in his arms then. Who would have guessed we were destined to be one?

When the piece ended we kissed, our friends applauded and then joined us on the dance floor. Joseph and Devon swept past us once or twice and then switched partners. She danced with Petey and he with Sasha. Devon had dressed them beautifully. Sasha was thrilled to own her first American party dress, Joseph explained to me during the evening. It was a pretty linen frock of warm bold flowers in deep rose colors. The long skirt was full with a big net slip and she wore pretty pink ballet type slippers besides. Petey wasn't as happy, I feared, in his new blue suit and big bow tie but Martha saw to it he had all the strawberries and chocolate he wanted to make up for it.

Victoria sat quietly at her table waiting for Allen to return. Michael had fallen asleep after the ceremony and he was putting him to bed. She looked as lovely as ever. Her porcelain white skin glowed from beneath her forest green gown.

Charlotte and Edgar and Chloe were busy socializing with Marie's two sons, Adam and Timothy. Chloe was without a date this evening but happy regardless. She had matured a great deal in the last year. Once so fearful of the future, her self-confidence and faith had grown considerably.

Hannah's elementary school teacher Summer Flowers was accompanied by her new steady boyfriend, a young Navy pilot named Ed Fox. Summer wore a beautiful gown of shimmering gold. Her ever-tanned complexion brought out the beauty of the luminescent silk. She and Miriam had grown to be great friends while working together on school projects, an added delight for Hannah, who loved them both.

Noah Adams spent most of the evening with Miriam; the two of them had become a couple. He was good for her, charming and gentle and kind. She, who had suffered so much, was now reaping the good fruits of happiness she deserved. Noah, besides being good to Miriam, treated Hannah like a daughter, giving her love, and stability and protection—all the things children need to live and grow and thrive. In addition, Miriam and Hannah gave Noah something he cherished: a sense of belonging and the family he never knew.

Hannah seemed very mature for being only eleven—almost twelve. She smiled shyly when Timothy asked her to dance and joyfully they stepped out onto the marble floor. I believe I even saw her blushing.

Marie and Thomas were not surprised to see Timothy, their youngest and most lighthearted teenage son on the dance floor. Adam, the elder of the two, was more involved in school activities according to Marie; he was also developing an interest in the world of politics. He spent the evening engrossed in the political discussions underway between John and Abby Anderson, our neighbors and some of our other legislative friends.

Chris and I greeted Woody Stevens who affably introduced us to his steady girlfriend, Zanna; her Polish last name, we were told, was too difficult to pronounce. We learned from him that she had flown to California from Washington, D.C. just to attend our wedding. Woody briefly gave us her history, which included the fact that she worked in D.C. for a prominent architect. He was obviously proud of her; perhaps their relationship had taken a serious turn. Today was after all Valentine's Day!

Noah happily introduced his associate and friend to the rest of the family and our guests. She appeared to be a very pleasant young woman—sweetly shy and unobtrusive.

Morgan and Clare Elliott joined us on the dance floor several times as did Patricia and Patrick. Once Allen returned to the ballroom, he and Victoria joined the growing throng of bodies enjoying the orchestra and the festivities.

Christopher and I took turns dancing and socializing with our guests. The ballroom was dressed in elegance tonight. Perhaps it was simply my frame of mind but it seemed more dazzling than my memory could recall. It was distinguished by its decorative fan vaulting plasterwork, which began half way up the inner wall, over the fireplace and spread across the ceiling. Nothing could be more beautiful.

The night air was cool and refreshing. Devon and I stood outside on the balcony talking for a while and Christopher spent some time dancing with Chloe.

The orchestra was wonderful—the music slow and romantic. The fireplace burned softly while its fiery red embers were colorfully reflected in the windows throughout the room. The chandelier lights above had been dimmed when the table candles were lit. The small sparkling flames created a dreamy vision of loveliness while the aromatic scent of roses perfumed the air.

I watched my groom dance across the marble floor, his daughter floating in his arms, until the music ended. A young man approached, and he and Chloe waltzed off together. When Christopher joined me on the patio, Devon excused herself and went in search of Joseph.

"She's beaming tonight," I whispered softly in his ear.

"Not my little girl anymore," he replied somewhat sorrowfully.

"They do have a way of growing up! But it's wonderful to see her so happy and content. They all are," I said as I glanced around the ballroom at our children.

"Yes, I think so!" He agreed.

"I see you relinquished Chloe to Dylan. What's he like?" I asked.

"He's a nice man, very decent. His father and I were friends when we were boys. Dylan wanted to be an actor and so I agreed I'd help him out a bit. He's very good really and hasn't needed much help. I made a few introductions for him and talked to my agent to help him get started. The rest of his success is all his own."

"Any reason why he and Chloe shouldn't go out or be friends?" I asked, eyes twinkling.

"None at all," he replied, "although I hate to see her get involved with any industry people. I guess I've seen too much of the shallower side of Hollywood. I know it isn't something I want for my daughter, but she will have to make that decision for herself."

"All we can do, Chris, is love, guide and pray. They have to find their own way in life the way we did. Chloe is an intelligent woman, she'll choose wisely. Don't worry."

Christopher looked into my eyes, held my face tenderly in his hands and kissed me gently on the lips. When the music began again, we danced together around the patio floor and then rejoined our guests.

The wedding cake was wheeled into the ballroom shortly before midnight. It was four tiers high and was topped with two red roses cast in a crystal globe. The bottom layer was Chris's favorite— a light rum cake with custard filling. The second tier was my favorite—chocolate with raspberry filling. The third tier was a magnificently light sponge cake. Knife in hands, we cut into the cake together and took turns feeding one another. I playfully dabbed icing on my groom's nose and laughed at the result. He did the same to me. The photographer snapped a quick picture of the two of us with frosted noses. It became one of our favorites.

At the stroke of midnight, James Hamilton, the best man, stepped forward to the microphone to pronounce a final blessing.

"Friends," he began eloquently, "Rachel and Christopher have asked me to thank you all for coming tonight to celebrate their marriage. It has been our good fortune to be able to participate in this special occasion," he said, facing the happy onlookers. "I know I speak for each one present here tonight," he spoke heartily, looking around the room and then toward us, "when I say, may you both be richly blessed. May you grow old together and live in happiness and peace all the days of your lives."

Tears streamed down my face. Christopher reached into his pocket and retrieved his handkerchief and tenderly wiped them away.

"Tears!" he said, smiling, "On our wedding day?"

"Tears of rejoicing!" I replied. He kissed my forehead tenderly and placed his arm around my shoulder.

Before the evening ended, Edgar stepped up to the microphone.

"We have the honor of presenting the bride and groom with a special gift," Edgar said as Charlotte quietly seated herself at the piano. "They are to have the final dance of the evening." He motioned us to the dance floor with his hand and then took his place on stage in front of a cello.

The lights of the ballroom were dimmed as the music began. Placing my head upon my groom's shoulder we swayed gracefully together as a lovely arrangement of "The Swan" filled the ballroom. It was from *The Carnival of the Animals* by Camille Saint-Saëns and was one of our favorites. The warmth and vibrancy of the cello was skillfully accompanied by the subtle sounds of the piano—like two souls joined harmoniously together. Our hearts were filled with the delight of the romantic moment; we tightly embraced and then kissed one another when it ended.

We waited until our departure from the ballroom to toss my bridal bouquet into the small but eager pool of single women hoping to catch it. Ecstatically, Miriam reached up as it magically fell into her hands.

We then said good night to our family and friends and headed off to our bedroom.

⌐ Chapter Ten ⌐

My Beloved Is Mine

Christopher and I walked quietly along the hallways that led to the central foyer and then climbed the stairs to our new home together—my second floor apartment in the northwest corner of the estate.

When we reached our room, Christopher opened the door and then gently picked me up in his arms and carried me over the threshold. Still holding me closely, he kissed my lips tenderly and carefully put me down. We glanced around the sitting room; the fireplace was lit and glowed softly. Candles throughout the chambers sparkled as they emitted their feathery romantic lights. The fragrance of freshly cut roses floated in the air. On the coffee table in front of the couch there was a crystal bowl of succulent red strawberries and whipped cream and a pot of hot aromatic herbal tea—something we both loved before bedtime.

Christopher's wardrobe had been moved in during the day and his bedclothes were now hanging in his private dressing room. I excused myself and headed for my own dressing room where

Martha was quietly waiting. She helped me out of my gown and took down my hair before silently disappearing through an exterior door.

I removed my slip and stockings and stepped into the willowy sage green peignoir that had been a special gift from my dear friend, Marie. My hair fell over the sensuous folds of the soft translucent satin adorned exquisitely with a white Chantilly lace covering. Small satin-heeled slippers fitted my feet snugly. I turned out the light and made my way toward the bedroom.

Christopher waited for me there, dressed in satin pajamas and a jacket. The stereo played softly in the background selections of our favorite compositions and a gentle ocean breeze blew in from the partially open tower doors.

Christopher held me tenderly in his arms and kissed my lips. We moved as one gently swaying with the music.

"I am the rose of Sharon, and the lily of the valley," I whispered ever so softly into his ear.

"As the lily among thorns, so is my love among the daughters," he replied, his cheek softly touching my own.

"As the apple tree among the trees of the wood, so is my beloved among the sons. I sat down under his shadow with great delight, and his fruit was sweet to my taste. He brought me to the banqueting house, and his banner over me was love."

Christopher swept me up into his arms, kissed my lips and carried me off to bed.

And so we became one flesh.

We awoke early the next morning and lying in bed together, I removed the Bible from my nightstand drawer and we continued to read parts from the Song of Solomon, one of our favorite books in the Bible. He read as the Beloved, I the part of the Shulamite.

I, the Shulamite said, "My beloved is gone down into his garden, to the beds of spices, to feed in the gardens, and to gather lilies. I am my beloved's, and my beloved is mine: he feedeth among the lilies."

Christopher, my Beloved responded, "Thou art beautiful, O my love, as Tirzah, comely as Jerusalem, terrible as an army with banners. Turn away thine eyes from me, for they have overcome me: thy hair is as a flock of goats that appear from Gilead. Thy teeth are as a flock of sheep which go up from the washing, whereof every one beareth twins, and there is not one barren among them. As a piece of a pomegranate are thy temples within thy locks."

Martha had brought us a tray of hot tea to drink and we each had a cup while we continued to read together and then we took time to pray. Christopher and I had talked at great length before we married about how we wanted to live as a couple and we had pre-determined we would begin each day with Bible reading and prayer. Today was the first day of our new life, our new journey together, and we began it just as we promised we would live it, putting God's word first.

When we got up we both dressed in traveling clothes and then joined our family for breakfast. Our honeymoon flight to the small ranch we now owned in Williams, Arizona wasn't scheduled to leave until two in the afternoon.

We sat with Christopher's parents who would be traveling north with Chloe. She was looking forward to their visit to her quaint little apartment. Their visit with their granddaughter would last for the two weeks we would be away. I believed they would have a great deal of fun sightseeing together and was almost sorry we would not be joining them. But they would all return to Winthropes again and we would have more time then to get to know one another more intimately.

My own three girls planned to spend a few days visiting with one another before returning to their respective homes. Victoria, Allen and Michael were also going north for a short visit with old friends and would return once again just before flying back to England. Devon, Joseph and their two little charges would be gone before we returned but we hoped to visit them all in Atlanta sometime during the year. Charlotte and Edgar we saw regularly as they lived the closest.

Marie and Thomas and their sons left right after breakfast and I cried when we said good-bye. A dearer more loving friend I had never known.

We kissed each member of our now combined families and climbed into the Suburban. Patrick drove Martha, Christopher and me to the airport in Santa Barbara where we boarded a chartered flight that would take us to the airport in Flagstaff, Arizona.

Southern California had been warm and sunny when we left, with a few puffs of clouds overhead. It was much cooler in Williams. The elevation was over seven thousand feet and snow was typical this time of year. The captain told us the weather there was currently clear and the daytime temperatures would be around forty degrees.

As we approached the Flagstaff airport we could see the snow that draped the entire area. I was delighted when we stepped off the plane and out into the cold, crisp air—it was invigorating and absolutely lovely. We thanked the crew for the splendid trip and headed across the tarmac toward the terminal.

A car had been arranged for our use prior to our arrival. After locating it, Chris deposited our baggage in the back and took his place in the driver's seat. Martha climbed into the backseat and I got in the front next to Christopher. He started the car and headed out onto the highway. We traveled along the road for some distance before coming to a private driveway that Christopher slowly turned into. He stopped in front of a locked gate and got out to open it. Once on the other side, we drove slowly down a gravel road through a densely wooded area until we came to a clearing. There, for the first time, I viewed our honeymoon cabin. It looked just like the tiny model Christopher has given me at Christmas.

There was snow on the red ground and on the tall fir trees that dotted the front of the property. A quaint winter wonderland scene—just like those so vividly painted by landscape artists or illustrators of storybooks. The cabin was built in the shape of an L and had two stories. There was a beautiful front porch, which was furnished with rocking chairs and small end tables.

Chris put our bags down near the front door and removed the key from his pocket. He went in alone, turned on the lights and returned to where we were standing. He forcefully swept me up into his arms and carried me inside. It was breathtaking. Entering through the front door we took a few steps forward and then three steps down into the living room. It was very open and airy. A huge stone fireplace filled one wall. Across from the front entrance was a wall of wood beams and glass, which looked out into the dark green forest of trees that was our backyard. I sighed, "Oh, Chris! It's wonderful!"

Martha quickly found her way to the kitchen located next to the living room on the other side of the staircase that ran up to the second floor. A small breakfast nook was built off one end of the kitchen. It extended out onto a long wooden deck in a semi-circle. A pair of glass doors opened out onto the wooden deck that was arrayed with an assortment of rustic patio furniture. A small but formal dining room was next to the kitchen. Two doorways connected it with the long hallway that ran through the downstairs. At the end opposite the living room there was a small study next to which was a bathroom. The only bedroom downstairs was large and had a small attached sitting room with a lovely wood fireplace. Martha quickly settled in there.

Christopher put me down and went back outside for our luggage. I excitedly walked upstairs. At the top of the staircase was an open sitting room bathed in sunlight that poured in from the skylights above. Directly over the kitchen area, the sitting room had a small circular outdoor balcony the size of the breakfast nook below. To one side of the sitting room was a spare bedroom. On the other side were the master bedroom and an immense bathroom, which could be accessed from either area. I walked around in a circle from the sitting room through the bathroom to the master bedroom and back into the sitting room again. It was a vision of loveliness.

I went back into the master bedroom located just above Martha's bedroom below. A fireplace similar to the one in her room was situated in ours. I walked to the end of the room and sat down in one of the rose-patterned chintz-covered chairs. In the middle of the room there was an antique four-poster bed made of carved cherry wood with a lace spread and matching canopy. All the floors in the cabin were wood and in the bedroom a lovely hunter green carpet was spread under the bed and covered most of the room.

Tiny steps went up to the bed because of its massive size. There were nightstands on both sides of the bed with crystal lamps and mauve shades and a tall chifforobe in the corner.

In front of one of the windows was an antique writing table. I walked over to see what treasures it contained. On top there was a small set of cubbyholes filled with Victorian writing papers and envelopes. There was an old-fashioned hurricane lamp of frosted crystal and in the center of the desk was a picture of Christopher and me in a silver frame. I opened the top drawer to see what was inside. I was amazed at what I discovered. There were vintage writing implements made of ivory and silver. Silver ink wells with matching pens and tiny candles for sealing wax along with several seals. One had my new initials R.A.E. and another had a single rose. I found blotting paper, ink erasers and powder. The man was positively amazing.

At the end of the room, where I was sitting, were two chairs, both covered in floral chintz, and a small couch dressed in a deep rose-colored fabric. These surrounded a small oval table, attractively decorated with a hand-crocheted lace doily and a pot of vibrant dried wild flowers. All were placed warmly in front of the fireplace. The walls were decorated with dark green wallpaper gaily painted with pink roses.

Along one short wall was a handsome banquette. Sheer curtains surrounded this long upholstered bench, which was brimming with lace-covered pillows. A perfect place to relax and snuggle up with a good book, it too looked out into the forest below.

I heard Christopher ascend the stairs carrying our bags. I walked into the small sitting room, which was predominantly decorated in warm golden tones. A lovely beige carpet flaunting delicate daffodils dominated the room. Two tall urns stood on either side of the balcony doorway and held potted ferns. All the furniture was white wicker with pale green and white striped cushions. The walls were divided in two by a white chair rail; the bottom was painted soft yellow and the top was beautifully covered with ivory wallpaper sporting tiny sprigs of fluffy white puschkinias. The room glowed.

"Darling," I said, when Christopher reached the top of the stairs, "the cabin is magnificent. I *never* expected it to be this big or this beautiful."

Christopher set our bags down and came to where I was standing. Looking down into my eyes, he placed his hand upon my face and kissed me ever so gently.

"I'm pleased that you like it. I wanted it to be very special for you. Do you like the décor? I had a set designer plan each room with your tastes and interests in mind."

"Really!" I said, astonished. "You are amazing, Chris!"

"Actually, I think it's just good fortune," he replied. "The nature of my business is such that I am constantly in contact with terribly creative people. I just have the good sense to employ them." He smiled, and I could tell that he was pleased.

"The desk in our bedroom is filled with wonderful Victorian writing implements. Some, I've never used before." I laughed.

He bowed at the waist. "Madame, as long as we live, I will endeavor to make your every dream come true!" he said with great theatrics.

"And I, also!" I responded, and curtsied in turn.

He kissed me sweetly on the lips and together we took the luggage to the bedroom to unpack.

In no time at all we were settled into our honeymoon cabin. Chris started a fire in the fireplace and Martha prepared a sumptuous dinner. The next day we drove into the city of Williams and looked around the town. Chris wanted to take me to his favorite eatery, The Pine Country Restaurant. He wasn't kidding when he said they made the best pie he'd ever eaten. The tiny restaurant was packed with customers but we found a small table near the window and ordered lunch. Pies filled one glass-lined refrigerator case in the front along with other magnificent desserts. We both ordered slices of chocolate peanut butter pie for our dessert. The pieces were close to four inches tall and the crust was deliciously flaky and light. We brought a slice home for Martha who had to admit it was better than her own!

⌒ Chapter Eleven ⌒

Upon the Craggy Mountains

Christopher was right. Northern Arizona was beautiful and in time I knew I would grow to love it here as much as he did. Our home was actually on the outskirts of Williams, which was situated in the southern part of the Kaibab National Forest. It was called the "Gateway to the Grand Canyon" as it headed the major entrance to the national park, which was about sixty miles north.

There was so much we wanted to see and do together but we realized there just wasn't sufficient time so we concentrated on hitting the high spots until we could come again. We spent a few days visiting nearby Flagstaff, only thirty miles east of us. Flagstaff wasn't really a small town, but it had the pleasant feel of one. There were plenty of places to shop and a variety of nice restaurants to eat at. There were museums, art galleries and numerous parks to enjoy.

Northern Arizona University had a nice campus and Chris was interested in finding out more about their drama department and what productions they might be working on. In quiet conversations between the two of us, he shared a desire to spend some time teaching small acting seminars—if not here in the future, then perhaps at the university in Santa Barbara when we returned home. He had already promised Chloe and some of her college friends and professors that he would visit the Stanford campus in the spring and take part in a round-table forum of questions and answers revolving around his industry. He was looking forward to being something of a mentor for young people wanting to enter his profession, hoping to help them avoid some of the undesirable pitfalls.

It snowed several times the first week of our vacation and I loved the powdery beauty it left behind. The Arizona Snowbowl Ski Area was packed with skiers and snowboarders who were out enjoying the winter sports. We played it safe, avoiding the possibility of incurring any broken bones, and enjoyed ourselves making snow people and having an occasional snowball fight. We even took a delightful sleigh ride one day through the beautiful Coconino National Forest whose elevation was around eight thousand feet. Traveling to Flagstaff from Williams and back again, we were awestruck by the magnificence of the San Francisco Mountain Peaks, which were currently covered with a blanket of glistening white snow.

We spent two days enjoying the Grand Canyon. We rode the Grand Canyon Railway's train ride into the heart of the national park. Leaving our car at the station, we left the depot around nine in the morning. We boarded the observation car, which consisted largely of glass and allowed us a stupendous view of the surrounding pine forests and mountain plains that we rode through.

We arrived at the canyon shortly before noon. Our trip took more than two hours but we enjoyed the scenery as well as the live entertainment. The Harriman coaches were from the 1920s and had been nicely restored. They were pulled by a vintage 1950 diesel locomotive engine.

When we arrived at the original rustic Santa Fe Railway Station, a historic two-story log depot, just steps away from the canyon rim, we were ready for lunch. Our guide met us at the depot. Chris had hired a professional to escort us around the canyon during our two-day excursion.

The El Tovar Hotel, built in the early 1900s, was where we would be staying overnight. We enjoyed lunch at the Bright Angel Lodge before taking a tour of the South Rim of the canyon. Later that evening, we showered and changed our clothes before enjoying a delicious dinner at the Arizona Steakhouse, recommended by our guide as one of the finest places to eat on the rim.

The next morning we were up early and had a light breakfast before continuing our sightseeing. This time we were off on a hike. The Grand Canyon was made up of many layers of exposed rock, which were absolutely magnificent. A variety of colors were represented in its formation—buff colored limestone, white sandstone, red shale and redwall limestone that was actually rose colored. There was also purple and green shale. Its charm and grandeur went beyond adequate description. We looked across the deep gorge below us through which the Colorado River ran and beheld such splendor we thought we were viewing an artist's landscape. It didn't look real!

Christopher and I left our guide for a while so we could walk together alone taking in the cool, crisp air, and enjoying the glory of God's magnificent creation.

"Christopher," I said as we strolled along hand in hand, "what do you think of when you look at the mountains?"

"Hmmm," he murmured, "I can't say that I really think of any one thing in particular. I just relish the beauty. And you?"

"Oh, I see so many things," I declared. "The picturesque mountains are indescribable—something you have to see to really appreciate. And then standing in front of them, looking down over the rim, I feel somewhat miniscule in comparison. But, instead of feeling insignificant because of my size, I feel a sense of wonder."

Chris put his arms around my shoulders and standing behind me, we savored the moment together.

"Do you see the finger of God?" He asked.

I looked around to see what he was referring to but was perplexed.

"Where, in particular?" I asked.

"In the canyon," he replied. And then taking his right arm and extending it in front of us, he moved his index finger from right to left in a long swirling motion. Finally, I understood.

"You mean, like a child playing in the mud, God took His finger and parted the mountains!" I stated.

"Something like that!" he replied.

I thought about the story of Job and his conversations with God. I could understand now the meaning behind the words he spoke when he said God cuts "out rivers among the rocks."[2]

"Mmmm, yes," I agreed. "Funny to visualize though, isn't it?" I smiled as the image flowed through my imagination. "Do you know, it may seem crazy but I think that makes me feel…more secure, somehow?"

"Really! In what way?" It was his turn to pose a question.

"I'm not sure I know," I replied as we separated and continued our journey along the rim. "Perhaps…because as you so clearly pointed out, the fingerprints of God are visible in creation. His attributes are openly revealed in the world around us; everywhere we look we see displays of His handiwork. It assures me that *He is* and that makes me feel secure."

I bent down and picked up a pinecone lying on the cold ground. It was covered with small dabs of dried sap. Chris had taken a seat on a bench nearby, quietly enjoying the view. We were getting to know each other better. Every conversation we had gave us more insight into the other's heart and soul. This was part of becoming one—knowing each other more intimately.

I tossed the pinecone back down upon the red soil covered in places with patches of the last fallen snow. Looking around once again, I asked my husband, "How is it possible that so many people can't see that God exists? I must confess it amazes me!"

"Well, possibly because most people see what they want to see. If they don't see God, it's not because they can't, but rather because they choose not to."

"I just don't understand it. Perhaps, it's because I grew up believing in God. And yet, it grieves my heart to think so many don't know Him…or, even as you say, choose not to believe that He exists. Where does that leave them? Not knowing how much He cares for all of us. If I didn't know God, it would make me feel…desolate, I think."

Standing behind him, I leaned over and kissed his cheek. His face was cold, so were my hands. He left his spot on the bench and taking my hand in his, once again we continued our walk, looking out across the deep colorful gorge ahead.

"Unfortunately," Christopher began, having taken time to contemplate my remarks, "many people have bought into the lie that there is no God. Evolutionists have been fairly successful in their attempts to convince mankind that we are nothing more than evolved animals—apes to be specific. And in their desire to rid us of all thoughts of creation by a Creator, they teach that our prehistoric ancestors were originally idolaters, worshiping gods made of wood and stone. And that only after a period of time did they develop their monotheistic beliefs—that there is only one God. Actually, it was just the other way around. God created us—in the beginning—to be monotheistic. Men, not wanting to give God the glory He deserves, created gods of their own making, gods that they could control and manipulate. You see, Rachel if men accept the concept of "One True God" then they are obligated to worship Him and Him alone. How can they then, in good conscience, worship and serve themselves?"

"But you don't have to be an atheist to be selfish or self-serving!" I replied.

"True! History proves that continuously. However, men still desire to suppress the truth of God's existence, even if only within. Regardless of what they believe, God Is. Besides which, He not only holds them guilty—without excuse for withholding worship, but He also calls them fools."

We walked for more than an hour, just talking and relishing our time together. So often I wanted to try to reach across the great abyss that separated us from the other side of the mountains and touch them, to see if they were real.

Our guide returned us to the train depot before three in the afternoon and we boarded the parlor car for our return trip to Williams. The journey home gave us ample opportunity to visit with other passengers and just relax from our whirlwind, two-day excursion.

We reached our lovely cabin in the woods just in time for dinner. Martha had made a delicious corned beef and cabbage dinner with sweet carrots and boiled potatoes. The freshly baked barley-herb bread was hearty and, smothered with butter, it tasted as good as it smelled.

We sat by the fire after dinner and told Martha all about our trip to the canyon. She had enjoyed her time alone and spent it working on new creations in the kitchen. We enjoyed a sample of her creative genius for dessert; it was a delicious apple rum pie topped with lightly sweetened whipped cream that she served with hot spicy cider. Weary from the long and busy day we retired to our room upstairs to spend the remainder of the evening relaxing in seclusion.

Early the next morning, after showering, I sat down at my desk in my dressing gown, to write a few postcards to mail to the children. Christopher lounged nearby on the banquette reading the newspaper. Relating our exciting days trip into the canyon was easy—there was so much to say. Movement in the forest below distracted me from my writing and I looked up to see a deer feeding in the woods.

"Chris!" I squealed with delight, "Look!" A young buck joined the lonely doe. They grazed for a short while and then they bounded off together, disappearing into the tall trees.

I smiled at my husband and he smiled back. I walked to the banquette and lay down next to him. He wrapped his arms around me and held onto me tightly. His rough beard brushed against my hair and lightly scratched the side of my face. It made me laugh.

"What's so funny?" He asked.

"Your beard," I replied. "It's itchy. Better shave!" I admonished.

"I will…later." He laughed. "I love you, Rachel. I'm so glad we found each other," he said giving me a hearty hug.

"Me, too!" I kissed my husband's lips gently and said, "The wilderness is behind us, Chris. We've come into the Promised Land together."

He closed his eyes for a moment, and I could tell he was searching his memory for a line, something he did often.

" 'Thou shalt no more be termed Forsaken; neither shall thy land any more be termed Desolate: but thou shalt be called Hephzibah, and thy land Beulah: for the LORD delighteth in thee, and thy land shall be married.

" 'For as a young man marrieth a virgin, so shall thy sons marry thee: and as the bridegroom rejoiceth over the bride, so shall thy God rejoice over thee.' So spoke the prophet, Isaiah."[3] Chris said, reciting the Scripture passage from memory.

"Beulah…it's such a unique name, don't you agree?" I asked.

"Yes, and it means 'married,'" he replied.

"How interesting," I sighed. "Beulah…"

The snow began to fall lightly outside the window, covering the red patches of earth while the dark green forest was quickly dusted with powdery pearls of frozen ice. Chris stacked more wood on the fire and we snuggled together in front of its burning embers. I closed my eyes while he read to me—feeling no longer forsaken, I too was Beulah.

~ *Chapter Twelve* ~

A Stairway to Heaven

Our lovely honeymoon ended too quickly and I knew Christopher was as sorry as I was to close up the house and return to our home in California. But our family would be waiting for us and we couldn't possibly disappoint them by delaying our return. Our present commitments were locked in, so we began making plans to enjoy an extended visit to what I now secretly called our "Beloved Beulah," later in the year.

When Chris locked the front door I felt the strings of my heart pull a little. In such a short time this lovely forest retreat had come to feel like home. I almost cried as we began to retrace the path we had taken two weeks earlier, back toward another sanctuary we also called home. The short trip down the gravel driveway ended as it had begun at the gate near the main highway, which took us back toward Flagstaff. The airport was much busier than when we arrived and I noticed more than a few people staring at us as we passed through the terminal to the airplane. The weather was lovely at noon when we boarded our charter flight home. Martha took a spot in the rear of the jet where she could relax on one of the comfy couches and quietly read a novel.

Chris and I sat together in the front of the aircraft just behind the galley. We played a game of cards at a small table between us while we nibbled on raw vegetables, crackers and cheese. One of the pilots joined us for a few minutes and told us all about the Gulfstream III we were flying in. He mentioned that we were cruising at a speed of approximately 530 miles per hour and that our altitude would be nearly thirty thousand feet for most of the journey.

The interior of the jet was beautifully decorated in a teal green and dark purple. The large stuffed chairs we were sitting in were cushy and very comfortable. We could swivel around in them so we were able to look out the windows and enjoy the view of the cities below us as we talked.

The clouds came and went as we flew across the sky and I marveled at one remarkable formation that reminded me of a puffy stairway to heaven. I pointed it out to Chris and turned to mention it to Martha but she had fallen asleep.

"Can you imagine a multitude of angels climbing up and down on that heavenly ladder?" I asked, softly, not wanting to awaken my friend. "It reminds me of the story of Jacob; his night spent under the stars with only a stone for a pillow. He saw God's angels ascending and descending—doing His bidding here on earth!"

"Rachel," Christopher laughed, "you have the imagination of an artist! You should have been a painter."

"You wouldn't say that if you'd ever seen any of my art work," I laughed in return.

"But honestly, doesn't it look as though the lowest cloud is gently resting on that hill in the distance? It's so close to the ground that you could almost step up to it and then simply climb the ladder of clouds upward until your reach heaven. One, two, three…six, seven, eight clouds," I said, "just like a scale of music."

"A scale of music!" Chris remarked with amazement. "What made you think of that?" he asked.

"Oh…I don't know really…maybe because the notes start out low and climb higher and higher while repeating the octave every eighth step of way. I think it must be one of those subconscious things that sit in the back of your mind until something you see or do brings it forward. Papa used to talk about the steps man takes to reach God—he often said they were like an octave of music.

Christopher smiled. "Really!" he exclaimed. His beautiful gray eyes sparkled like glistening gems. He sat back comfortably in his chair smiling.

"What?" I asked.

"Nothing," he replied, "just waiting."

"Waiting for what?" I asked again, laughing.

"Your explanation," he replied jovially. "The steps to heaven, I'm curious. What are they?"

I took a few moments to compose my thoughts while I tried to recollect my grandfather's words.

"The stairway to heaven, he often told me, is something like an octave of musical notes. The first note is the key and the most essential in order to find success. Fortunately, God has placed it suitably low enough for any one to reach, like the first step on a stairway.

"He made up an acronym for me, to help me to remember each step. He said the stairway to heaven brings H-A-P-Y-N-E-S-S.

"*Humility* is the first step. Humility defers to another, in this case, to God. We must acknowledge a poverty of spirit, our lowliness of personhood and our utter dependence on God to save us. The only way we can inhabit the kingdom of heaven is by knowing God personally. In order to do that we must lay down all we are and all we possess and submit ourselves totally to Him. Pride is the natural enemy of humility. So, the only way we can submit to God is by His grace, which comes through faith given as a free gift."

"Then you're ready to climb up to the second step?" he asked. I nodded.

"The second step on the stairway is something unexpected," I said. "It's *Anguish*."

"Anguish?" Chris responded.

"Yes, anguish, a grief for sin—no man truly grieves over his sin until he comes into a right relationship with God. How can anyone know what offends God until they begin to know who He is. Once we do, we realize that our sin causes Him grief and that we must confess and turn away from it.

"*Perseverance* is the next step on the stairway but it is more difficult to reach. It requires meekness—self-discipline—learning to be patient, learning how to endure the trials and tribulations of life without seeking to retaliate. It requires the crucifixion of the flesh."

"Hmm," Chris uttered, "extremely difficult to achieve, self never dies easily!"

"Yes, you're right, but if and when we put self to death, something wonderful happens. A secret *Yearning* springs up within us. This is step four."

"Yearning! Really!" Christopher sat forward in his chair, totally engrossed in the conversation. "For what?"

"For the love of God above all things; to seek after holiness to please Him. Love is one of man's strongest desires and in searching for it he can become misguided, confused and terribly lost."

"So man, in desiring God's love above all others, actually keeps himself from becoming ensnared morally because the longings of his heart, or his affections are focused on God and won't become perverted. Is that right?" Chris asked.

"Yes, that's the idea. We should desire holiness because God is holy. The stairway to heaven changes direction between step four and five. You see the first four steps to heaven are all focused on us in relation to God. The fifth step introduces a change of sorts; it focuses on us in relation to God, which in turn affects our relations with others and shows us our needs. Our *Need* of mercy, the fifth step on the ladder enables us to become channels of God's mercy to others—it helps us show kindness where once we might have been cruel."

"So you truly understand the admonition to *do unto others!*" Chris surmised.

"Precisely!" I agreed. "When we truly walk in kindness, we see things differently. Have you ever thought about the inconsistencies of mankind? We want justice for the other guy but mercy for ourselves? Compassion changes us and eases us into keeping a new set of ethics; the next step up the stairway is therefore *Ethics*. The internal set of guidelines that keep us morally pure and hopefully free from the things that will weaken or pollute. You know only the truly pure in heart can see God and those who do see God find *Serenity* in their lives, which is the seventh step. When we are at peace with God we will strive to maintain peaceful relationships with others and promote harmony wherever we go."

"And what is the final step?" Chris asked.

"The eighth note, the final step, is similar in some ways to the first. It is to be *Set free.* Only those who know and enjoy perfect freedom are capable of making choices. Forgiveness sets us free and enables us to do the same for others. It asks us to give what has been given but it does not demand—we are free to choose. We are asked to freely love and pray for and forgive those who hurt us physically, mentally and emotionally—in order to inherit the kingdom of heaven."

"What an amazing man your grandfather must have been!" Chris said with admiration.

"I wish you could have known him, Chris. He was larger than life in so many ways especially in my memory but he truly was a humble and self-effacing man. Any of his friends would tell you the same. You know, in many way you resemble him—not physically—but mentally and spiritually, I think."

"Thank you," he said modestly. The clouds had long since passed by and Martha was awake once again. She had listened without comment and only nodded her head in silent agreement. Her thoughts reached over toward mine and I remembered her words the evening we were married.

"He's a good man!" she said, as she buttoned up my wedding gown, tears in her eyes. "So much like your dear grandfather that I'm sure he's looking down from heaven, nodding his approval."

We smiled at one another; it was a fact that pleased us both.

~ *Chapter Thirteen* ~

A Love That Endures

Patrick was waiting for us at the airport along with a multitude of reporters who had undoubtedly gotten wind of our arrival through someone at the Flagstaff terminal. Christopher very politely answered several of their questions and we even posed for a few photos until Patrick retrieved our luggage, and we headed for home.

Our trip to the estate was relatively brief and, upon our arrival, our family and the chorus of everyone talking at once affectionately greeted us. It was wonderfully noisy. The house was bubbling with the gaiety that comes forth from happy hearts relishing the delights of loving relationships. Each person was eager to share in the happy adventures of another. The warmth of the sun was invigorating after the cold snowy days in Arizona but as I walked through the large front doors and into the parlor I thought fondly of the days we spent at Beautiful Beulah and I eagerly anticipated the time when we could go back for another visit.

Devon had unexpectedly changed her plans and, using the remainder of her vacation time, she lengthened her visit with us in

California. She was radiantly happy in her new role as surrogate mother and we were excited to have her home for an extended period. Joseph flew back to Georgia because of his work and Charlotte and Edgar had returned to their home days earlier but would probably be back later in the evening. Chloe flew down for the weekend with her grandparents and was in high spirits sharing the events of their brief sightseeing tour of Northern California.

On Saturday morning, Chris and his father, along with Allen and Edgar, headed over to the Anderson's ranch to go riding—an event they planned prior to our honeymoon departure. They wanted time to enjoy themselves and the sport they loved and I sought after time alone with the female members of the family. Martha and I made plans well in advance for an afternoon of fellowship and a lovely ladies' tea. We discussed the menu together and Martha took care of the arrangements, leaving Sophie a long list of instructions to be carried out during her absence. She wasn't disappointed with the results upon her return; neither was I.

Victoria loaded Michael in his backpack, and she and Devon took all the children on a short nature hike early in the morning. They did a little exploring and while Sasha picked a few wildflowers for her room, Petey collected as assortment of colorful rocks to bring back home. These they shared as Martha fed them lunch in her BIG kitchen, one of their favorite places, and then they were quietly tucked away in bed for a long afternoon nap.

Martha relished being home once again, busily working in her kitchen finishing the preparations for an assortment of delicious dishes. Patricia was occupied with dressing the dining room table in lovely pastel colors and decorative embellishments.

The long oak table in the smaller dining room was set with a white cloth and each place setting had a different colored pastel napkin. There were shades of cool pinks, dusty blues, tranquil violets and vibrant yellows surrounded by pewter napkin rings designed to look like Victorian teapots. The place card holders were replications of miniature teacups, also made from pewter, which held small bits of parchment with each lady's name written in calligraphy. Flower blossoms surrounded the hobnail dishes and in the center of the table was a lovely bowl of shimmering, floating pastel candles. The room was heavily perfumed with the fragrance of a spring bouquet of flowers, which gaily decorated the sideboard.

We were having a number of guests: Sarah Edwards, our pastor's wife, Zoë Pascal, a nurse from the hospital who was working diligently to help her with Tabitha's House, Abby Anderson, our neighbor and her daughter-in-law, Anne and of course Summer Flowers, Miriam and Hannah. I was happy that Isabelle was feeling well enough to join us and along with Victoria, Devon, Charlotte, Chloe and Clare, we made a nice menagerie.

Pleasant chatter filled the dining room as the ladies casually conversed while Patricia and Sophie served the first course: cold strawberry soup with a scoop of heavy whipped cream floating in the middle like a small island. Perched beautifully on top of the cream island was a large juicy strawberry skillfully sliced like a fan with a sprig of tangy mint in the middle. Almost too beautiful to eat, it was nonetheless, delicious!

Our main course was grilled chicken Caesar salad with croutons and freshly grated Parmesan cheese. Buttery croissants melted in our mouths with each delectable bite. Sophie served drinks of lemonade or ice tea and dropped cubes of frozen raspberry or lemon ice into glasses, whichever might be preferred. An interesting touch I thought. When lunch was over, we all retired to the parlor for dessert and conversation.

Entering the room last, I was pleasantly surprised to see how our tiny group had situated themselves. There was a great disparity in ages among my guests, Hannah being the youngest, almost twelve. Clare and Isabelle and Abby were all in their seventies while the rest of the group was in between; the younger women were predominantly in their twenties.

Sarah was sitting on one of the big sofas in front of a window with Abby, Miriam and Zoë, while Clare sat next to Chloe and Victoria in the big comfy chairs nearby. Devon and Summer sat on the sofa nearest the fireplace close to where Isabelle sat rocking in her chair while Charlotte and Hannah quietly perched on ottomans in front of her.

I took an empty chair in front of one of the windows central to the room to listen to the variety of conversations going on around me. All talk ceased abruptly, however, when Sophie came into the room pushing a lovely teacart carrying one of Martha's elegant desserts. A tall, triple layer clove and raisin cake with mocha-caramel icing sat beautifully in the middle of the cart surrounded by a platter of small butter cookies. Underneath, there were cups and saucers and two large pots of hot currant tea. As soon as Sophie sliced the magnificent cake, the fragrance of spicy cloves filled the room and enticed the palate. I couldn't resist the temptation to sample a small piece…and I wasn't alone.

Sophie served everyone with grace and speed and quickly returned to the kitchen for more tea. I welcomed the opportunity to silently watch Hannah as she interacted with the other women; she was growing into a delightful young lady. The conversational topics ran a gamut of subjects until we came to a favorite that caught the attention of everyone in the room—true love! Oh what an effusion of comments and opinions that topic evoked, and it elicited an abundance of stories that my friends sought to share. I didn't say much because I rather enjoyed listening as the younger ladies shared their beliefs and, when they were finished, I encouraged the elder ladies to comment.

"I have been married almost sixty years," Clare began slowly. "Our marriage has been a mixed blessing, sometimes wonderful…and at times…almost *unbearable!*" she said, with a sparkle in her eye. "My husband, Morgan, is a good man, I have been fortunate in that respect. But marriage is difficult…it takes more than love to make a good marriage…it takes a great deal of commitment and work…and more often than we like, an abundance of sacrifice."

All eyes around the room focused on Clare who took center stage. The young women especially were fixated on her dialog, attentively listening to our refined guest share her experience of love and life and marriage in general.

"I still remember so clearly the first time I met my husband…why, he was only a boy…and *very* young at sixteen," she said, her mind fixed on their first encounter. "He was tall and gangly and thin…too thin. And his hair was always tousled and messy but to me, a young waif of a girl at fourteen, he was delightfully charming.

"His father had died and he and his mother had come to our small village to live with her sister, who was our neighbor. We became friends, good friends…love came later on. I must admit I was even a little surprised when he asked me to marry him. I was only seventeen and a bit afraid of men I think…the world was very different then, and women too, but love is still wonderful no matter what and first love is especially so.

"My parents were receptive to our engagement but wanted us to wait to marry until I finished school. Morgan agreed that would be wise and also wanted to save a little money for a nest egg, so we waited. When we finally did marry, we had a small ceremony with just our families and a few close friends. I wore my best blue dress; he wore one of his father's old blue suits. I remember it like it was yesterday.

"Our first home was a tiny cottage—barely big enough to turn around in but we had it to ourselves. I'll never forget our first night together. I was excited but terrified! He carried me over the threshold into our new little home. On my table I had a lovely pair of silver candlesticks, given to us by my mother and dad; a hand-stitched quilt his mother had made covered our bed. We received a few other small wedding gifts…the candlesticks we still have. We ate bread and cheese by candlelight and in front of the fireplace and when we were done—he sweetly carried me to bed.

"We were both so new to love—awkward and clumsy…and terribly immature, I must confess…in the beginning. But our love was simple and pure and our lives were uncomplicated. We were honest with each other—we felt no need to put on airs or pretend. We *learned* the meaning of true love in *time* because true love doesn't happen overnight, it weathers every storm and matures throughout a lifetime."

"What are the earmarks of true love, Grandmother?" Chloe asked, quietly. "How can you know love will last a lifetime?"

"*True* love, Chloe is a conscious decision to love even the unlovely, forever. Therefore it must be both unselfish and committed.

When two people are devoted to one another, they seek to serve and meet the needs of the other while working through difficulties and differences still allowing each one the freedom to be themselves."

"Clare is right!" Abby chimed in. "It's selfishness that breeds so much discontentment; too much of 'what's good for me,' instead of 'what's best for us!' Eventually it kills the love inside of you."

"Do you think that's why we have so much divorce today?" Victoria asked, intensely interested in the experiences of these elderly matrons.

"Well, Victoria," Clare began once again, "I think it is at least a contributing factor. After all, why do marriages end in divorce? Because ultimately, one of the two parties believes they are unhappy. What do they call it today? Irreconcilable differences! Don't misunderstand me; there are times when marriages do need to end. Whenever there is abuse, or repeated infidelity…there are dangerous people in the world. But that doesn't account for the great majority of divorces today."

"People want instant everything!" Abby added. "They don't want to work at marriage—every worthwhile relationship requires work, takes time, energy and personal investment. Why else would we be here today? It's pleasant getting together for lunch and fellowship—this is one of the perks of investing time in our relationships with one another. But how about when we feel we need to confront one another, to help someone grow or meet a challenge they are facing? That can be difficult and uncomfortable, but when we care, we confront and offer assistance. Friends help friends grow in a positive way. Marriages should be the same only better."

"Confrontation is always difficult," Sarah said, "but necessary in close personal relationships and if done properly, productive. Love must be honest enough to confront."

"I hate confrontation!" Charlotte sighed with a shrug. "I'm not very good at it, I guess."

"And I'm *too* assertive when I confront someone," Victoria confessed, "and often I end up in an argument. It's frustrating."

"I ran away from confrontation because of fear!" Miriam shared. "It drove me to find courage in alcohol but that only made things worse for me." The room filled with conversation as individuals in their small groups shared about their experiences with love and the problems they encountered when they tried to confront.

Silence came only when Clare once again began to speak and share her experiences.

"If you want your marriage to succeed, you must always be honest and truthful…using as much tact as possible," she said with a smile. "After all, dishonesty only leads to confusion and frustration…people often disagree—that's inevitable. But to be able to disagree without becoming angry or combative is something else. You must learn to do so without erecting walls of bitterness and resentment. These lead to separation and can destroy any relationship." Clare spoke from experience and then took time to reflect for a moment before continuing on.

"And, you shouldn't expect your spouse to be everything you need in life, we need a variety of relationships to be healthy and happy. Remember, no one person, especially your husband, is solely responsible for your happiness or unhappiness.

"Be realistic…young love is usually passionate but it must grow and mature in order to survive. Your husband should also be your friend."

"Too many young people are in love with the idea of being in love!" Summer Flowers admitted. "One week they love one person, the next it's someone else. I think parents are greatly responsible for rushing their children into adulthood long before they're ready."

"I agree," Zoë said.

"Some people treat marriage like that, too," Devon, said. "Constantly changing partners when the romance dies or their feelings change."

"We all have a tendency to treat new things better than old. Like getting a new car or a new house, we want it to sparkle and shine and when the thrill of the newness disappears, so does the devotion," Sarah responded. "It's a shame we treat people like that."

"Why does that happen?" Chloe asked, looking around the room for an answer.

"Well," her grandmother began, "we are all mysterious in some way. When you are courting someone, as we would say in my day, you dimly see who he or she truly is. But once you marry, the person is seen more clearly. What we don't realize, I think, is that it is in part, their mystery that attracts us to them in the first place. We love them for who we think they are…that is the immature part of love. But, as I said, mature love grows and learns to love the person for they who they truly are, good and bad. Really, for better or worse, as we promised."

"So the real question, girls," Victoria laughed, "is how do we keep those home fires burning?" The match was lit once again and conversation filled the room. Sophie reappeared with the teacart and offered fresh tea to those desiring it.

Isabelle, who had been silent up to this point, quietly listening to the discussion around her, finally spoke.

"All love requires some passion to thrive…whether it is love of a spouse, a child, a friend, or even our love for God. Indifference sounds the death toll of love. If love is to survive and grow…then we must remember to do the things we did in the beginning, when love was new and fresh."

~ *Chapter Fourteen* ~

The Gift

*T*he estate grew quieter over the days that followed as one by one our family departed for their homes. Only Clare and Morgan remained at the estate for an extended visit. How wonderful it was getting to know them and seeing Christopher through their eyes, learning of his boyhood pranks, hearing about his adolescent accomplishments. Every evening, weather permitting, we strolled out back in the woods, just as I had as a young girl. Life just couldn't be better!

Christopher and Morgan went out riding with the Andersons regularly, and Clare accompanied me to my various charity events. Currently busy working to raise funds for Tabitha's House, a home for battered women and their children, we were always in search of new volunteers or new donors to lend their support to this worthwhile endeavor. Providence frequently smiled upon us and graced us with our petitions.

Sarah Edwards was the driving force behind the project, which she had begun a year earlier. She was now striving to make the home a joint venture that would be supported by the churches in the area.

Her kind and tender heart easily touched the compassionate natures of many, which fortunately propelled them into action. Even the house we were using to provide needed shelter for women and children in explosive situations was donated. A wealthy businessman generously bestowed the facility to the charity, provided the community would maintain it.

The necessary renovation work had been completed and the building was now habitable. Although Sarah had acquired enough support from local churches and wealthy benefactors within the community to help maintain the home on a monthly basis, we knew we needed to find ways to raise funds toward building a nest egg for future developments.

The first Tuesday of each month we designated for the new board of directors to meet to plan and discuss the ministry and its needs. Sarah had been named director and Zoë Pascal, our friend from the hospital, had volunteered to be her assistant. Dr. Luke, a local pediatrician, and Mr. Ronald Lee, a lawyer, along with Summer Flowers and Marie Kim, both elementary school teachers, served in advisory positions with Miriam and myself.

Clare, Miriam and I drove to the tall brick and stucco building located in an older section of town that had become a symbol of hope for the battered families that were now residing there, all victims of spousal abuse. The building had been newly painted after being renovated and completely landscaped with beautiful trees and plants. There was a small yard with swings and even a game area. A wooden signpost hung near the front door with the words, "Tabitha's House" painted brightly over a colorful rainbow—a symbol of hope for their future.

We met in the director's office, which was located on the first floor to the left of the front entry. Miriam brought a large basket of fresh pastries from our restaurant kitchen for everyone to enjoy and Zoë had ready a large pot of steaming hot coffee. We all helped ourselves before being seated, ready to discuss current issues.

Sarah briefly gave us a run down on any new occupants and then we covered expenses, work projects, new supporters and any other business that we as a group needed to cover.

"While we are doing well financially," Zoë began, when all other business was concluded, "we still need to find other sources of income. It is part of our goal to become as self-sufficient as possible."

"Are there any suggestions?" Sarah asked.

"The schools do a number of fund-raising events all year long," Marie Kim said, "We could probably do the same here."

"Could we try to produce something unique that we could sell?" Mr. Lee asked.

"That's an idea!" Miriam exclaimed. "But what?"

"I don't think we are capable of producing much on our own…at least not at this time I'm afraid," Sarah replied. "Although I am open to any suggestions."

"Many years ago when our church was looking to raise money to build a new Parsonage," Clare began somewhat hesitantly. She glanced around the room and with all eyes on her she continued, "we printed a small but rather lovely cookbook. Each member of the church donated a family recipe. It was fairly successful."

"I've been approached by several people to do a cookbook for the restaurant," I added. "So, I guess that's a viable possibility. Cookbooks always seem to sell."

"I've had a number of people at the inn ask for recipes for some of our specialties," Miriam said, her enthusiasm mounting. "A cookbook would be a great idea. Noah could give us a reasonable projection of costs and since we are already preparing to sell our own merchandise through catalogs and the Internet, I don't see why we couldn't include the cookbook with a note that the proceeds go to charity."

"Perhaps we could ask some of the school kids to do the art work? Or even design the cover?" Marie Kim suggested.

"Oh, a contest might be fun," Summer exclaimed.

"Sounds like a good idea!" Dr. Luke said in agreement.

"I'm sure Chris and I could gather a few "celebrity" recipes to include," I interjected. "Could generate some additional interest!"

"Is everyone agreed then?" Sarah asked and everyone present raised their hands.

"Then I am going to ask Miriam and Rachel to proceed first with the projections and some preliminary plans for the cookbook itself. I'm sure everyone here is willing to help out if necessary. Just let us know if you need anything." All the members of our small circle concurred.

"The last measure of business to discuss before we part company today is something on a personal note," Sarah said, her voice more quiet and reserved. With a smile on her small pixie face she proudly announced she was expecting another baby.

"Congratulations," Zoë burst forth exuberantly, as she gave her friend a big hearty hug.

"My practice continues to grow," Dr. Luke said with a laugh.

"I'm so happy for you, Sarah!" I added, amidst a flurry of hearty echoes of the same sentiment.

"When is the baby due?" Summer asked with excitement.

"Not for awhile," Sarah responded, "I just found out that I'm about ten weeks along. John and I are very excited and just shared the good news with our family over the weekend. He'll be making an announcement at church next Sunday. Unfortunately, I'm going to have to curtail some of my activities. Most of my free time is devoted to my work at church and here at the shelter but I won't be able to continue to do both, indefinitely."

"Are you going to resign from the board of directors?" Zoë asked anxiously.

"Well, not immediately," Sarah replied. "I will remain on the board in an advisory capacity as long as I'm wanted but I was hoping that someone else might take over as director. John and I have both been praying about it and we have decided to ask you all to do the same. Having a baby will take up a good deal of my time, and we both feel that it's important for me to be at home with our children."

"We don't need to reach a decision right away, do we?" Ron asked.

"No, that won't be necessary. But we will have to make a decision some time in the near future. It needs to be someone who will have the time and the desire. We want the best person possible. Think and pray about it and we'll discuss it again next month."

"Thought about a name for the baby yet, Sarah?" Zoë asked.

"Well, John wants to name the baby Jude if it's a boy; if it's a girl than we'll name her Jemima." Sarah replied.

"Jemima? That's a lovely name, Sarah!" Summer Flowers responded.

"Yes, I've always liked it. It means 'dove.'"

Our tiny group continued to chat for a while sharing other news and then disbanded, each of us returning to our personal lives and duties. I dropped Miriam off at the inn, and Clare and I drove up the hill to the estate.

We decided to take a walk before lunch and headed outside and up the hills toward the orchards. The weather was beautiful and warm and the air was filled with the fragrance of orange blossoms. A tiny California ground squirrel scurried across the path in front of us and quickly climbed a tree.

"You are very fortunate, Rachel, to have been raised in such a lovely place; the weather is so delightful!" Clare said as she carefully climbed the dirt trail upward.

"I don't think I could imagine living anywhere else, ever again!" I responded wholeheartedly. "Although I do love our new home in the forest. I hope you and Morgan will consider taking a vacation there with us. I think you'd love it as well. Still…there is nothing like the ocean! For me, there never will be."

"I can understand why you love it so. Even the turbulent waves can be restful, can't they?" She stated with a knowing smile.

Clare understood what I had always known. The majesty of the grand mass pushing across the horizon, the strength and unlimited power the water possessed, the peace of the waves as they lapped upon the shore…the grandeur of it all.

We walked for half an hour before stopping for a rest. We had reached the top of a small hill and could gaze upon the ocean from where we stood.

"I can remember bringing my girls here when they were small, before my grandparents died," I began, "to visit them and to explore the ocean. Devon in particular loved to dig in the sand. Victoria hated getting dirty but enjoyed sunbathing and Charlotte was delightful just dancing to the music of the waves. My children are all so uniquely different and I think that's wonderful.

"Devon always insisted on bringing a pail and a small shovel on our excursions so she could collect things. We'd walk along the sand together, looking for shells and pretty rocks. She's find dead crabs and bury them and loved playing with sand fleas, called them 'Poppers.' Always the inquisitive one, she still is I guess. I used to laugh and say, 'Mother doesn't want you to bring any of your little critter friends in the house, Devon!' Lord, I have so many wonderful memories of my life here. Devon called it 'Papa's ocean' simply because it was in front of Papa's big house."

"It's sad for us when they grow up and move away, isn't it?" Clare remarked, her mind apparently sifting through a lifetime of memories of her own. "Christopher was such a wonderful child—so eager to please…warm, charismatic and amiable. No wonder he lights up the cinema with his presence. He's very regal looking, so much like Morgan; they have the same enigmatical persona." Her eyes sparkled as she spoke of the man who had been her husband for many decades. "Our lives go through a series of beginnings and endings," she said, contemplatively. "The ending of one phase brings a mixture of both happiness and sadness while the beginning of the next often delights us with eager anticipation, as well as fear and trepidation."

"When Charlotte got married," I began, "I went through an array of emotions. Joy and happiness for her and the new life she was beginning with Edgar, but regret too. I think I felt I was being left behind, in some way. My baby was leaving her childhood, and in some ways, me, as she moved forward into her marriage and new home. I guess those are the times when we really begin to face the fact that we're growing old."

"Ah yes, youth does ultimately fade away. Our hair turns gray and wrinkles appear. And then we don't move as quickly as we once did. Our memory grows dim and we suffer from terrible bouts of forgetfulness." Clare sighed a bit. "But, aging isn't terrible and we senior citizens even have certain advantages that youth lacks. Regardless of the inevitable physical changes our bodies undergo, we are fortunate in that we gain the wisdom and maturity that only comes with time and experience. Growing old shouldn't be so distressing or at least, it doesn't need to be. We should be more concerned with the perception people have of the elderly; too many view us in a very negative way. Why, when Morgan and I were young, we were taught to respect our elders; we even revered them for their wisdom."

"The world moves a lot faster today than it once did, doesn't it? Technology has changed the way we live; television and the movie industry along with the print media and the Internet are all at least partially responsible for fostering a culture that has become obsessed with youth, beauty, pleasure and riches."

"Yes, that may be true, Rachel. But I believe Solomon said it best when he wrote, 'there is no new thing under the sun.'⁴ History proves that's a fact. What disturbs me tremendously is the growing incivility occurring in our society. In the past several decades it appears people are becoming more intolerant of our differing beliefs and too often we treat one another in a rude and discourteous manner. So many are lacking a moral compass to guide them in a positive direction and the end result is the destruction of lives. We actually have children killing children and it's horrendous!"

Clare was visibly troubled; I felt her anxiety as well.

"In the past five decades we've seen many things change here in the United States, Clare. I'm sure you've seen the same in Great Britain!" She nodded her head as we walked toward home. "What do you think has been the most detrimental?" I asked.

She didn't respond at first, I could tell she was thinking deeply about my question. When she finally replied, her answer took me by surprise.

"Perhaps, it is something as simple as selfishness," she said, sincerely. "People just don't concern themselves with the rights or feelings of others. And selfishness really stems from a greater evil; people want to be their own god."

Clare and I walked in silence. Her words rang out in my ears and I felt blessed to know this seasoned woman with keen insight and understanding. She was a true believer in the Word of God, which clearly taught the underlying truths of all social evils. The Psalmist summed up succinctly when he wrote,

> The fear of the LORD is the beginning of wisdom:
> And the knowledge of the holy is understanding.
> For by me thy days shall be multiplied,
> And the years of thy life shall be increased.[5]

Chapter Fifteen

Hannah and the Tea Party

*I*n April Miriam's daughter Hannah turned twelve. Her tall angular body was beginning to develop and mature. Her bronze face wore the bloom of youth and glowed like the glistening rays of the sun—the result of so many afternoons spent enjoying the delights of the ocean shore. Her bright rosy cheeks were speckled with tiny brown freckles while her platinum gold hair, which was like spun silk, fell gracefully from her pretty head downward past her slender waist. Her period of transformation was interesting to watch—so young and playful one day and serious and mature the next.

Miriam and I had discussed the plans for her birthday party. Hannah wanted a Victorian Tea this year, and we decided to use one of the large banquet rooms in the Tea Cottage to make the event more authentic. Hannah loved the idea! One quiet Saturday afternoon, the three of us sat down together and planned the festive celebration.

Winthrope's Cozy Tea Cottage had been in business for more than a year and had become more successful than I had ever dreamed possible. While many considered the conversion of the rustic horse stable into a charming restaurant a stroke of genius, I preferred to think of it as divine inspiration.

The stable had always been a place of enchantment for my brother Riley and me; like The Castle above that eventually became my home, it was filled with mystery. I loved the old stone building with its tall walls and heavy oak doors. The scent of horses and leather still lingered…or perhaps, it was just the memory.

The converted stalls made quaint private dining chambers and the old tack rooms located at either end of the building had been efficiently transformed into small kitchenettes and storage areas. On the west end we had removed the walls between some of the stalls to create large rooms to accommodate large parties.

All of the stalls had an exterior window, which had been replaced with decorative stained and clear glass. The wrought-iron mangers that once contained hay now bloomed with potted plants. Water buckets were still located in each corner but were now filled with small trees. The tall horse doors had been entirely removed for easy access and in front of each dining chamber were large oak cabinets, which displayed a variety of beautiful tea services gathered from all over the world. I had spent thirty years collecting them; the first was the most precious because it had been a gift from my former husband's beloved grandmother.

While the renovation had made the stable an enchanting place to visit and a prosperous business, I had to confess that much of my enjoyment came from being able to decorate the private dining chambers. First, a theme was developed for each room and then we embellished it with lovely works of art and décor, preferably but not always from the Victorian era.

Hannah loved The Sea Chamber. It was imbued with the character of the ocean. There were several oil paintings of young ladies in old fashioned bathing attire—some were lounging under big umbrellas enjoying the sun and others were peacefully strolling along the shore. There was one of a young boy playing with a tiny sailboat at the water's edge that reminded me of my brother. A series of ocean side watercolors hung from large blue ribbons along one wall. There were ceramic angels holding conch shells on the sideboard used for serving while pewter plates of vintage lighthouses lined one of the shelves on the walls. A lovely pastel of sandpipers at play in the surf was another favorite of mine.

Hannah chose invitations with a Victorian Tea Cottage theme and addressed them herself to all the invited guests. Since most of her close friends had younger or older sisters, she decided to invite them as well, and asked Chloe, my stepdaughter, whom she admired greatly, to attend as her "big sister."

"Well, Hannah," Miriam asked several days before the big event, "How many of your friends have responded to your invitation?"

"All of them!" Hannah replied, her mouth grinning from ear to ear. "My friend Candi is bringing her younger sister Clarissa; Joanna is bringing her younger sister Jackie and Angélique is bringing her older sister Amanda."

"And Chloe is arriving Friday night!" I filled in.

"That makes eight, I guess," Miriam said.

"No, nine!" Hannah corrected. "Don't forget we invited Miss Flowers also. And with you and Aunt Rachel, that makes a total of eleven."

"The room has several tables in it, so, we can either use them and have your guests seated throughout, or we can bring in two large tables and put them together to make one long one. Which would you prefer?" I asked, speaking to Hannah but looking at Miriam for her assistance in the decision.

"It would be nice if we could all be together," Hannah replied timidly, "but I don't want you to have to go to so much extra trouble, Aunt Rachel. You've been so wonderful to allow me to have all my friends here."

"Oh, it isn't any trouble at all, Hannah, believe me. And there isn't much I wouldn't do for friends as wonderful and dear as you two. Besides, it's one of the perks of owning a restaurant. You get to have things your own way!"

"So, one long table for the tea!" Miriam said, making the final decision. "And we need to finish the details for the luncheon." Once again, the three of us went over the details of the menu, the games and the décor until we were sure everything was just as Hannah wanted. Her eyes sparkled with delight as she finished the plans for what would be her first big party.

Chloe arrived on Friday night as promised and after dinner she showed me the lovely dress she had purchased as a birthday gift for her young friend. It was a lovely summer frock of pale pink cotton muslin—reminiscent of something a southern belle might wear. A wide band of sheer pink tulle went around the shoulders. It had a square neckline and fitted bodice with a full skirt.

"The last time I came to visit, I saw her admiring it in a catalog and so I asked Miriam if it was okay to buy it for her," Chloe explained.

"I think it's lovely. And pink is her favorite color, too."

"What are you and Dad giving her?" Chloe asked, nonchalantly.

"Well, that's still a surprise!" I said, refusing to divulge the secret.

"Come on, Rachel!" Chloe pleaded, her interest piqued. "You can trust me with the secret, I won't tell! I promise!"

"*Nope!*" I replied, remaining firm. "You'll find out tomorrow along with everyone else." I smiled at Chloe who grimaced at me until she broke out laughing.

The young ladies arrived promptly at noon and were escorted with great pomp and ceremony to their private dining room. The table was beautifully adorned with a powder blue tablecloth topped with silver-gray place mats. The place cards were actual seashells; each young lady's name had been written inside with pretty blue ink. We used our simple white china for the luncheon service. Miriam and I had located and purchased attractive individual teapots with matching cups and saucers, decorated in a pretty rose chintz pattern with a pale blue background. We ornamented the handles with stiff white ribbon and filled each pot with an assortment of flavorful teas. These, along with tiny teaspoons embellished with roses, the young ladies would take home as a gift from their hostess.

The center of the table sported a lovely floral creation of water reeds and calla lilies in a sand-cast ceramic pot. There were also large conch shells holding sugar cubes bedecked with tiny flowers and small pots of cream placed along the middle of the table. Elegant crystal vases held honey sticks, which could be used for sweetening. Candy confections in the design of seashells were ornately wrapped in cellophane and ribbon and sitting at the top of every place setting. The table was enchanting and the girls were bursting with excitement as they located their place card and sat down.

Hannah and her mother had worked together creating a menu everyone would enjoy. The luncheon began with hot bowls of creamy potato-cheddar soup topped with crisp bacon pieces. Fresh fruit was served along with an assortment of dainty tea sandwiches. Miriam had been teaching Hannah a great deal about the art of cooking and the guests were extremely impressed with their creations. The cucumber and cream cheese sandwiches were pleasing on a light sourdough bread; the cashew chicken on a hearty grain bread was a favorite of the younger girls; and the older ladies delighted in the creamy shrimp and onion salad served on small croissants. Mmmm...everything was scrumptious!

Hannah chose chocolate and butterscotch scones for dessert...Miriam's specialty. They were among the best I've ever eaten and the girls declared them to be delectable! Some were cut like pie wedges and others were circular; all were served with English cream and fresh raspberry curd.

The girls chatted gaily throughout the meal and enjoyed the Victorian word games Hannah prepared for them to play until it was time to open gifts. She received lovely presents: a pen and pencil set, a pretty scarf, stationary and perfume, and a new diary from Summer. The dress from Chloe was a big hit. She adored the beautiful Victorian doll Miriam had given her and promised to treasure it always. I waited patiently to present the gift that Chris and I had chosen.

After all the other gifts had been opened and enjoyed, I brought out a small but bulky parcel. A golden cloth covered the light crate now gaily decorated with a big blue ribbon. Hannah looked puzzled until she lifted the cloth covering...and then her eyes sparkled with delight. There was a small wire door in the front of the crate, which she opened immediately. Her hands went searching inside for the contents—with a squeal of joy she removed the tiny, chocolate ball of fur.

"Your mother has agreed to allow you to have a pet!" I said, happily. "And Uncle Christopher and I looked around for one we thought you would grow to love. We hope you like her!"

"Oh, Aunt Rachel, thank you!" Hannah said enthusiastically. "And thank you too, Mom. I've always wanted a dog of my own. And she's such a beautiful shade of brown!" Hannah said, giving her new pet a hug.

"She's a pretty cocoa brown!" Summer said, giving the tiny poodle a stroke.

"Cocoa brown?" Hannah repeated. "Wouldn't that be a wonderful name? Miss Cocoa Brown! I love it. That's what I'll call her: Miss Cocoa Brown." Hannah repeated it several times, affectionately stroking her new companion.

The girls all huddled around little Miss Cocoa Brown and everyone wanted to hold her. The party ended on this happy note and Hannah graciously thanked all of her guests for coming. Before we left she gave Chloe a kiss for being her big sister for the day, and I got a warm hug for giving her such a lovely gift. But her sincerest thanks and affection were reserved for Miriam, the truly wonderful mother that she loved so dearly.

~ *Chapter Sixteen* ~

The Beauty of Diversity

Chloe and I walked up the long winding driveway leading to the estate; it was always exhilarating. The briny smell of the ocean filled the crisp spring air as gulls circled overhead searching for food. Chipmunks scrambled among the bushes and into the surrounding trees. It had been a pleasant day. Hannah's birthday party had been a fun-filled success.

Christopher was out of town for a few days working on some business related to his newest movie and had taken Morgan with him. Clare remained at home with us; she enjoyed her time at the estate and wanted to see as much of her granddaughter as possible before returning home.

Chloe reached the front door first and headed toward the parlor where Clare and Isabelle usually sat in the afternoons, chatting, drinking tea and enjoying something delectable from the kitchens. Martha was in her glory cooking and baking for our household guests, constantly creating new recipes.

"Mmmm, smells good in here!" Chloe said entering the parlor through the large open doorway.

"We are enjoying the most delightful pot of vanilla maple tea!" Clare said, as Chloe bent close to give her grandmother a kiss on the cheek.

"And chocolate covered walnut brownies, as well," Isabelle added. "Would you like some?"

"Oh, no thank you, Isabelle. I couldn't possibly eat or drink another thing. How about you, Rachel?" Chloe asked as I sat down on the sofa in my favorite spot. Little Baby came alive from under the chair where she had been snoozing and I picked her up to hold in my lap.

"No thanks!" I said cheerfully. "I'm full as well. We had a lovely time at Hannah's party. What wonderful friends she has!"

"Well, tell us all about it," Clare said, while sipping a cup of the aromatic tea. "Isabelle and I were just talking about it. Tea parties are always so much fun for young girls!"

"Tea parties are enjoyed by most women, I think, regardless of age," I responded. "But you're right, these young ladies certainly had a good time."

"So did I!" Chloe chimed in while making herself comfortable on one of the big comfy chairs nearest her grandmother. Once settled in she began to share about the party, the food and the games and the gifts and what fun it was for her, being Hannah's big sister.

"I guess we can both relate to the loneliness of being an only child," she said, speaking of Hannah's dilemma of wanting a sister to share things with. "I always wanted to have a sister…I guess, now, God has blessed me with several. Your daughters, Rachel, are all older, so I have big sisters, and with Hannah being younger, I get to play the role myself. It's wonderful having a *big* family!"

I smiled. Remembering my own lonely childhood I understood her feelings completely. Families were much more important than people realized and having siblings was a great advantage—at least I thought so. Naturally, people don't always get along and it's no different with families. Brothers and sisters were often as different as night and day but, regardless of their differences, they could be a loving system of support. I realized that more and more because of my children. They didn't always agree but they loved each other tremendously and that was all that mattered.

"And Hannah has a wonderful assortment of friends," Chloe continued, "and they all seem so different...but they appear to get along famously. I guess contrasts can and do complement."

"Yes, I think that's true when the contrast involves temperament and personality, Chloe. Remember, Hannah and her friends are still children; their lives and backgrounds may be different but when they come together at school or in a social setting, their minds aren't concentrating on anything more strident than what they look like or how others think of them. All children want to be liked and accepted, just as adults do. But while I may be attracted to someone on a surface level, as an adult I would find it somewhat difficult to be in a close relationship with someone whose basic principles and ideologies were vastly different from my own."

"Ahhh, the simplicity of childhood!" Chloe murmured, with feigned chagrin. "Regardless, Hannah has great friends." She laughed out loud, and pulled her feet up under her chin as she began to tell Clare and Isabelle about each girl at the party.

"Of course, all the girls were sisters, but it was interesting to find out that they aren't all related by blood. Cándida and her sister Clarissa are biological sisters; they're from Guatemala, and they are really beautiful girls. Their hair is long and dark black and they have the most beautiful green eyes with long and curly lashes. They were very soft-spoken and polite.

"Then, there were two French girls, Amanda and Angélique. They were half-sisters, apparently they have the same mother but different fathers. Their mother is French and speaks five languages; can you imagine speaking five languages? So many Europeans do, of course, I know that. Not me, I just don't have the knack, unfortunately. The girls don't look very much alike. Amanda is tall and regal looking, has very Romanesque features, I think. While the younger girl, Angélique, has a very round, rather cherubic looking face. Her name is absolutely perfect for her.

"Then there's Joanna and Jacqueline—who insists on being called Jackie…she's the younger. They're both adopted but look a great deal alike. Tall, thin with reddish blonde hair and lovely blue eyes. Joanna has a sharp wit and is extremely outgoing. Jackie is engaging but a little more of an introvert. I think Miriam said the family came from Ireland about a year ago. I don't know all the details but they have lovely Irish accents."

"Oh, you're right, and I forgot to tell Martha that Miriam found out that they come from County Cork, which is where she hails from," I quickly added.

"Oh, there's a lovely cathedral there, in Cork, Ireland," Clare interjected. "Morgan and I have visited the area several times; it's called St. Fin Barre's. And I believe Cork Harbor is said to be one of the best natural harbors in Europe."

"It sounds as if Hannah's friends really are very diverse," Isabelle declared.

"Yes, they are, beautifully so," I affirmed, "but then, children are often more able to cross the cultural and ethnic boundaries that adults fear to traverse. And while I admire many things about my dear friend Miriam, one of the things I admire most is the way she has taught her child to love others. Regardless of what they have been through, and you know Miriam and Hannah have not had an easy life, they know how to love people unconditionally!"

Sophie Anastasia walked into the room just then to let me know Christopher was on the telephone waiting to speak to me. I left the parlor and went to the study nearby to take his call. I was sorely disappointed to hear that he would be away from home longer than expected but accepted the sad news as graciously as possible.

When I returned to the parlor the ladies were still gabbing and I decided to have a fresh cup of the vanilla maple tea that Sophie had brought while I was gone.

"Bad news?" Chloe asked. "Let me guess! Dad is going to be gone longer than expected! Right! They always do that to him. Tell him his commitment will be one week and then work to extend it to two. Things change, but then nothing really changes! Does it?"

I laughed, "I guess in some respects you are right. People like your father endeavor to please whenever possible, especially when his working a little longer or a little harder helps others. If his movies sell, people benefit. It means more people have opportunity to work and make money. Your father doesn't just think of himself. He is a big star and his name and support attracts people and projects that provide employment for a great many. He always considers his actions in light of what it will mean to others; he's a very responsible man. Anyway, he is disappointed that he won't be home to see you, especially since we have a special gift for you."

Chloe looked at me with a surprised expression on her face. "A gift for me?" she asked, a smile appearing on her face. Chloe loved surprises.

I left the room and went to the rear of the estate and to the kitchen to retrieve the package being kept there for Chloe. She jumped up in excitement when I walked into the room carrying a crate with a cover and a bow; it was almost identical to the one we had given to Hannah earlier that day.

"Your father and I thought you would enjoy this gift as much as Hannah," I said as I placed the crate in front of her seat.

Chloe sat on the floor and quietly removed the crate cover. Inside was another cuddly ball of fur. When she saw Chloe's face she quickly began to whine and yelp to be let out of the cage. Little Baby scurried down from the sofa and onto the floor to investigate the new puppy and was just as eager to meet her. Chloe opened the door of the crate and the puppy tumbled out onto the floor. She went right up to Baby who growled a bit but the puppy ignored her. Instead, she patted her face with her paws in a playful way and when Baby figured she was safe, she licked her face. All was well between the two.

"Rachel, she's wonderful!" Chloe exclaimed. "I can't tell you how much I've wanted a puppy…and she's just perfect. Oh, thank you, so much. You and Dad are just super."

"You're welcome, dear. When we went to get the puppy for Hannah we just couldn't resist getting one for you also. She's a little lighter in color and a tad bigger."

"She's sort of the color of root beer! Isn't she?" Chloe said. "And a bit sassy, too."

"Like Sassafras!" I proclaimed, "Which used to be an ingredient in root beer. Although I'm not sure that it is anymore."

"Sassafras! What a wonderful name, Sassy Sassafras! That's just what I'll call her. Suits her!" Chloe said, and she picked up the puppy for everyone to see.

Christopher and I spoke on the phone again later that evening, just before I retired to bed. Chloe had called him during the day to share her surprise and express her gratitude. I could tell he was pleased.

We talked over the events of the day, as we always did. He would share his news and concerns and I would share mine. Separate but together—regardless of space and time.

Chapter Seventeen

A Political Party

John and Abby Anderson had planned a large political fundraiser for Memorial Day weekend. They were promoting Frank Crosby, a new political candidate who had recently retired from the Navy and returned to settle in the local area from which he hailed. He had outstanding credentials and was endorsed by many to run for the United States Senate. We were eager to help him gain private support for his upcoming election.

An African-American in his late forties, Frank was a graduate of the Naval Academy at Annapolis and had served in the Navy for thirty years. He and his wife, Jennie, were warm and conscientious people who were ready to continue serving our country via the political arena. Chris and I had been to dinner with them on several occasions and readily agreed to assist Frank in his run for the senate.

A dinner party to help raise funds was scheduled in Santa Barbara at one of the larger hotel banquet rooms. Chris was slated to be a guest speaker and we called upon several of our friends, many

119

of whom were political activists, to assist in entertainment. Morgan and Clare were extremely excited to be included.

Shopping for the event was always half of the fun. Clare and I drove into Santa Barbara for the day and had a wonderful time trying on gowns. She told me they had been active in town politics when they were younger but this would be their first big political fundraiser. Naturally, she wanted to look, as Chloe might say, "smashing!"

Since the event was political and being held on Memorial Day weekend, we decided to look for something "American," that is, in red, white or blue. We visited several stores and tried on a multitude of lovely gowns before finding what we wanted.

Clare's tastes tended to be more conventional than my own so I wasn't surprised by the classic evening gown she chose. The lightweight royal blue satin was stunning with her complexion. The long fitted sleeves were made of Chantilly lace and the bodice was artfully covered with it as well; the waistline was asymmetrical and gathered slightly on one side.

"Morgan always said blue was very flattering to my complexion!" she declared while admiring her figure in the dressing room mirror. I agreed.

A beautiful gown made from a stiff flame red silk taffeta caught my eye and heart's desire. The full-length sheath silhouette was form fitting without being too tight. The strapless dress featured a wide band of white silk taffeta across the bust, which set it off nicely. I chose a shawl of white organza to wear with it and white satin heels.

The weather was agreeably warm and comfortable for the holiday weekend; May was often unpredictable. The event was listed in the social columns of most papers and promised to be highly successful as well as entertaining. We left the estate early enough to arrive at the hotel in time for hors d'oeuvres in the VIP suite, which gave us an opportunity to greet all the speakers and special guests. Morgan joined in with most of the men while Clare contentedly remained in the background. It pleased her simply to be included.

We entered the grand ballroom around 7:30 P.M. I was pleasantly surprised to see several television crews setting up for interviews in the hotel lobby and figured they were the result of the extensive newspaper coverage the rally had received. Frank Crosby was not as well known as his opposition—but hopefully, tonight's reception would change all that.

Chris, as one of the evening's guest speakers, was seated at the table on the platform with John Anderson, Frank Crosby, a congressman and two entertainers. Clare, Morgan and I sat at a table on the main floor with Abby Anderson and Jennie Crosby. Across from us at the same table were Jennie's brother-in-law, also a military man, and his wife, and John Anderson, Jr. and his wife. I sat quietly observing everyone around me; Chris's parents were as proud of him as I was! It showed in their beaming faces.

The dinner was delicious and elegantly served. We began with a course of cold broccoli soup. The evening's entree was fresh salmon served with a sauce of pureed asparagus and small white potatoes with baby carrots that had been roasted in butter and herbs. Dessert was colorful blueberry pie, with vanilla ice cream and an American flag on top.

The speeches went well and were kept short and concise. The orchestra had entertained during dinner and was now set up to perform once again for dancing. The room was abuzz with happy people. Chris and I enjoyed a few dances before he left me to talk politics and strategy with his friends. Many of the tables were empty; people seemed to be either clustered together talking or gaily dancing. When Chris went off to speak to his friends, I returned to my table and joined the only other person there.

"Your mother and father-in-law seem to be having a wonderful time!" Jennie Crosby said to me as I sat down.

I turned to watch Clare and Morgan as they danced together, their faces alight with smiles.

"They certainly are, Jennie. I'm so happy they were able to come. Can you believe they're in their late seventies? They amaze me," I replied, rubbing my sore feet.

"I hate breaking in new shoes! They always make my feet hurt."

"Oh, I know. I can't wait to go home and put on some comfortable slippers!" We both laughed.

"And I've been meaning to tell you all night," I said softly, "that I think your gown is stunning."

Jennie was wearing a very chic white sequined gown. The front had a high loose collar, which framed her lovely face and short curly black hair highlighted with just a touch of gray. The gown draped smartly down her tall lean figure; the back of it was cut in a deep V to the waist where it was embellished with a red silk rose.

"Thank you, Rachel," she beamed, "I was afraid it might be a tad too bold but Frank loved it and I really wanted to make a good impression."

We continued talking for a while and she told me a little about her life as a Navy wife until one of the hotel waiters interrupted us with a message.

"Excuse me, there is a telephone call for you, Mrs. Crosby," the waiter said quietly; it was hard to hear him above the music from the orchestra. His back turned toward me, he continued politely, "You may take it in the VIP lounge." He turned and left as abruptly as he had arrived.

"Will you excuse me for a moment, Rachel?" she asked. "I need to take this call."

"If you are going to the VIP lounge, I'll go with you," I said. "I'd like to freshen up a bit."

We walked together across the ballroom floor and I waved to Christopher who smiled back as I walked out of the room. The VIP lounge was some distance down the hall from the ballroom but on the same floor. It was empty when we arrived. The telephone was on a small table in the middle of the large room. Jennie went to answer her call and I headed toward the bathroom to freshen up my lipstick.

"Hello! Hello! Operator, is anyone there?" I heard Jennie ask. I walked to the bathroom door and looked into the suite where she was standing.

"What is it?" I asked. "Is something wrong!" I said somewhat alarmed. Jennie turned around to face me.

"How strange!" She said. "There's no one there!" She turned again and placed the telephone back into its cradle. Just as she did, the room exploded.

The force of the explosion sent me reeling backward. I was thrown against the cold bathroom wall—stunned; I sank to the ground. Debris was falling from the ceiling; something heavy hit my shoulder and tore into my flesh. Pain ripped through my arm and set me on fire. I was wedged into a corner of the room and couldn't move. Something from above fell down and landed just in front of me in the darkness. I could hear water running somewhere but it was too dark to see anything. The air was filled with dust and it became difficult to breathe…another rumbling from above…a plank fell from the ceiling and hit my head…and then…and then…I heard voices…and I saw a light. Oh, it was the most beautiful light…*Christopher!* I called. *Where are you?*

~⌒ *Chapter Eighteen* ⌒~

The City of the Great Light

"*O*h, my!" I cried in delight. "How lovely is this place!"

My eyes, which had been completely enveloped in darkness, were now exceptionally clear. My vision wasn't hazy or even blurred; I could see everything clearly. The sky was brilliantly painted a bluish green color and it sparkled like a precious jewel. It radiated resplendently and it clothed me with a feeling of warmth…and peace…oh, such a sublime sense of peace.

It couldn't be real, I thought. It must be a dream. I closed my eyes and slowly reopened them. Everything was the same…it was real but unknown to me. Lying in a meadow, peacefully contented with my surroundings, my soul began to awaken to my new environment. A scent of lavender filled my conscious mind and I rose to my knees to look for the source. Behind me, I saw multitudes of the lush evergreen shrub growing, its light purple flowers imbued with the rich fragrance I found so delightful.

Slowly, I stood to my feet and looked around. Fields upon fields of beautiful flowers loomed about me as far as my eye could see. I strolled through the luscious lavender singing softly—without a single care—until I came to what appeared to be a broad golden highway. There was no one around—not a single person came in sight as I stepped upon the glistening glass surface.

Happily I strolled down the peaceful highway enjoying the lush beauty of the countryside. I climbed up a small hill to see what was ahead; my heart leapt within me when I caught sight of a bright light shining in the distance.

"How beautiful!" I uttered to myself. And then I realized the light was emanating from a city…a city on a high hill…a city with a Great Light. It seemed somehow vaguely familiar; had I been here before?

Attracted by its beauty, I headed toward the source. A field of yellow buttercups caught my attention and I stopped to admire them. The ground trembled slightly and for the first time since my arrival I heard a noise; it was the sound of something beating like thunder. I looked across the meadow in front of me and suddenly an endless host of striking white clouds appeared on the horizon; it was thundering in the distance. Strange, I thought to myself, as I looked overhead, not a cloud in the sky above; out of curiosity I ventured closer.

I crossed the highway and stopped to admire a bed of pretty primroses—red and white in color, they attractively lined the pathway that I traveled on. Across another meadow of the most colorful poppies I ran toward the thundering clouds—fearlessly filled with excitement and eager anticipation. The clouds also moved in my direction and as they did they began to take on form. These weren't clouds at all, I realized. Amazed by their magnificence, beauty and number, I was enthralled at the sight now standing in the meadow before me; thousands upon thousands of pure white horses grazed in the fields of flowers. The breed was one I did not recognize. They stood tall like a Thoroughbred but were more powerful. Elegant like a finely trained Lippizaner, they had manes and tails, which flowed like strands of luminous silk. Awed by their majestic splendor, I simply watched them roam freely and then bound away producing another burst of thunder until they were out of sight.

When the last of the horses disappeared from view, I returned to the golden highway and continued my journey.

I traveled for what seemed like miles without growing weary until I happened upon a very singular grapevine. Leaving the main road once again I walked into the field where it was growing. Nearly six feet tall the strong woody vine grew alone, propped up by what appeared to be the remains of an old tree. Its leafy branches like tendrils grew around and were spread about the branches and the trunk. It flourished and was abundantly filled with large clusters of dark red berries. I removed one cluster to eat—the juicy pulp of the globular fruit was rich and sweet. Gloriously fortified with energy never before experienced; I continued my journey toward the city of the Great Light.

The day wore on as I walked joyously toward the light that beckoned to me. Drawing closer with every step, new objects garnered my attention. I was fascinated by a tall structure that loomed ahead of me. Brilliantly glistening in the light, I was overwhelmed by its tremendous height and beauty. The golden highway that I was on led directly up to the magnificent wall that stretched high into the sky. The wall was stunning, comprised of diamond-like gems it was crystal clear so the city of the Great Light could be seen through it.

I approached the immense gate of translucent pearl, which opened inward toward the city. As I did, a man stepped out and appeared in front of me and asked my name.

"Rachel Arielle Elliott!" I answered happily as he searched through a large book for my name.

"Welcome!" he said having found it and then he disappeared.

Eagerly I walked across the gateway that allowed me to enter into what I thought was the outskirts of the city of the Great Light. Passing by the open gate my eyes focused upon its precious substance. Close enough to touch it, my hand skidded across the lustrous pearly structure. Magnificent! Intrinsically, I knew this was a very costly gem. This one pearl alone must have cost the city a great price.

The center of the city loomed in the distance and I walked steadily toward its radiant light. Glancing behind occasionally I eventually came to realize that the walls surrounding the city were longer than I had envisioned. There were other gates besides the one

I had entered through, each with a road that appeared to proceed toward the city's center.

Peacefully walking along the golden highway, a noise drew my attention to a group of pine trees situated not far from the road. I left the path once again to investigate and was delighted to catch a glimpse of a group of deer. They quietly chewed on the verdant grasses growing on the forest floor and were not startled by my appearance. I walked closer to a small doe; she watched me approach and sauntered nearer, even allowing me to stroke her silken fur without fear. I smiled and then walked away when the doe rejoined her happy little family.

During my journey I encountered several different types of trees, all more beautiful than any I had ever seen. Their leaves were refreshingly aromatic; they emitted a fragrance unknown to me but their perfume was like a healing balm to my senses.

When I left the tiny forest and returned to the road I was surprised to see in the distance what appeared to be a hillside of homes—magnificent homes. These houses were not made with human hands; they were too glorious. They varied in color but each structure was similar in shape, some were denser than others, but all were attractively robed in garments of splendor. A lamp of prismatic beauty hung delicately in every window. The rooftops were ornamented with gold and bedecked with jewels.

Eagerly, I rushed ahead, hoping to meet up with one of the city's inhabitants. But the streets were empty when I reached the small hillside community. Walking through the center of town, I was perplexed to see the same name written above the doorway of each home. The Great Light drew me forward and, leaving the small town behind, I continued my journey onward. Once, looking back, I thought I saw the faces of a multitude staring at me—what an enigmatical place!

Farther and farther I walked; the city of the Great Light, seated high atop a mountain, could be seen more clearly with each step. In no time at all I reached the base of the mountain, which was surrounded by a magnificent garden. The picturesque beauty evoked memories of another time and place—it was Paradise.

~ *Chapter Nineteen* ~

A Majestic Throne

*E*cstasy swept over me as I continued down the golden trail, which led directly to the garden entrance. There I stopped to breathe in the fragrant bouquet of sweet perfumes. The lush foliage was resplendent with flowers in bloom, several unrivaled in splendor anywhere on earth.

A tall circular fence covered by hearty berry vines extended around the garden's border. Luscious raspberries grew wild. I picked a few to sample and found the fruit succulent and juicy; they melted in my mouth like cotton candy. Beneath the fuzzy vines the walls glistened in the light. Pushing aside the stalwart branches my eyes fell upon an unknown sight; the wall was constructed of a beautiful but hard substance—shimmering emerald.

Once inside the garden, I wandered among the verdant vegetation. There were many types of berries growing along the lengthy wall. The green and yellow gooseberries were tart but delicious nonetheless. There were rich tasting blueberries, red-fruited loganberries, deep purple blackberries and even a very rare orange colored raspberry among a diversity of other fruit-bearing plants I couldn't identify. I tasted some of every variety as I ambled along and then ventured further into the garden.

Leisurely strolling from section to section I marveled at the order of the garden. Some areas were merely ornamental and reflected the graceful beauty of an Elizabethan parterre; other sections were abounding in all types of vegetation. One path led to another and then another. The floral gardens were skillfully filled with a variety of flowers, colorful shrubs and small trees. My pleasant stroll led me around the mountain's edge. A small spring appeared to encircle the garden; it had spokes like a wheel that ran through the sections, abundantly nourishing the flora.

The air was invigorating and fresh wherever I walked but, as I left one section and entered another, the scent of roses filled my senses. I looked around but the garden was mostly green shrubs and trees. Strolling toward the fragrance I found myself entering the hub of this wonderful Paradise. There, on a small hill swathed in a bed of baby tears, was one Solitary Tree, covered with the most unusual but beautiful "Iceberg" roses, the whitest variety I had ever seen. Mesmerized by its beauty, I approached it with reverent awe; it was majestic. Touching one of the buds I was surprised that it felt softer than velvet—each blossom was a perfect creation without a single blemish. And there were no thorns! The bark was crimson brown; the leaves glistened like emeralds. Carefully, I plucked one of the buds and tenderly held it in my hands. Overwhelming love rolled over me as my spirit was filled with a new sense of revelation.

A new vision directed my journey through the gardens as I followed the circular path that wound around the base of the mountain. A noise in the bushes ahead of me caught my attention and I stopped momentarily to see a small baby lamb as he quickly scurried down the golden trail. Quietly, I pursued my gentle companion as he left the garden and headed up the hill toward the city above. The lamb moved too swiftly for me, and in moments he had disappeared in the dense foliage. Where had he gone?

The sound of running water led me farther upward and before long I came upon a mountain stream; the water was crystal clear.

Standing at the water's edge, I looked around; once again the lamb appeared. He approached the shallow stream and took a drink and then he bounded upward. I continued to follow.

As we climbed higher upon the mountain the sound of rushing water grew stronger until we reached some sort of plateau. Out from among the tall trees, my new vantage point afforded me a different view of the water's source. Above the plateau was a steep promontory; this high peak jutted out fiercely into the river that ran beneath it. Cascading streams falling off of the high mountain ahead of me in several different directions were feeding the river itself.

Here on the plateau the water pooled on the flat land before running down the hillside. Thirsty for the first time since entering the enchanted garden, I decided to take a drink of the inviting water. I walked toward the small pond, bent down and put my hand into the water. Startled by my reflection, I stopped to look more closely. My face appeared in the water—the same but different somehow— it was younger and more beautiful. I touched my cheek; it felt as soft as a piece of silk.

Standing at the water's edge, I looked intently at the vision now staring back at me. Funny that I never noticed my clothing had changed. Actually, my attire had been completely insignificant until now. Why wasn't I wearing my evening gown? What had brought me here? Questions filled my mind but try as I did, I simply couldn't remember. I looked at my reflection once again; I was now dressed in a captivating white gown. It was made of the finest linen—and around my waist was a belt of twisted gold. My long hair was draped down my back; its auburn colors more vibrant than ever before. A crown of colorful roses graced the top of my head.

"*Where am I?*" I heard myself say with wonder.

"Rachel!" A familiar voice called out to me. I looked around but saw no one.

"Papa!" I cried, "Is that you?" The voice did not answer.

The light refracting off of the falling waters created a prismatic rainbow, and then once again, the tiny lamb appeared moving ever upward. Journeying on the path toward the mountain I forged ahead, climbing steadily through the forested area until I reached the top. I turned to look back at the valley below and was mesmerized with delight. The greenery of the garden vines glistened brightly like an emerald rainbow; its berries, like little facets of colored light, twinkled gaily.

On top of the mountain the river ran next to the golden pathway. Diligently pursuing the river's source, I pushed on faithfully. The sweet sounding melodies of tiny birds filled the air and for the first time I noticed other small creatures scurrying around the mighty evergreen trees of the forest. At the river's edge ahead of me, a family of deer was quietly drinking and nibbling on the hearty grasses. Incredibly, my presence didn't appear to alarm any of the creatures that inhabited the forest.

Quite unexpectedly, I walked out from among the forest of evergreen trees into an orchard. The river continued to flow next to the golden highway but all along its edge I saw row upon row of colorful trees. Apples, oranges, pears and many other different types of fruit trees were all growing together.

Fruit abounded everywhere on the first tree I approached. Rich, succulent and beautiful fruit gaily colored the magnificent tree they grew on. More than enough to feed thousands upon thousands of hungry travelers, the fruit was irresistible. Without thinking, I reached up and plucked a piece from a low-lying limb. I lifted it to my mouth to take a bite…and then stopped. Thunder struck and a beam of lightning flew past me; startled, I dropped the fruit and it rolled away.

Intrigued, I quickly ventured forward past the rows of trees growing by the river's edge until I came to its source. There I saw a magnificent marble stairway; it rose high into the sky above. At the top was a Pillar of Smoke centered on a Golden Throne of Fire, which beamed forth the Great Light; it radiated like the brilliance of a ruby encrusted with diamonds. The Smoke fell around the Throne like the majestic robe of an Eternal King.

Awestruck, I fell to my knees—my heart pounding within, I clutched the rose in my hand to my breast. I was filled with a sense of reverential wonder. I remained still in front of the Throne. I saw no one and heard nothing except occasional peals of thunder and balls of flaming fire, which streaked forth from the Throne above.

Secure in the fact that I was indeed safe, I chanced to look behind me as a blazing ball of fire streaked by. When it was far off into the distance I could see the semblance of a shape. It looked like a man, dressed in a glistening white robe, flying through the heavens. I rubbed my eyes and looked again but he was gone. Unbelievable!

I stood to my feet and, without fear or trepidation, I stepped upon the stairway. The lamb appeared and as he did, I saw a face gentle and serene, like that of a Man. I walked up the stairs comforted by this heavenly countenance. After taking several steps I came to the realization that the stairway was really a bridge, linking the temporal structure below with the eternal structure above. It appeared also that the Throne itself was the source of the life-giving river, which flowed freely and abundantly, feeding everything beneath.

The thunder and lightning seemed to increase while the fragrance of incense filled the sky as I climbed higher and higher into the heavenly kingdom and for the first time I heard the sound of singing. The most magnificent voices bellowed out an anthem of praise and thanksgiving and I found my voice giving way to the chorus and cheerfully joining in with the melodious singers. Almost to the top, the Throne practically within my reach, a voice called out to me from below.

"Rachel!" it cried. "Don't leave me."

"Christopher!" I replied, recognizing the voice of my husband. "Where are you?"

"Rachel!" He called once again. "*I love you!*"

I turned and looked around for the face of my beloved. There, across the bridge in the valley below I saw him, for the first time. I reached out my hand toward his, we touched, and at once, my spirit rejoined my body, and I woke up.

Chapter Twenty

An Earthly Tabernacle

My mind was fuzzy and confused when I awoke from my dream. Amazingly, my hand was tightly clenched shut. When I opened it I found one single white rose bud.

Hesitantly, I shared with Christopher my experience in the City of Great Light. My mind had difficulty sorting out what was real and what was not. Had I died and gone to heaven or was it really just a dream? Chris was constantly at my side. When I asked him about the rose bud he was surprised. He never even noticed it until after I woke up. Did God send me back? Was my work here as yet unfinished? I couldn't answer those questions; I only knew that in my heart I longed to see more of that glorious kingdom.

Jennie Crosby, I sadly learned, had been killed instantly in the bombing. Several hotel employees and guests were also seriously injured; fortunately, there was only one critical injury. My wounds were not as bad as they could have been; I had a broken arm and a concussion. A laceration across my forehead, in my hairline was already mending, but my right eye was black, swollen and sore, and there were many small cuts and bruises covering my body.

Police detectives spent several hours interviewing me, once my mind had cleared and I was able to describe the events that led up to the bombing. Technically, the FBI was now in charge and they believed, as we did, that the attack was directed against Jennie Crosby in an attempt to get to her husband, Frank. My presence in the room at the time had been purely coincidental. Nevertheless, Christopher determined for safety's sake to hire a security firm to guard our property and us until the facts could be sorted out and proven. In the meantime, we endeavored to do whatever was necessary to find the culprits responsible, and see them brought to justice.

The funeral for Jennie took place at the end of the week. Christopher and I, Morgan and Clare attended together, along with our newly acquired security guards. Numerous state and local politicians and even representatives from the White House appeared to pay their respects and condemn this senseless act of violence. I wasn't surprised that the bombing had made world headlines and that reporters had flown in from all over the globe. We had been overwhelmed with requests for interviews but Christopher declined all for the present and had his publicist work with Wesley in handling the press.

On the morning of the funeral, the large Baptist church the Crosbys attended was filled to capacity. The old red brick building was bathed in floral arrangements, while Jennie's white casket, covered in delicate pink roses, her favorite, sat silently at the front of the church. Pink candles were burning in tall candelabras at either end.

The funeral was being televised across the nation and as Christopher and I walked down the long aisle toward the casket, I stopped to place a single white rose on the lid. We then sat down in the pew reserved for us.

I was somewhat angered at the throng of people both inside and out who thought of nothing more than headlines. Perhaps this was part of the problem. Insensitivity to people and their feelings made us dispassionate. Where did it come from? Why was America becoming a land of violence and hatred? What could we do to remedy what appeared to be an escalating problem?

Pastor John Edwards and his wife Sarah sat in the pew ahead of us. They were good friends of Jeremiah James, the senior pastor of this lovely old church. Next to them Frank Crosby and his family sat silently. Tears ran down his eyes, which were focused on the casket in front of him. Silently he waited for the moment he would say his final farewell to his beloved wife, Jennie. My heart ached for him!

The sound of the pipe organ filled the spacious building and then faded away as Pastor James stepped up to the tall pulpit on the left side of the church; all conversation ceased. Jeremiah was a small African-American man in his late fifties; he looked much younger, only a few strands of hair graying at his temples spoke differently. Tenderly, he opened up the pages of a well-worn Bible and he read:

" 'I am the resurrection, and the life: he that believeth in me, though he were dead, yet shall he live: And whosoever liveth and believeth in me shall never die.'"[6]

"These are words of comfort spoken by our Lord and Savior, Jesus who is called the Christ, our Beloved Messiah. He too wept over the loss of a dear friend.

"Our hearts are heavy," he began somberly, tears glistening in his eyes, "and they are bound together in pain…for we are grieving the loss of our dear friend, Jennie Crosby. And while we will miss her dearly, we take joy in the knowledge that today, she is sitting with the angels, in heavenly places." A chorus of hallelujahs rang out from church members.

"Life is a vapor…it is really nothing more than a brief breath of air. And while we mourn the loss of our dear sister, Jennie, we have come here today to celebrate her life and remember her for the good woman she was. Jennie was a woman of great joy. She gave her best; she served her husband, her friends and her community with diligence and with grace. She gave without expectations; she loved unconditionally; she forgave freely. She was a blessing to all whom had the pleasure of knowing her even a little."

Pastor James spoke well of Jennie, divulging to the audience the intimate knowledge he had of this extraordinary woman. The sound of sobbing filled the church when one after another of her close friends stepped up to the podium to tearfully share moments from her life. Sarah Edwards was the last person to speak. Slowly she walked to the front of the church and ascended the platform; her petite frame was dwarfed by the immensity of the room. Silence fell over the audience.

"Jennie Crosby and I were good friends and I loved her dearly," Sarah began calmly. She was a gifted speaker; eloquent and demure, she spoke from the heart and her audience was noticeably affected. "I don't believe I've ever met another woman who loved life as much as she did. Today, I'd like to honor her memory, by sharing with you all just a small portion of her heart." Sarah glanced over at Frank who nodded his approval as tears streamed down his face.

"Jennie celebrated life; she had a great respect for people, regardless of race or creed. She knew that every person matters; that each of us has been divinely created and blessed with a unique gift to share.

"Jennie treated each day as a new beginning with new opportunities to do good. She wanted to impact the world in a positive way; she lived every day knowing it might be her last, endeavoring not to waste one precious moment. She rejected strife, bitterness and self-pity because they lead to destruction. She had problems and experienced pain just like everyone else, but she refused to allow them to hinder how she lived each day. Instead, she chose to learn from her mistakes without constantly looking back and in so doing she avoided becoming their victim. She knew that life has to be lived one day at a time—today is all we can be sure of because tomorrow is guaranteed to no one.

"A few weeks ago Jennie and I attended a women's luncheon together. She was the featured speaker; it was her last public address and I'm so thankful now that I was able to attend. Her words left an indelible print on my soul. I'd like to share a portion of what she said at that meeting." Sarah closed her eyes momentarily as if searching the memory of her mind for just the right words.

"Jennie looked around the fancy ballroom brimming with a montage of beautiful women nonchalantly sitting in gorgeous clothing and she said, 'Ladies, how lovely you all look today. You sparkle like diamonds and glitter like gold; my, oh my, don't I feel old!' Everyone laughed out loud at her charming little rhyme. Jennie continued, 'Aging gracefully is a topic few seem to relish speaking about. Actually, growing old is natural and not to be feared. And if we didn't live in such a throwaway society, perhaps we wouldn't dread it at all.

" 'What is the body anyway? It's something of a suit of clothes—a house of sorts. The body is an earthly tabernacle—destined to fade away? Honestly, girls we're nothing more than cleverly constructed dust!'"

"Well, the room erupted in laughter again and I knew Jennie had captured the attention of every person present.

" 'Oh, you know I'm right,' she continued. 'Of course, some of that dust looks pretty darn good, but most of it needs plenty of work and continual repair. And the truth is, most of us, if given the opportunity, would love to just slip off this old dusty suit of clothes and step right into a newer model. One that requires a lot less maintenance, one that won't grow old and wrinkled and worn out. Well the Good News is, ladies, that one day, we will all own just such a garment. We will dwell in a new tent—a new home in fact, one not made from earthly dust but one that will be specially fitted for us by God Himself.[7] This is what the Lord meant when He said,

" 'In my Father's house are many mansions: if it were not so, I would have told you. I go to prepare a place for you. And if I go and prepare a place for you, I will come again, and receive you unto myself; that where I am, there ye may be also.' "[8]

" 'And ladies, the truth is we spend just a little too much time on these old fading tents, forgetting that they are only containers. Receptacles designed to hold our living essence; the Spirit of a Holy God. Let's work on making that the most beautiful part of our being.'"

"This was Jennie's message; this was Jennie's life. It was not without difficulties. She simply chose to accept the good with the bad; to work to change what she could change; to learn to live nobly with what she could not. Day by day, week by week, year by year, she celebrated life and lived it with dignity." Sarah quietly stepped down from the platform and returned to her seat while Pastor James returned to the podium.

"Today, we pay our last respects to our dear friend Jennie and we say good bye. Death can be tragic; it needn't be in vain. Our hope is that as we leave this place today, we leave it as people changed…perhaps challenged to begin a new way of life. Challenged to rise above hatred; challenged to love the unlovely; challenged to forgive the unforgivable; challenged to extend mercy to those who do not deserve mercy. For in giving to others, we receive unto ourselves."

The pastor stepped down from the pulpit and the choir began to sing "Amazing Grace." At the end people began to file out of the church and we followed, walking somberly to our car to drive to the cemetery.

The prayers at the internment were the traditional "ashes to ashes and dust to dust," that we hear so often and never really contemplate until we are touched by the grief of death ourselves. I personally was struck by the truth that my life had continued while Jennie's had come to an end. Providence continued to watch over me and to guide my life; my journey would go on. But Pastor James was right; I left the church changed. Jennie's death had affected me, perhaps more so than even her life, as good as it was. Why? I asked myself silently while we drove home along the highway. I found a simple answer: Because it compelled me to alter my own course of direction.

~ *Chapter Twenty-One* ~

Changes, Times and Seasons

A few weeks after Jennie's funeral, Christopher left with Morgan and Clare to accompany them on their return trip home to England. He had delayed several business meetings and cancelled engagements because of my accident and its investigation and refused to depart until he could be better assured of my safety. He was able to leave once security was in place at the estate and, regardless of my reassurance that I would be all right, he was determined to condense his trip and return quickly.

"I'll be fine, Chris!" I declared, just before he left for the airport. "I'm on the road to recovery; my broken arm is healing and I'm surrounded by a flock of mothering hens!" He laughed, kissed me on the lips and flew out the front door to join Morgan and Clare who were already in the car outside. I waved at them as they drove down the long winding road to the highway. It took only moments for them to completely disappear.

My arm ached and was the cause of considerable discomfort but I couldn't complain. I had been extremely fortunate. The wound on my head had left only a small scar and was barely visible under my thick auburn bangs. My black eye, bumps and bruises had practically disappeared.

The investigation into the hotel bombing continued and I was interviewed and re-interviewed by the FBI and other officials a multitude of times. During one visit, photographs of several different men were produced for me to look through; would I be able to identify any? I wondered. How much of the waiter's face had I seen? Would it be enough to make a positive identification?

Flipping slowly through a small packet of pictures supplied by an agent, I stopped abruptly. "This one!" I said, surprised, but without hesitation.

"Are you sure?" the agent asked.

I looked at the photograph again, this time more carefully. "Yes, he's the one who called Jennie to the telephone. I'm positive," I replied with ease. "I wouldn't say so if I couldn't be sure." The agent was pleased; he had been hired just two weeks prior to the bombing and was their key suspect. Finally, they had a bona fide lead they could pursue.

Frank Crosby telephoned often to see how I was and during one conversation he let me know that he had decided to continue with the election.

"It's what Jennie would have wanted me to do," he stated sadly. "And if elected, I'll do whatever I can to change the direction of the country. I know that I won't be able to do it alone…but I believe God will be with me."

"Thank you, Frank," I said, knowing it would be difficult for him. "Don't worry, you won't be alone. We will continue to pray for God's mercy…perhaps He will intervene and heal our land. And we will do all we can to help as well. I promise!"

Christopher, regardless of his determination to return quickly, was gone for weeks, much longer than he had planned. While I reassured him that all was well at home I still missed him tremendously. Summer was here; the roses planted throughout the estate were in bloom and I longed for his companionship on my nightly walks amidst the fragrant flowers. The rose gardens, surrounding the gazebo just beyond the Tea Cottage, were fabulous; they were among the most spectacular in the county. Landscaped beautifully in what had once been our old horse paddocks were the ruby red rose trees that Christopher had given me for a previous Valentine's Day. They were magnificent.

The Tea Cottage was open to visitors all year but the lovely terraced gardens below it were only open in the summer. Tall white colonnades with heavy wooden planks running overhead made a lovely gazebo. Verdant foliage grew up alongside the colonnades and hung loosely over the tops of the wood. The sunlight filtered through the openings and glistened on the quaint cobblestone floor. It was a charming place and increasingly popular with local residents. White wrought iron tables and chairs filled the dining area. Flowers spilled over the planters and hanging pots that abounded throughout the gazebo, while the fragrant perfume from the roses filling the gardens nearby permeated the air.

Wherever I went my new security guards followed; they hindered my personal life and I was beginning to feel suffocated by their presence but there was nothing I could do. Christopher had been very insistent about the need for our protection, especially now during the criminal investigation into the bombing. I sometimes wondered if life would ever be normal again.

Lunching with Noah and Miriam under the vine-covered gazebo was a pleasant diversion; today in particular we enjoyed the bright summer sun and a cool ocean breeze. We sipped on cherry cokes and devoured delicious pita sandwiches filled with turkey, avocado, tomatoes and sprouts. I even indulged in a raspberry tart drizzled with chocolate for dessert. It was heavenly.

Conversing about the growth of the business was natural and as we ate we talked about our different endeavors. The new kitchen was almost finished and Noah was preparing to move into his larger office. He and his assistant, Woody, continued work on our first catalog and had sample baskets now on display in our boutique in the Tea Cottage. Miriam and I were engrossed in the Tea Cottage Cookbook to raise funds for Tabitha's House; it was more fun than work and rewarding as well.

"There's Hannah!" Miriam said as she watched her daughter exit the Victorian and look in our direction. Hannah waved at us and we waved back as she hurried up the hill with Miss Cocoa Brown, to take their afternoon walk along the edge of the orchards.

I quickly scanned the surrounding area, concerned for Hannah's safety even though I knew that security was posted inconspicuously around the estate compound.

"Miriam," I said, hesitantly, "I'm not so sure it's completely safe for Hannah to go walking alone anymore."

"Don't worry, Rachel. We got her a cellular phone, which she carries with her and she knows that she isn't to go very far from the house. We've told her to be careful."

"I spoke with security as well," Noah said, "to let them know what time each day she would be out walking; they're watching her wherever she goes, Rachel."

"Still!" I sighed, words choked back in my throat.

"We've spoken to everyone on staff at the Tea Cottage and the Victorian," Noah said, "emphasizing the need for extra safety precautions as well as security. And we've had the head of security go over reporting procedures and they've also given training. I think we are as safe as can be expected, Rachel. There isn't much else we can do."

"I know," I said grievously. "I just want to be extra careful. Hannah is so young! Perhaps this isn't the best place for her anymore." It pained me to say so.

Noah looked at Miriam and then at me.

"What?" I asked.

"Rachel," Noah said, quietly, "I've been meaning to talk to you about this for a while now."

"No, let me!" Miriam interjected, smiling at the blond curly haired man she sat next to. His tan face smiled back and taking her hands in his, Miriam said quickly,

"Noah and I are getting married!"

"Oh, Miriam," I cried out, "I'm so happy for you." I gave her a hug with my one good arm shielding the broken bone in the other one from harm. "And of course for you also, Noah. Does Hannah know?"

"Yes and no; at least she knows we are making plans but that we haven't set the date. We spoke with her about it because what we decide affects her life as well as ours and we wanted her approval. We asked her not to discuss it with anyone until we spoke to you and Chris first…especially about work." Miriam hesitated and from the look in her eyes, I could tell she was facing a difficult dilemma.

"We've found a little house up the coast that we would like to buy." Noah said. "It's right on the ocean and something that we think Hannah will love. I won't be far from work but Miriam…" He stopped. The problem wasn't hard to anticipate.

"Won't be able to continue working at the Inn," I finished for him. "Miriam, that's okay. Did you think I wouldn't understand?" I asked.

"Oh, Rachel," she said with a huge sigh, "you've been so wonderful to me and to Hannah…to all of us really, Noah as well. This is the first real home we've had for a long time and I think the first place where I have ever been truly happy. We didn't want you to think we were ungrateful for the opportunities you've given us. We'd never do anything to hurt you."

"Oh, Miriam, don't you think I know that? Why, it's only natural for you to want to settle down and make a home for Noah and Hannah. I think it will be wonderful for all of you, especially now. I'm sure Hannah must be terribly excited and I'm surprised she was able to keep such a well guarded secret," I said with a laugh.

"Oh, that has been no easy task, believe me," Miriam answered with a huge smile. "Hopefully, the wedding will take her mind off Miss Summers; you know she's getting married and moving overseas. Hannah is happy for her but sorry to see her go. I know how she feels because I'll miss her as well. And…I think it makes her feel a little insecure," Miriam said almost mournfully.

"It's always hard to part with people you love," I replied. "Especially when you're young…I'm not sure if it's easier as we get older or if we just become more aware that life moves on and somehow we learn to adjust to it. In time, Hannah will too."

"Yes, she will," Miriam responded somberly. "Fortunately, Miss Flowers will be here for a while since her fiancé is in the Navy and not scheduled to depart until the fall. So, they will be going to her home in San Jose first to be married and then they will be leaving for Europe afterward. I think he will be stationed there for two or three years. I've thought about giving her a little bridal shower before she goes if you don't mind."

"What a wonderful idea! Of course I don't mind and I'll help you with anything you need. We can have it here in the gardens if you like or you can use one of the larger rooms in the cottage. Just let me know."

"Oh, Rachel, thank you. You're always so generous; I wish there was some way I could repay you."

"Miriam, friends don't incur debts; your friendship has been all the gift I could ever want or need." Tears began to stream down from her large blue eyes and mine were filled to overflowing as well. "Why are we both crying?" I admonished. "This is a time to be joyful. What plans have you made for your own wedding and what can I do to help?"

"Well," Noah began, "the house can be ours in about sixty days I think. We'll need to make a few changes and I guess that could take up to another month and then moving in shouldn't take long. So, we thought a small wedding around Thanksgiving would be good. We decided not to have a large reception, just cake and punch at the church after the service. We want to spend our honeymoon in the Cayman Islands and we hoped that Hannah could stay with you while we do."

"Of course she can!" I said enthusiastically. "Christopher and I will plan something special for her while you are gone. Just leave it up to him! He's terribly creative." Simultaneously, we looked around the grounds at the dozens of flowering roses he had purchased and we laughed.

"But can we trust him?" Miriam chuckled.

"Well, that remains to be seen!" I responded with delight.

One of the waiters walked to our table and I asked him to bring each of us a cup of fresh coffee; mocha caramel was the flavor of the day and it was delicious.

"Do you have any thoughts about your replacement, Miriam? I'd like you to suggest someone from our current staff if you can.

Otherwise, Noah will have to begin to set up interviews. Or, maybe," I snickered, "I should call Sarah Edwards. She has an uncanny ability to find real treasures...diamonds in the rough." Miriam and I both smiled. How could either of us ever forget our first meeting, arranged by our dear pastor's wife?

"Well, Rachel," she began, contemplatively, "I think there's another rare jewel here, right under our noses. I know Noah agrees and I think even Martha would approve."

"Really!" I said. "Who?"

"*Sophie!*" They replied in unison, chuckling.

"She's a little on the fiery side," Noah said, "but one of the hardest workers I've ever seen."

"And she learns fast," Miriam chimed in. "She's really very talented and I think she could be a special blessing to you... and... that you could be a blessing to her."

"Really?" I asked, sipping my hot cup of coffee. "In what way?" I asked, quizzically.

"In the way you bless everyone, Rachel! With the unconditional love and acceptance you give so freely to everyone you meet. Just think about it," she said with a smile. I replied that I would.

~ *Chapter Twenty-Two* ~

The Highway of the Heart

Christopher was still in London the following week when Miriam and I met together in my office, now located in the downstairs study, to discuss the future. Her engagement to Noah had been announced and the simple diamond engagement ring she wore was lovely. Hannah proudly shared the news with everyone at her school and she was ecstatic when Miriam and Noah took her to see the new beachfront home they were buying for their new family.

"Rachel," Miriam said, continuing our conversation about her final days as manager of the bed-and-breakfast, "I'll be able to stay on as manager until someone is trained well enough to take over, you know that! And even after you've found a permanent replacement, I'd be glad to fill in anytime you need me to. I don't plan to retire completely, although I would like to shift the focus of my attention elsewhere."

"Well, I am still contemplating your recommendation of Sophie. You are right about one thing; she is definitely a hard worker. I spoke to Martha and Patricia about her work here and they both gave their approval."

"Well, that's good, isn't it?" Miriam replied, sipping a cup of herb tea.

"Yes, it is. But they also both agreed that she has a temper which needs to be curbed," I said. Miriam raised her eyebrows a little, something I found she often did when expressing either mercy or patience.

"She's still young!" She commented sincerely. "But she has tremendous potential." Miriam sat very still for a moment, her mind in contemplation. "Something appears to be holding her in bondage, Rachel. I don't know what it is, but I believe once she's freed from it, she'll blossom like a rose…. and honestly, I think you're just the person to help free her…"

"Hmmm! Another butterfly concealed in an old cocoon, huh?" I laughed but Miriam only smiled and nodded her head. "Well, we'll see. Being manager is a big responsibility and she is young. I need to pray about it and talk to Christopher once he returns home. And then, I'll have a conversation with Miss Sophie Anastasia.

"Now, about your plans for leaving," I began, switching subjects. "Do you want your last day to be before or after the wedding? How long do you want to stay?"

"Well, I was thinking I'd stay until the week before Thanksgiving, if that works out for you. Then, I'll have time to move my things into the new house and get Hannah settled so when we return from our honeymoon, everything will be ready for us."

"Okay," I replied, "that sounds like a workable plan. As a special wedding gift from Christopher and me, I am going to pay you through the end of the year. And I want Noah to take the month of December off as well. His assistant, Woody, will be able to handle everything while he is gone."

"Oh, Rachel," she cried, "Thank you so much! Thank you for just everything." Miriam's eyes glistened with teardrops of joy and my heart was glad and sad at the same time.

"I'll miss you, Miriam. More than you will ever know, I will miss you both. I love Hannah, and I love you too."

"Rachel, it isn't the end of our friendship," she whispered.

"No!" I replied, "It's the beginning of a new phase of our friendship. And we'll still see one another, but things change, Miriam. People move about; they come and go into and then out of our lives. I've had to learn to live with that—losing the people we love as they journey along fulfilling God's destiny. It isn't easy to let go…like Hannah losing Miss Summers, it makes us all feel a little insecure."

"I know! I'm even a little afraid of getting married again, even though I believe life with Noah will be wonderful. I think I'm a little apprehensive about leaving here. My heart is torn in two directions," she said, hands raised pointing away from each other. "I love Noah and I love this place…it's hard to explain because I'm not sure I understand myself but I guess I feel as though I were born again here. Prior to coming to live here, I was like a little caterpillar trembling inside of a dark cocoon afraid of the outside world…I was filled with so much fear…and I had little hope of a bright future for me or for Hannah then. Now, everything has changed…my journey through the darkness has ended. I've spread my wings and am flying high into the future and the hope that God, in His infinite mercy, has seen fit to give me. And now I want to do whatever I can to give back to others what I have acquired along the way.

"I wasted too many years!" she said somberly. "But I'm not going to let the past victimize me any longer. I have a burning desire in my heart now, to make a difference in this community. One person can really make a difference, Rachel. That is something I learned from you, perhaps it will be your greatest legacy, whether you realize it or not. You invested your life into mine; now I will invest my life into others."

"You've always had a servant's heart, Miriam," I said with admiration. "Only now you have the ability to use it."

"I hope so…because now that I won't have to work, I want to be able to use my time and talent in a way that profits others; I've already spoken to Noah about it. I just wanted to ask your opinion first before making a final decision. Rachel, I think I am going to talk to Sarah Edwards about taking over her position at Tabitha's House. What do you think?"

"What a wonderful idea, Miriam." I smiled. "God is amazing, isn't He? Here we were, wondering who would be able to step in and fill Sarah's shoes managing Tabitha's House and He had already set you aside for the task.

"My Papa used to say that we should follow our dreams. He told me that God has a unique plan for each of us…sometimes we get off course and muddy it up a bit but he believed as I do that when we commit ourselves to Him, He guides us down the paths of His choosing. Then He gives us the desires of our hearts because He puts them there to begin with. The Lord will give you the grace you need to walk down the highway of the heart, wherever it leads. As far as Tabitha's House goes, there couldn't be anyone better suited to serve there, than you."

"Thanks, Rachel. I certainly hope so."

We enjoyed our time together, made some plans for the bridal shower she wanted to give for Miss Flowers and talked of her own wedding as well. We scheduled time to go dress shopping for her bridal attire.

I knew I was going to miss Miriam and Hannah a great deal. But even I realized their leaving was a part of God's plan for me also. My parched days of walking in the dry valleys of loneliness were, for the moment anyway, past. Who knew where the future would lead me? People would continue to come and go in my life; of that I was certain. My years of suffering had taught me a great deal and one thing I found to be especially true—the stronger in God I grew, the easier the trials were to undergo. Of course, I also realized that joy on earth would never be complete and that all my hopes and dreams would only be fully realized in heaven.

A visit to my doctor the following week confirmed what I knew inside, that I was healing. The cast on my arm could be removed shortly and then I would be going to physical therapy to strengthen the muscles. The scar on my forehead was a lasting reminder of the bombing incident that had taken Jennie Crosby's life. The greatest frustration we were all facing was that no one had been apprehended for the crime, even though the police and the FBI were pursuing several suspects.

When Christopher finally returned home he plunged head first into fund-raising activities for Frank Crosby, who was doing well in the polls, support for him was gaining every day and it appeared he had a very good chance at being elected.

August passed without much notice and while I was busy with therapy on my arm, Christopher continued to assist Frank in his campaign. They worked well together; Chris's celebrity status opened many doors where Frank was then able to get his message of reform out to the public.

The murder of Frank's wife had been televised around the world; it made him more newsworthy than ever. Many of the networks were now broadcasting his speeches and debates as his popularity increased and he gained in the polls.

One Friday night when Chris and I were at home alone we watched Frank on a cable news network, as he defended several of his political stands. The interviewer asked,

"Mr. Crosby, don't you believe that your value system leans too far to the right for you to be able to properly govern the liberal voters of California, many of whom believe you to be intolerant of those who oppose your viewpoint?" His answer was brilliant.

"My wife and I both dreamed," he began somberly, "that one day we would be an integral part of a New America, one in which any man or woman, regardless of race or creed, would be treated with equal dignity and respect.

"The Founding Fathers in 1776 wrote in the Declaration of Independence words, which many of us still believe. They said,

> We hold these truths to be self-evident, that all men are created equal, that they are endowed by their Creator with certain unalienable Rights, that among these are Life, Liberty, and the pursuit of Happiness.[9]

"People have immigrated to the United States for hundreds of years to find this new and better way of living, to have freedom of expression as well as freedom from persecution.

"There are those who seek to attack my system of values and others who have tried to accuse me of being intolerant SIMPLY because I hold conservative views based upon the teaching of the Bible. When, may I ask, did it become a crime in America to be a conservative? When did it become a crime to believe in moral accountability? Why," he continued, "am I and others like me, demonized in the press and labeled as intolerant solely because we have differing opinions? Does tolerance reach in only one direction? My wife was murdered because I am a strong conservative running for public office. Is this the type of America we want? I am a decent, law-abiding man. I have spent most of my life in service to my country. I still believe it is the greatest country on earth. But it is time for change. If others believe that as I do, I hope they will consider voting for me."

Frank answered direct questions about his ideas and expressed himself well, always in a clear and articulate manner. His opposition was fighting a fierce campaign attempting to discredit him whenever possible; fortunately, Frank was a man of virtue. He lived what he believed and no one could prove otherwise. People believed him and his numbers in the polls continued to climb upward.

In September, there was a slight break in the bombing case, which gave us hope. The FBI agent in charge of the investigation informed us that one of their key suspects was now in custody. After following up on an anonymous tip, a hotel busboy had been pursued and finally apprehended in Seattle, Washington. When interviewed, he denied having any prior knowledge of the bomb. He said that he had been recruited and paid well to stand guard in the hotel hallway keeping everyone away from the VIP suite. When the bomb went off he panicked and ran. Fear drove him into hiding until he heard of the death of Mrs. Crosby; it was then he decided to leave the country. Realizing that people would be looking for him at the Mexican border he headed north instead. He knew his picture had been in the papers so he attempted to disguise his appearance. He purchased hair dye and new clothes in a small town south of Olympia, the place of the anonymous tip. According to the agent, it appeared he was telling the truth. Any additional information they gained only led to more dead ends, and frustration for justice settled in once again.

Chapter Twenty-Three

A Holiday in New York

Miriam and Noah were basking in the excitement of their engagement as they busied themselves making plans for the wedding. The house on the beach had been purchased and was now in escrow. News of their impending nuptials had traveled quickly among our small estate family and up and down the coastal area of our tiny community. They were quickly inundated with gifts and flowers from many of their friends and well-wishers.

Sophie was chosen as Miriam's replacement and was already in training for her new position. She didn't have Miriam's experience but she was energetic and diligent so I agreed to give her a chance.

Feelings could be so complex and mine at times were an indecipherable mixture. My heart grieved for my loss but rejoiced for my friends' gain; I knew they would all be greatly missed. My tender affections for them were similar to those that I felt when my own children married. They were now all living their own separate lives—some too far from the place I called home. Miriam and Hannah had filled part of the void I felt within when one by one my daughters married. I would indeed miss the fun and fellowship we had all shared living here above the beautiful blue ocean.

Fall had settled in quickly this year and the weather was more stormy than normal. We had unusual bouts of rain in both August and September; it reminded me of the year of El Niño and the terrible floods and devastation it had caused. I would never forget that terrible day when part of the mountain above Highway 101 broke loose and slid down onto the road below. A huge boulder pounded down the mountain and into a northbound truck. It skidded across the highway and into Hannah's school bus, which was traveling in the opposite direction. The heavy earth cascaded downward like a giant waterfall and the mudslide of dirt and rock quickly covered both the immobilized truck and bus under its slimy ooze. Christopher, Miriam and I had been following closely behind, after returning from a food delivery to the local mission. Propelled into action, Christopher was the first to reach the stranded bus and managed to save not only the children, but the injured passenger of the truck as well. A shiver ran through my spine every time I thought of him jumping out of the rear bus window just before it finally collapsed under the weight of the heavy earth.

Today, it was cold and wet and windy. I sat in front of the big fireplace in the parlor, my favorite retreat, reading a mystery by Agatha Christie. Lightning and thunder had filled the sky intermittently all day. Christopher was away, working on a new film, this time in Montana. I had grown quite used to his coming and going and occasionally, we traveled together, so I could be with him while he worked. But my concern for Isabelle and her failing health made it difficult at times for me to leave. Another bout with pneumonia kept me close to home to watch over my childhood nanny and beloved friend.

When the old grandfather clock in the corner chimed, I looked up and was surprised to find it was already noon. I put my book aside and headed out into the kitchen where I knew Martha was busy preparing lunch. She had a tray all ready for Isabelle, which I myself took upstairs to her room.

Isabelle slept lightly and I didn't want to startle her so I knocked lightly on the door before entering.

"Come in!" she said in her slightly squeaky voice.

"How do you feel?" I asked, as I entered and placed the tray on the table nearest her bed. She was warmly clothed in a soft flannel nightgown gaily covered with pink roses while mounds of her satin comforter surrounded her frail body. Patrick maintained a warm fire in her fireplace for her. Even though the house had been completely renovated with gas heating, the large old rooms could still get chilly. The fire flickered softly behind the ornate metal grate and kept the room comfortably warm. The curtains were open slightly and outside the gray skies streaked first with flashes of white lightening followed by heavy peals of thunder. Boom! Boom! It rang out loudly.

"Do you think old Hendrick Hudson and his mates are playing a game of nine pins?" Isabelle asked, with a smile.

"Oh, they couldn't be this far west, Isabelle. Surely, they can only be found in the Catskill Mountains and then, on a summer's day." I laughed as I fondly recalled the story of Rip Van Winkle and the joyful trip we took to New York during one winter vacation.

I fluffed up Isabelle's pillows before placing her lunch tray in front of her and gently sat down next to her on her bed so we could talk while she ate her lunch.

"The thunder always reminds me of *Rip Van Winkle* by Washington Irving," Isabelle said, as she slowly swallowed a mouthful of the split pea soup from the bowl on her tray.

"Papa did love to read it on rainy nights like this, didn't he? And *The Legend of Sleepy Hollow* was a favorite of mine also; he always read with such realism that he made the stories come alive. I'm glad that Papa encouraged us to read so much," I said, "and to play board games as well. I wish parents spent more time today enjoying those types of family recreation."

"Mmmm, I agree. At least you continued the practice with your girls while they were growing up, Rachel."

"They loved reading the Nancy Drew mysteries," I laughed. "Guess they got that from me, I enjoyed them as well. I think reading helps children learn to develop their imagination while learning to think for themselves…and playing games teaches good sportsmanship and something of the need for community…more or less how to work together harmoniously."

"And it was such good fun!" Isabelle said emphatically.

"So many happy evenings in front of the fire listening to Papa's resonant voice. I can still hear him in my mind," I said reflectively. "You know the saying 'less is more' is really true. People have more things today, but less time to enjoy them; we're all *too* busy filling our lives with things that really don't matter a great deal. I believe we all enjoyed life more when everything was simpler, including pleasures, with more time together to share them."

"Do you remember the wonderful trip we all took to New York, Rachel?" Isabelle asked, almost reading my mind.

"Of course!" I declared. "How could I *ever* forget seeing the Statue of Liberty for the first time? It was inspiring." I walked over to Isabelle's library of books, housed on the bookshelf nearest her small writing table and removed an old photo album that I knew was nestled in among her well-worn collection of classics.

"How's the soup?" I asked, returning to my comfortable spot on her bed.

"Delicious!" she responded with more enthusiasm for eating than I had seen in a while. "And the corn bread is yummy, too," she added while munching on a bite, "Martha is such a wonderful cook. This whipped honey butter she makes is always so light and fluffy, it's scrumptious!"

"You must be feeling better," I said, smiling and happy to see her so cheerful.

I flipped open the old album carefully and turned the dog-eared corners of the pages until I arrived at the section that began our trip to New York. There she was, Miss Liberty! Standing tall and beautiful in New York Bay. We had taken pictures of her while on the ferry; the lady's strong right arm holding the torch of freedom high into the skies for all to see.

"It was overcast that day, and although it didn't rain, it was cold!" I said, pointing to the first picture. The dark clouds hovered over New York Bay.

"Typical for New York in December, Rachel. I remember feeling so proud when we walked through the visitor's center there on the island. Having come from France myself, so many years before, it

meant a lot to me. This beautiful gift had come from my native homeland to the people of the United States my new adopted country.

"The sculptor, Frédéric Bartholdi, designed the statue after the
Colossus of Rhodes. I didn't know that until our visit; or that the
seven pointed headdress she wears stood for the seven continents."

"And the pedestal the statue stands on is unique in its configu-
ration too," I remarked, admiring the beauty of it while allowing my
mind to gently flow backward in time.

When Isabelle finished her lunch I placed the tray on the coffee table so we could continue to look through her photo album
together, commenting on each picture as we took a pleasant little
journey into our past.

Grandfather had taken the three of us, Grandmother, Isabelle
and me, with him to see the sights of New York, the birthplace of my
mother, just a few years after the tragic death of my parents and my
only brother, Riley.

We spent a few days in the city, seeing the sights. I enjoyed the
movie and stage show we saw at Radio City Music Hall and our visit
to the Empire State Building, made eternally famous as a ren-
dezvous for lovers in the movie, *An Affair to Remember*. I loved the
day we spent at Rockefeller Center, which was so beautifully decorated for the Christmas holidays. A magnificent tree hovered over
the statue of Atlas and was gaily lit with bright colored lights and
dusted with the white flurries of a freshly fallen snow.

Grandfather had taken several pictures of St. Patrick's Cathedral because of its Gothic architecture; I still had them in one of my
own albums. Isabelle's photos showed the beauty of its tall spires
which towered over three hundred feet into the sky. An impressive
Gothic structure, it is also one of the world's largest cathedrals.

Turning another page of Isabelle's photo album was like turning a page in a history book, only this was a chronicle of our history—Isabelle's and mine. There were pictures of Central Park, the
Bronx Zoo and the botanical gardens. I had forgotten how many
things we had crammed into our three weeks' visit.

When our holiday in the city came to an end, the four of us
headed north to spend several days in the Hudson River Valley; the

area was rich in history, the Hudson itself having played an important part in the American Revolutionary War.

We stayed in Tarrytown, visiting such sights as Philipsburg Manor and the Old Dutch Church, which was not only the oldest church in the state of New York, but it had received its name from Washington's Irving classic tale, *The Legend of Sleepy Hollow*. Sleepy Hollow Cemetery, which was adjacent to the church, had the graves of the renowned Irving, William Rockefeller and Andrew Carnegie among the Old Dutch family names—some reputed to be the inspiration behind Irving's characters.

Visiting Sunnyside, the delightful home of the author, had been a special highlight for us. Having so often enjoyed his stories, we wanted to see the place that inspired him.

The snapshots of Sunnyside were old and faded, as the others had been, and somewhat yellowed around the edges, but that did not detract from the enchanting and picturesque riverside home. The seventeenth-century stone cottage, which Irving purchased in 1835, was enlarged and remodeled to suit his tastes. The stepped gable entrance was covered with wisteria.

The guides who took us through Sunnyside were dressed in mid-Victorian costumes and offered visitors freshly baked cookies from the kitchen. The house was decorated for the Christmas holidays. A lovely fir tree stood in one corner of a room gaily bedecked with long strands of popcorn and small colorful candy canes. Garlands of greenery and scarlet ribbons hung from the doorways, and filled the rooms with the scent of fresh pine.

Irving's magnificent oak writing desk stood out in a room filled with shelves of books. On top were his writing implements, along with some Moorish daggers, which he obtained during the years that he lived in Spain.

I loved his bedroom, which was relatively plain. A small table with a picture and some books sat against one wall. The four poster bed was covered with a white canopy and a navy and white patterned coverlet; a candlestick burned brightly on the end table.

Inside the dining room, the table was set for a feast. Decanters of wine, a basket of fruit, candles burned along the center of it, sprigs of evergreen and holly berries decorated each place setting.

Page after enchanting page, we strolled down memory lane together. The next big stop on the journey was West Point, a most extraordinary and imposing military post and our nation's oldest service academy. The academy, which stands along the beautiful Hudson River, was most impressive. We were greatly surprised as well as being thrilled, when we were allowed to sit at the back of the Gothic-style Cadet Chapel while the heavenly choir of angelic voices rehearsed. It was the end to a perfect vacation.

I closed the book, kissed Isabelle on the forehead and dimmed the lights for her to take a nap. It had been a wonderful afternoon, one I would never forget.

Chapter Twenty-Four

Isabelle's Story

While Patricia and Patrick were out shopping, Martha and I ate lunch together in the sizeable old kitchen that had become one of our favorite places for fellowship. She made me a delicious turkey sandwich on fat slices of grilled San Francisco sourdough bread. It was piled high with fresh green sprouts, plump portions of juicy red tomato and ripe avocado. It was delicious! Soft chunky oatmeal raisin cookies were served for dessert, which I ate wholeheartedly with a cup of nonfat-latte.

Christopher called after six that evening, and I was, as always, anxious and pleased to hear his voice. The movie he was in the process of filming was with an experienced crew and a director he had worked with several times so things were going along well and were on schedule. I acquainted him with the details of my delightful afternoon with Isabelle and he was pleased to hear that she was feeling so much better.

A few days later, while out taking an evening walk in the rose gardens below the cottage, I stopped in at the bed-and-breakfast, for a cup of tea and to see how things were progressing with Sophie, the new manager in training. She was doing an exceptional job just as Miriam and Noah had predicted and I was sure that in time she would fit in fine.

Hannah was beaming about her mother's forthcoming wedding and couldn't wait to tell me the news of their lovely new home. The three of us sat together in the dining room while Sophie kindly served us dessert. Large pieces of German chocolate cake that Miriam had prepared that morning were elegantly served on the antique china we used for special occasions. Noah eventually joined our merry group when his work for the day was finished and I could see what a happy little family they would soon be. My heartstrings felt a big tug when I left the old Victorian, knowing they would soon be moving away. Not far away perhaps, but their lives were certainly moving in a new direction, and it would be an adjustment for all.

I walked across the new stone pathway, recently finished, leading from the Victorian to the Tea Cottage. Flowerbeds on either side of it dressed up the property, which once was covered only with gravel.

The Tea Cottage was as busy as ever. Our patrons were casually enjoying the homey atmosphere and the delectable treats and nourishing meals we took great pride in serving. We had expanded our weekend hours to include dinner, while during the week we continued to serve only breakfast and lunch and afternoon tea. Weekday evenings were reserved for private parties and special events.

Upstairs in the loft, a local artist was doing sketches; a number of his works were on display in the Tea Cottage and were for sale. We were now sponsoring several university art students; we allowed them to work on the premises, give exhibits of their craftsmanship and even supplied them with scholarships to help pay their tuition.

The server at the cappuccino bar was busy making an assortment of beverages and hot drinks and the room was filled with quiet laughter. I finished my inspection, said hello to a few friends from church that were drinking tea downstairs, and then walked back up the hill to the estate; my security guards always on duty in the background.

The front porch of the estate as well as the Victorian and the Tea Cottage were all cleverly decorated with pumpkins and hay and dried ears of colored corn for October and the harvest festival we would be hosting at the end of the month to help raise funds for Tabitha's House. Our committee was still diligently seeking ways to raise income for the home and we were succeeding in most of our endeavors.

When I entered the front door, I automatically headed for the parlor and the warm fire that was kept ablaze there on cold days. Isabelle was sitting in her rocking chair, working on her newest cross-stitch project. The work of art was of a large ethereal angel swathed in soft shades of blue kept floating in the air by a pair of delicate white gossamer wings.

"You look like you're feeling a lot better," I said, removing my coat and hanging it on an old wooden coat rack grandfather had fashioned years ago. I walked toward her chair, gave her a kiss on the cheek, and tucked her favorite woolen afghan tightly across her lap to make sure she was covered. Patricia appeared almost magically with a tray of hot tea and plates with dessert. Martha had been as busy today as always. Earlier I smelled the aroma of freshly baked chocolate chip scones emanating from the kitchen but I was too full to taste them.

Patricia poured tea for Isabelle and me and then served her a scone filled with raspberry curd. The chocolate and raspberry flavors blended nicely together, Isabelle said.

"Mmmm," I sighed, "they smell heavenly, Isabelle!"

"Oh, Rachel," she laughed, "You say that about everything!"

"Really?" I asked, smiling. "Well…maybe I do," I laughed. "I guess I just appreciate the simple things of life, Isabelle."

"Yes, you do!" she replied. "I wish more people could understand what you have always known, Rachel; ever since you were a little girl you have always had a humble, down-to-earth sincerity. You are unpretentious and uncomplicated; you have an open heart that gives easily and generously. Regardless of your circumstances and your wealth, you have always been a well-grounded individual and a blessing to my life. I want you to know that now, more than ever, dear. I have loved you like you were my own child, Rachel."

Tears streamed down my cheeks and my heart ached as I walked over to Isabelle's chair and gave her a warm hug.

"And you have been a second mother to me, replacing the one I lost so long ago, Isabelle. You've touched my heart and my soul and I have learned a great deal about true love and friendship from the example you always provided."

Now it was Isabelle's turn to cry and we both reached for tissues to wipe away the tender tears of our affirmation of love one for another.

I refilled our cups and sat close to my friend in front of the fire as we talked about the past and the years we had shared as a family.

Isabelle had spent most of her life with us. I knew her history almost as well as I knew my own. Her father had died in 1928, leaving her and her mother, Lena, alone. They came to America together in 1929 aboard the *S.S. Patria*; Isabelle was only eight then. They lived in New York with my grandparents where Lena worked as a domestic, helping my grandmother. When our family moved to California years later, Lena and Isabelle came also. Lena died when Isabelle was in her teens but she remained in my grandparents' care until she finished high school and then stepped into her mother's position, caring for the estate, as its premier domestic. It was all she ever wanted.

"Isabelle," I asked demurely, "have you any regrets that you never married?"

"Oh, no, none at all," she laughed lightly. "I know most girls dream of getting married and having their own homes and families when they are young, but I never did. I dated a little when I was in school but I just never felt the desire or the need to get married. Unusual, I guess, but not as uncommon as most people think.

"Marriage is a wonderful institution, Rachel, because it was given to us by God; the family was His ideal for raising children. Mothers and fathers both bring unique qualities to childrearing and each should be allowed to parent in their own ways…as long as they are also God's ways." She smiled with a little twinkle in her eye.

"But for me, I have always felt complete being alone. I have never desired marriage and I believe I am complete in my relationship with

God alone. Singleness is not for most people; I believe it's a divine calling. But it has its advantages, you know. It has allowed me more time to serve the Lord by serving others; this has given me great joy and satisfaction!"

"I know that you and Grandmother were always busy caring for others…doing good works that so few people ever knew about; making meals for the sick, providing care packages for the elderly and the poor. Don't you believe I learned by example? It is one of the greatest teachers!"

"Yes, you are right. My dear mother was a generous soul too…regardless of how little we had to eat…she could always make room for one more. How fortunate we are to have learned the blessings of generosity. So few understand that it really is more wonderful to give than to receive!" she sweetly affirmed.

"Yes," I sighed, "Because it is through giving…that we receive as well!"

~ *Chapter Twenty-Five* ~

A New Song

Christopher was extremely busy on his new movie and working long hours. I joined him on location for a short weekend visit and then flew home. Still hampered by my bodyguards and the need for protection, we both agreed it was best that I refrain from any inordinate travel where I might put others and myself at risk. It was difficult being separated for such long periods of time—especially since he was unable to travel home periodically. Now he had to fly overseas for filming in Italy and France and would be gone another month. If all went well he would be home by Thanksgiving and we would have the holidays together.

Slowly, the affairs at the Victorian began to undergo a slight metamorphosis under Sophie, our youthful manager, who had new ideas and fervor for change. The air was filled with the spirit of transformation, which often fills the hearts of a new regime. Her ideas were generally sound and innovative and Noah and I both gave her room to experiment and mature. It was all a part of the process of growth and development.

Frank Crosby succeeded in gaining the senate seat he competed for on Election Day and Chris called from France to congratulate him. His victory party was inspiring but bittersweet because of Jennie's absence. Her violent death had been so tragic; the perpetrators continued to elude the authorities and this only made the grieving process more difficult. There was, however, if nothing else, a feeling among many, that it had served as a catalyst—a wake up call to many, that we were a country desperately in need of reform. Frank, we all hoped, would be just one of a multitude of new leaders who could assist us in ushering in that transformation.

Thanksgiving weekend the weather was cool and crisp. It was on a bright and sunny November day that Miriam and Noah became husband and wife. Their simple wedding ceremony at the church was a highlight to the beginning of the winter holidays. Miriam wore an elegant two-piece beige bridal suit trimmed in lace. Sarah Edwards, the matron of honor, and Hannah, her attendant, wore something similar in a powdery chocolate brown. The colors enhanced the natural beauty of their fair complexions. Miriam and Hannah wore their long blonde tresses neatly wrapped in an upswept bun encircled with autumn flowers. Sarah also wore a wreath amidst her short pixie-like curls. Noah and his best man, Woody, wore dark brown suits. Noah, whose skin was always darkly tanned, looked as handsome as a movie star; his curly blonde locks sparkled in the bright sun.

The ceremony was short but fit the two of them perfectly. They expressed their love and commitment to one another, exchanged rings, said their vows and kissed. Hannah smiled affectionately at the two people she loved most in the world. I cried.

Chloe, Charlotte and Edgar had all come home for the long Thanksgiving weekend. Having them with us was always fun, and Chloe and Charlotte's presence would lighten the burden I personally felt at losing Miriam, another beloved daughter, so to speak.

Sophie sweetly volunteered to oversee the serving of the refreshments at the reception and had several of our employees assist her. Now acting solo in her new position as manager of the bed-and-breakfast she was doing well. Miriam's training and influence were definitely having an effect on Sophie whose demeanor already appeared somewhat calmer. The change was remarkable given the short period of time they had been working together.

After the ceremony, cake and cookies along with punch, tea and coffee were served in the small church hall. The table was decorated following the autumn theme Noah and Miriam had chosen, and the cake was deliciously adorned with candy flowers and leaves in burnt oranges and yellows and browns.

When it came time to toss the bouquet, all the single girls lined up in a tight little bunch together; anxious eyes kept focused on Miriam and when the flowers soared through the air, Sophie came up the winner.

While the bridal party was busy taking pictures, I sat and visited with Zanna Stevens, Woody's new wife. The tall, dark beauty of Polish descent looked almost regal dressed in a light peach colored linen suit. During the summer months left behind now in time, I had learned a great deal about this tender young couple.

Zanna and Woody had been good friends for years; that much Noah had told me. The rest of their story remained a mystery until Zanna and I finally met.

"Our paths diverged," she explained one day, while we enjoyed a hot cup of tea at the Tea Cottage, "when I went on to do my graduate work at an Ivy League university on the east coast. Woody was working in Westwood by then and neither of us was contemplating or ready for marriage. When I graduated, I was offered a position at a prestigious architectural firm in Washington, D.C. and I took it.

"We both dated other people on and off but nothing ever developed and we continued to correspond as friends. It's funny I guess…we just felt so comfortable with one another that the distance between us never seemed to matter. It wasn't until I flew back to Los Angeles for your wedding that we realized how much in love we were. Our engagement followed and we were married in June at my grandparents' home in Kansas."

Her portfolio was small but her recommendations were impressive and, aided by nothing more than an introduction from myself, she was interviewed and then hired by Mr. Lloyd. His architectural firm was pleased to have her on staff at his very busy office.

At the end of the wedding festivities, a waiting limousine conveyed the bridal couple to a hotel in Santa Barbara. Early Sunday morning they would begin their journey to the Cayman Islands; there they would spend their honeymoon basking in the sun, playing in the surf and leisurely relaxing while enjoying the beauty of the tropical paradise. Hannah would spend the week with us at the estate.

Christopher and Edgar and Hannah and Chloe busied themselves in the parlor with a game of Monopoly after church services on Sunday while Charlotte enchanted us with a musical concert at the piano. Isabelle and I listened intently to all our favorites; beginning with Rachmaninoff's Prelude for Piano, Opus 23, No. 2, in F sharp minor, (Largo). She followed with pieces by Debussy, Mahler and Mussorgsky. Her precision and intensity in her performance had grown considerably over the years. Listening to her play always moved me backward in time. My eyes envisioned a sweet young girl of five at the beginning of her musical career—a young rosebud waiting to bloom. Now, the woman had emerged from the shadows of youth and the rose had fully matured; she was a beauty to behold.

Patricia came in at four o'clock to announce that dinner was ready. The fragrant aroma of pot roast and potatoes filled the air. We ate hungrily; the fall weather always seemed to excite appetites more profusely. The pot roast was so tender that it easily melted in my mouth. Baby potatoes, carrots and peas filled our plates and flaky croissants smothered in butter disappeared like magic. Hannah and Chloe devoured their dinner amidst laughter and the gaiety of story telling. Afterward, Christopher drove Chloe to the airport for her return trip home.

Charlotte and Edgar departed as soon as dinner was over; I was sorry when they left, knowing they wouldn't be returning for Christmas this year. Edgar's grandmother was not well. Suffering from Alzheimer's, she had grown worse over the past several weeks. Edgar's parents said that she was very thin and her appetite had almost completely faded away. Her doctors warned it would only be a matter of time before she succumbed to her disorder. Charlotte and Edgar knew they needed to travel to Seattle to spend Christmas vacation with his family—perhaps the last they would all enjoy together.

The rhythm of change beat strongly on the door of my heart. Varying harmonies were floating around in my subconscious; I could almost hear a faint melody line being added and I sensed that before long, a new lyric would be sung in the grand opera of our lives. Regardless of what it might be, I had to embrace it. Yes…a new song was definitely in the air.

∽ Chapter Twenty-Six ∾

The Secret Passage

During her brief but pleasant stay with us, Hannah and I enjoyed daily walks in the gardens or orchards after she returned from school. She was a great companion, always so carefree and conversational. One minute she was the picture of maturity and exhibited all the character traits of one of her favorite storybook heroines. The next she was the typical girl next door—a shy giddy adolescent. She had always been tall but had grown considerably taller this past year and now towered over me by at least four inches.

Walking around the estate grounds was pleasant even with a continual string of companions at our heels. Hannah loved to walk with Miss Cocoa Brown, and I resigned to take Little Baby with me occasionally, although I had given up any hope of her ever walking on a leash. Her legs were too short to keep up with us and so she ended up in a designer tote bag for dogs and was carried along quite happily.

Hannah talked incessantly of school, boys and of the new home they now owned on the beach. Her mother's happiness gave her immense joy; I also sensed that she felt an inner freedom to finally pursue her own secret desires. We often discussed books— reading was a pastime we both enjoyed immensely.

"Have you finished reading the copy of *Pride and Prejudice* you received for your birthday?" I asked.

"OH, YES!" She replied with great enthusiasm. "And it has quickly become my favorite of all Jane Austen's books. I must admit that I like Jane Bennet best of all the sisters; and that I hope to fall in love with a man as nice as her Mr. Bingley! They were an amiable couple!" she declared with a laugh.

"Just so!" I replied. "And I fear I am a great deal like the young Eliza Bennet, who in her youth was much too quick to judge, although time has taught me better that people are not what they often appear to be."

"And Lydia! Goodness, she was such a foolish young girl to elope with that horrible Wickham."

"Yes. Everyone was taken in by his charming ways and they were much too eager to listen to his rebuffs of poor Mr. Darcy."

"Well, Mr. Darcy is rude in the beginning. And it's so easy to think the worst of people we don't like."

"True, and something we must guard against. Perhaps this is part of the moral of her story? We don't always think about the pain we may inflict on others when we judge them too quickly…and that we are capable of being deceived by someone as charming as Mr. Wickham!" I asserted. "Did I tell you that Christopher played the part of Mr. Darcy once? It was early in his career, in a stage show in London."

"OH, I'm sure he was wonderful…and what a handsome Mr. Darcy he would make, too!"

We laughed and continued to chatter about other books as we headed for home. The sun was slipping quickly beyond the horizon and, as it did, the sky grew dark. We hurried back to the house and entered from the patio doors walking toward the kitchen. We grabbed a small snack to eat and then headed down the narrow servant's hallway on the first floor until we reached the library.

"Where are we going?" she asked with a whisper.

"Shush!" I said, putting my finger in front of my mouth. "Can you keep a secret?"

"Oh, yes!" Hannah responded, eyes glistening with excitement.

I closed the door behind us and went over to one of the bookshelves on the opposite side of the room. Reaching in between the books, I pressed a small hidden button. The wall opened magically. Hannah's eyes widened.

"A secret passage?" she asked.

"Yes," I replied, "of a sort. My grandfather had several passageways put in between some of the walls for a number of reasons. Initially, he thought they would be quicker for the servants to use, to expedite getting from one place to another. He also thought they would reduce the noise in the house. If he wanted to go downstairs at night for a book or a snack, he could do it quietly. They are rarely used by anyone but me. Patrick uses them on occasion, but Patricia is afraid they are too dark.

"Can you imagine how surprised Christopher was the first time I popped out from behind a wall? I can almost see his face—it was an ashen color!" Hannah and I both laughed.

We walked up a narrow staircase and then down a narrow corridor. I pressed a button in front of a door and magically it opened. We walked into my sitting room.

"This used to be my grandparents' room. When my brother Riley was alive, we would play hide and seek here in the castle when we came to visit. We never could figure out how Papa was able to disappear from one place to another. When I came to live here later, he told me."

"Its fantastic, Aunt Rachel!" my young friend exclaimed. "This really is a magic castle...I hope there aren't any ghosts!" She laughed.

"It isn't something you expect to find here, is it?" I cried. "Although many old mansions were built with secret rooms and panels for hiding things. My grandfather was a man of intricate dreams and visions. The estate holds more secrets than most people will ever know. Someday, perhaps, I will tell you more but for now, remember, it's our secret!"

"Oh, don't worry, you can count on me to keep quiet!" she said. "I promise!"

We left my room and headed across the hallway toward Isabelle's room to see how she was doing and to share a little of our day.

Before the week was out we had rain, which always made the estate a little damp. Hannah was sleeping in Charlotte's bedroom, which was nearest to the one Christopher and I now shared. It was the room I had spent my childhood in and I still loved it. Patrick kept a warm fire burning in the hearth, something I always enjoyed because it made the room cozier.

On Saturday night Hannah had a sleepover for her three dearest friends. Martha was wonderful. She allowed the girls access to her kitchen where she supervised them making homemade pizzas. These they devoured and then made their way to the study, which was equipped with a large screen television. Christopher purchased several movies for them to watch and as an added surprise; he obtained a copy of the BBC, A&E co-production of *Pride and Prejudice*, which they loved. Martha, being the old softie that she was, allowed them to make their own hot fudge sundaes for dessert. They took them upstairs where they retreated for the evening, to talk the night away.

I let them sleep in until eleven when Patricia was sent to rouse them from their slumber to come downstairs for breakfast. Four tired but happy girls sat at the long oak table in the kitchen eating pancakes and sausages and bacon and eggs. Martha made them each whatever their hearts desired and I knew she felt as I did that it was nice having children in the house once again!

Hannah had much to share with Miriam and Noah when they returned from their honeymoon and, while I knew she had enjoyed herself during her visit, I could see how happy she was that they were home. The three of them left quietly to begin their new life together. They were a family now—planted in a garden of love and I was sure only good fruit could come from it!

~ *Chapter Twenty-Seven* ~

A Voice from the Past

Chloe came home for Christmas on a Thursday evening, as soon as her last final was over and she had said good-bye to her friends. Christopher picked her up at the airport while I remained at home with Isabelle. In a flurry of excitement she bounced in through the front door heading for the parlor where she suspected we would be; her animated spirit was her truest expression of a sincerely joyful person. She was growing lovelier and more self-assured every day. What a difference from the fearful young girl she had once been.

On Friday, Charlotte and Edgar came for dinner—they had altered their vacation plans a little upon hearing that Edgar's grandmother was physically a little better. They decided to spend two days with us before heading north to Seattle for the holidays; if all went well they would stop in again on their return.

Our Christmas celebration with them was a few days early but enjoyable regardless. We had a simple but ravishing dinner of boeuf Bourguignon—beef and vegetables cooked in the French style my family had always loved, in Burgundy wine. We enjoyed a crisp green salad with a vinaigrette dressing and crusty French bread with herbed butter. Martha had made her famous Christmas fruitcake, which was unlike any other, and served it for dessert with an assortment of iced gingerbread cookies.

We opened the gifts we had for each other in the parlor, where a tall fir tree now stood gaily lit and adorned with sparkling ornaments. Patrick had found the perfect tree for the parlor—as always. Trees of varying sizes were purchased for the dining hall and foyer as well as for the Tea Cottage and the Victorian. Christopher and I had a marvelous time decorating the parlor tree with ornaments, garland, ribbons and lights. This was our first Christmas together as husband and wife and we meant to enjoy every moment. Happily, Chris was home for two weeks and we planned to spend most of our time together in pleasant relaxation.

Sitting on feathery cushions on the floor of the parlor in front of the fireplace, tenderly cradled in my husband's arms, I watched with joy as the children unwrapped their pretty packages.

Charlotte was first; she picked a large box covered in green foil with her name on a gold tag. Inside was the lovely tan colored wool crepe suit I had purchased for her. The A-line skirt was ankle length; the matching coat came just to the knee; it would look wonderful on her tall slender figure. In a smaller box she found a soft cashmere turtleneck sweater in a deep rust color. A perfect match for the suit; it would certainly bring out the copper highlights of her beautiful auburn hair.

Chloe opened a few of her gifts as well but some were saved for Christmas morning. She loved Charlotte's new attire and admired it greatly. Under the tree she found a large silver foil wrapped package with her name on it, which she opened with eager anticipation. Carefully, she removed the dark brown tweed pleated skirt and short matching jacket; her eyes lit up with delight and I was pleased. The pale ivory camel hair sweater that was its companion thrilled her as well. Lovely ornamental and unique pieces of jewelry had been purchased for each lady's ensemble and were unwrapped with as much joy and acceptance.

Christopher had been put in charge of buying gifts for the men of the family and chose to get Edgar a new laptop computer; software programs for composing music and reproducing musical scores were an additional bonus. Edgar was fascinated.

A variety of gifts were generously given and graciously received by all. We had purchased similar things for all of the children, keeping in mind their habitats and personal preferences. Devon and Joseph were spending their holidays overseas with his family. His sister had finally recuperated from her long illness and Alexandra and Petey would soon be on their way home. My heart ached for Devon; it would be difficult for her to let them go.

Victoria and Allen and dear little Michael were thoroughly enjoying their life in England—so much so that I thought they might never return. Uncle Edgar made good his promise to send his delightful little nephew his first musical instrument; a small snare drum with sticks was only the beginning, he assured us!

Our small ensemble relaxed quietly in front of the fireplace for the rest of the evening, sharing different thoughts and dreams. Little Baby was curled up in Christopher's arms, sound asleep and snoring loudly. We were amazed by how much noise she could make. Chloe took good care of little Sassy who had grown considerably since her last visit and whose color has lightened as well. She was an obedient little dog, and much better behaved than my little mischief-maker I was ashamed to admit!

Patricia entered the parlor in silence. Not wanting to detract from the conversation going on, she whispered to me that I had a phone call. "Excuse me," I said and leaving my comfy place on the floor next to my husband I followed her out of the room. As soon as we were out of earshot of the parlor door, she mentioned the name of the caller. Quickly, I headed in the direction of the study where there would be privacy; anxiety embraced my heart as a voice from the past reached out to me.

"Hello, Paul!" I said into the receiver.

"Merry Christmas, Rachel!" he replied. "I hope I haven't interrupted your evening."

"Not at all," I responded politely. "Charlotte and Edgar are here. We just finished exchanging gifts with them. I'm sure you must know they are going to Seattle for the holidays."

"Yes, she told me," he answered back warmly. I knew his relationship with the children had been improving because Charlotte had mentioned a perceived difference in his attitude toward them lately. "Rachel, I don't want to keep you from your family. Perhaps this was a bad time to call but…I wanted to tell you before Christmas that you were right…about me…about so many things." He stopped abruptly. The anxiety in my chest lessened a bit and I settled back into my chair somewhat more composed and ready to listen to whatever it was my former husband wanted to say.

"We haven't spoken much in the past year. Not since…" he hesitated. Was he thinking, as I was, of our last meeting? "But I thought you should know that I did take your advice about counseling…and I'm happy that I did." He sighed and a sense of relief seemed to set in…his tone was softer—less demanding. Had he changed?

He spoke openly of that night…that last dreadful night we had been together. He admitted using the pretense of family business to get me to meet him for dinner. He was convinced at the time that I still loved him and that in spite of all that had happened, even his marriage to Jessica, that I would return to him. I however was shocked by his declaration of love. Selfishly, he considered tossing Jessica aside in order to regain my affections. Angered by his thoughtlessness, I rejected his proposal and suggested he seek counseling. His profession of love became resentful when I walked away. We had spoken little since then. Now, his repentance seemed sincere—but could I trust him?

"I've been wrong about so many things, Rachel. I know that now…I'm sorry it's taken me so long to admit it. I lost you…and I almost lost Jessica too…because of my stubborn self-will…my pride and my conceit." He paused momentarily, "I hate to have to confess to my own arrogance; the truth hurts, but I've had to face a lot of things about myself this past year, in order to be able to change. It hasn't been easy and I still have a lot to do. But I wanted you to know how I feel and I've called mainly to tell you that I'm sorry and to ask for your forgiveness."

Stunned, my heart raced within; tears of joy steamed down my face. Paul, the Prodigal, had come home…not as a husband…that was impossible now. But as a Prodigal child returns to its Father, it was obvious that Paul had come home to God and it was wonderful!

"Jessica and I were separated for a while but we're back together again and I am, maybe for the first time in my life, endeavoring to make my marriage work the way God intended. I'm not sure if you want to hear that at all; I simply called to tell you that I'm truly sorry. Sorry for all the pain and grief that I caused you. I know you have forgiven me but I just needed to tell you personally how I feel.

"Rachel, I know there were times you probably doubted yourself and your role in our breakup. But believe me, the fault was predominantly mine. I refused to commit, I refused to work on our relationship…I abandoned you and I abandoned God. When I lost sight of Him, I lost my moral compass.

"Well," he sighed, "that's all I really called to say. I will always care about you, Rachel. Our life together is part of our past. I've let it go. Jessica and I are doing well together and I just wanted you to know that I have finally grown up."

"Paul," I said, so gently, "I wish you every happiness. Merry Christmas, Paul!" I whispered.

"Merry Christmas, Rachel," he replied, "God be with you!" He hung up his phone and I quietly placed mine into the receiver. I took a tissue from the box on my desk and wiped my eyes before returning to the parlor.

Christopher's eyes met mine when I came back but he said nothing and no one else questioned my absence or probed into my privacy.

Later that evening, when Chris and I were alone in our room, I told him of my conversation with Paul. He was reflective but silent, which wasn't unusual. He rarely commented about my previous marriage. He understood as I did that life often doesn't turn out as we hope or plan. His marriage to Juliet had ended in death; mine to Paul had ended in divorce. Both events were beyond our control.

The pleasant crispness of the cool evening entered the bedroom through the open balcony door, and the fragrance of the ocean filled the air. Silver beams of moonlit rays danced romantically on the walls creating interesting shadowy figures.

Christopher had the stereo on and was listening to several selections by Russian composers. He especially liked *A Tear*, a very sweet piece by M.P. Mussorgsky that I enjoyed as well. Already in bed, I nestled closely next to him; tenderly he caressed my hair, his lips lightly touching my forehead.

I turned my face toward his and gently placed my hand on his cheek. The moonlight reflected across his steel gray eyes; they were penetrating. What did he see when he looked at me, I often wondered? His love for me was passionate and tender and at times effusive, as if bubbling up from a well within. My love may have been less demonstrative than my creative partner's but it was nevertheless just as fervent. We had reached a comfortable place in our relationship where words were often unnecessary—perhaps the intimacy that lovers share enables them to understand things unspoken. A nod, a look, a glance all said so much.

Gently he pressed his lips against mine. Delight flooded my senses. The night passed sweetly as the moonbeams became sunrays and another day had begun.

Chapter Twenty-Eight

A Stranger in the Shadows

Chloe enjoyed her holiday at Winthrope's and spent most of her free time working at the Tea Cottage or helping Sophic at the bed-and-breakfast—a diversion she pursued wholeheartedly. Working at the Cottage was fun not only because it was dissimilar from her usual routine but also because she loved the activity, especially during the busy holiday season.

Donning Victorian attire, which was standard apparel for the waiters and waitresses who worked at the Cottage, Chloe performed well as a hostess and gladly assisted wherever needed. She relished wearing the costumed garb that made the Tea Cottage appear more authentic. The ladies usually wore long slate blue dresses with a small bustle and a white apron with matching cap. The gentlemen wore charcoal gray trousers, a white pinstriped gray shirt with black necktie, and a slate blue vest. However, in order to diversify a bit we had recently purchased costumes in several different styles, but in matching and coordinating colors—a benefit for our employees who had varying tastes. Everyone seemed to approve.

Garlands of greenery hung over the old stable doors—once the grand opening for the elegant animals that paraded in and out—now the main entrance into the Tea Cottage. Small white blinking lights surrounded each dining room window and a tall evergreen tree stood proudly in the center of the wide aisle, which separated the rooms on the north from those on the south. Beautifully wrapped packages lay beneath its lofty branches and the scent of pine permeated the wintry air. Sprigs of holly berries decorated the tables and mistletoe hung in each open doorway.

A visit to the Tea Cottage was a treat; it was a pleasant stroll in time to a simpler way of life. The atmosphere seemed charged with the electricity of childlike delight. Faces beamed vibrantly as hearts were stirred by the picturesque surroundings; so often they seemed filled with a sense of anticipation evidently repeated each time they came in. I knew that I felt it myself.

Chloe loved the hustle and bustle of the busy restaurant and enjoyed the camaraderie of the young people we employed, many from the local university. The season made the ambiance more pleasant than usual and many of our patrons exhibited a generous amount of holiday spirit and good cheer.

The chefs had been busy preparing many seasonal favorites; sour cream apple pie, along with a Scotch apple tart, seemed to be among the fall favorites. Yet, the traditional pumpkin and mincemeat pies seemed to sell just as quickly. My own desires leaned in the direction of the chef's holiday special—a delightfully moist white cake that was filled with almond flavored pastry cream and decorated with red and green marzipan candies. Chris preferred the extravagant four-layer ambrosia cake filled with orange marmalade and topped with mounds of fluffy coconut frosting.

Just a few days after Chloe arrived she took a day off from work and drove down to the beach with Sassy to spend the day with Hannah. It was my household staff's usual day off and even Christopher had disappeared for the day, having driven into Santa Barbara to finish some last minute shopping. Isabelle and I were content to spend a quiet evening alone listening to music. The weather had turned cold and it was drizzling outside and even a little damp within. We made ourselves comfortable in front of the fireplace in her room. The stereo played Handel's *Messiah* and while we listened, Isabelle worked on her cross-stitch and I busily finished crocheting an afghan for a new resident at Tabitha's House.

When dinnertime approached, I went downstairs to retrieve the meal Martha had thoughtfully left for us in the kitchen. Individual servings of pumpkin soup and Indian cornbread awaited us—all I needed to do was to heat it in the microwave. The soup was extremely delicious—the pumpkin was rich and smooth. We ate slowly savoring every delectable bite.

"I'm going to take the dirty dishes downstairs and make us some spiced tea, Isabelle. We haven't had that in a while, have we?"

"No, we haven't. It's perfect on a cold damp night like tonight." She rubbed her hands together.

"Are you feeling all right?" I asked with concern.

"Yes, dear. I feel fine," she said. I threw another log on the grate in the fireplace and then took the cart down the hallway to the servant's elevator.

The large old kitchen had a built-in fireplace with a spacious homey hearth. The kitchen had been renovated years earlier and updated with wonderful new appliances, but they had been installed so as not to detract from the old-world charm of the original design.

I took a copper saucepan from under one of the cabinets and filled it with clear water. Once boiling, I added some tea bags, a cinnamon stick, and a few whole cloves and allowed it to steep for a few minutes. After removing the pan from the fire I retrieved the tea bags and set them aside. Quickly I added cinnamon-flavored sugar and cranberry juice and then heated the beverage again. Finally, I poured the steaming hot mixture through a sieve to remove the spices and then into two large china mugs, which I carefully carried upstairs.

"Mmmm," Isabelle said, taking a sip, "this is wonderful. Thank you, Rachel."

"You're welcome," I replied and took a sip myself. "This is good!" I said, and picking up my yarn I continued to work on the afghan. "I love these colors! Hunter green, cranberry and slate blue; they look wonderful together." Picking up where I left off we talked while we sipped our spicy beverages.

Abruptly, the lights in the room went out and the music on the stereo grew silent. The fire from the hearth provided our only source of light but it was sufficient for me to see around the room. Putting my yarn aside, I went to Isabelle's desk and retrieved a flashlight I knew she kept in her drawer.

"Power failure again," I said without concern. "I wonder why the generator hasn't come on?" Walking toward the door in the dark, I turned to Isabelle and said, "I'll go downstairs and check on things. Stay right here. I'll only be a few minutes."

"Rachel!" Isabelle cried with alarm. "Are you sure you should go downstairs in the dark? Do you think it will be safe?"

"The security guards are just outside—don't worry. I'll be cautious," I promised.

Aiming the flashlight in front of my feet I carefully walked down the hall to the circular stairway. Maneuvering in the darkness really wasn't a problem for me; having grown up at the estate I knew I could find my way anywhere without much difficulty. And power outages were frequent occurrences here on the hill so they were never a cause for alarm. Even though the generator hadn't switched on I wasn't concerned, although I did wonder why the security guards hadn't checked in but it was feasible they weren't affected or aware of the blackout. California had been faced with growing energy problems and we had experienced some rolling blackouts. The staff had worked hard at reducing our usage of electricity and cut back on both the interior and exterior lighting as much as possible. Since the estate was on a separate system independent from all the other surrounding structures, no one but its inhabitants would know of the outage unless it was universal to the entire area.

Everything within the house appeared to be dark—pitch black actually—with the exception of the emergency earthquake lights throughout the hallways that ran on batteries. These acted as small guides leading me toward my destination downstairs. The main fuse box was located in the kitchen area, which I reached quickly without incident. The flashlight illuminated the box; all the fuses seemed fine. I picked up the telephone to call security and I was surprised that the line was dead as well.

The generator was our only recourse so I quickly walked toward the rear exit closest to the generator house. It was out back beyond the old oak tree; I hesitated when I reached the door. Should I go outside alone? The generator power should have switched over automatically when the electricity went out; for the first time I felt a twinge of fear. Something held me back. My hand touched the door handle while my mind searched for answers. Where were the security guards? I hesitated and peered out a window nearby; the battery-operated lights were on around the perimeter of the house but it was still very dark.

The sound of footsteps walking on the wet patio brought welcome relief! I was just about to open the door when I heard the faint tinkle of broken glass coming from someplace close by. Instinctively, I stepped back into the darkened hallway. Fear ripped through my heart; I listened intently for any sound. All appeared quiet. Slowly, silently, I walked toward the ballroom. Crunch! Crunch! Footsteps sounded on what I assumed must be broken glass and then ceased abruptly. Edging toward a window that faced the rear of the estate I looked out and saw the faint shadow of the man walking on the patio; identity was impossible. I remained as quiet as possible as I slipped away from the window; quickly I pressed my body up against a wall and noiselessly stooped down.

He was very quiet but I could hear him moving through the ballroom; there were at least two of them. One was inside and one was outside. Crawling along the floor I moved toward the kitchen and hid behind a large circular cabinet. Moments later, a small band of light streamed into the kitchen as the stranger appeared in the doorway. I stopped breathing as he ran the beam of light around the room. Apparently satisfied that it was vacant, he moved on.

"Rachel!" Isabelle's willowy voice called out to me from upstairs, "are you all right?" I held my breath tightly and said nothing not wanting to give away my location. The light quickly disappeared but the stranger did not move; perhaps he was waiting for my reply.

"Rachel!" Isabelle cried out again, this time her voice was filled with fear, "where are you?" The stranger slowly walked away from the kitchen and crept down the hallway moving in her direction.

Swiftly, as quietly as possible, I ran from my hiding place out another door toward the study. Once inside, I loudly slammed the door closed and locked it. Hopefully, I had made enough noise to draw him to my location. I hesitated to listen and then headed for the bookshelves. I reached in among the books and released the latch and the wall magically opened, as only I knew it would. I stepped inside and closed the secret panel. I waited another moment and could hear the muffled sounds of the stranger as he struggled with the door handle. I didn't wait to see what he might do, instead I ran quickly up the narrow staircase of the secret passage and then down the hallway toward my bedroom.

Having reached the doorway, I instantly pressed the latch and entered my sitting room.

Isabelle's room was nearby; I entered without making a sound.

"Shush!" I warned her. "Come with me quickly," I whispered as I helped her out of her bed and down the hall to my room.

"Hurry!" I said, "Get inside the wall." I snatched Baby from her basket and a blanket from my bed and quickly joined Isabelle behind the secret panel. Instantly the door closed but not before we heard the sounds of footsteps now rushing up the staircase as they echoed in the big hall.

"*Thank you, Papa!*" I prayed, silently once the door had closed. We moved down the narrow corridor as I directed Isabelle upward to the next staircase, which would take us to the third floor tower. There was a small niche there where I would hide her and the dog, while I ran to get help.

We climbed the stairs slowly. It was cold and damp inside the walls but I knew she would be safe here. Once we reached the tower niche, I had her sit down against the wall and I covered her with the blanket to keep her warm. Baby snuggled quietly in her arms.

"Who is it?" Isabelle asked, in a trembling whisper.

"I don't know. Only one is in the house but there's another out back," I uttered softly even though I was fairly sure we couldn't be heard through the walls. "But I need to get help before the others come home or someone might get hurt."

"How did they get past the security guards?" she asked.

"I don't know. Listen, Isabelle, you stay right here. Don't make a sound no matter what happens. I'm sure the passage that leads to the chapel is open; perhaps I can get outside without being seen. Then, I'll head on down the hill toward the Victorian. I will leave the flashlight with you. Don't worry!" I kissed her on the cheek. I felt tears stream down her eyes. "I love you, Isabelle."

"I love you too, Rachel. Be careful," she whispered as I headed back down the dark hallway.

As quietly as possible, I walked back down the stairway and through the corridor. I thought I heard footsteps on the other side of the wall so I stopped and listened until they passed. They were climbing the stairs to the third floor tower above. Quickly, I headed down the stairs and toward the back of the house. Another staircase made of concrete took me down into the earth; now I was beneath the house in a tunnel that ran next to the underground basement. There was a little bit of water on the ground and I stepped carefully to avoid slipping and falling but, in my haste, I stumbled and scraped my right knee and both hands. Regaining my composure I continued my journey until I reached the steep steps that led up into the chapel. The heavy trap door was bolted on the inside but it opened easily. I carefully pushed it up a little at a time. It was dark inside the chapel as I cautiously left my hiding place. Sliding out from the trap door I crawled under the altar located just ahead of it. Noiselessly I moved to the heavy oak doors and slipped outside into the shadows. It was still raining lightly. The house was completely black as I ran toward the orchards. The dirt road the farmers used was the safest route down the hill especially in the dark. I cut through an opening in one of the tall hedges and then stumbled and fell over something large behind it. There, lying in the wet dirt was one of the security guards. Placing my fingers on his neck, I felt a slight pulse. A sticky substance oozed from his forehead; it had to be blood.

I took off the sweater I was wearing and wrapped it tightly around his wounded head. There was nothing more I could do, so I left him. As swiftly as possible, I sprinted down the muddy orchard road, trying to keep from falling again. My arm stung with pain from my fall and now my ankle ached as well but I ignored it and pressed on.

Traveling quickly down the road, I was somewhat relieved when I saw a car parked on the shoulder of the road ahead. Only the parking lights were on but I could clearly see the outline of someone standing in front of it. Cautiously, I ducked behind the shrubs, and waited a moment before approaching. He appeared to be watching the house and the highway as well. What could I do now? If he was one of them, there might be others.

Without a sound, I stepped back into the darkness. My mind raced as I prayed for direction and then turned quickly and headed back up the hill toward the garage. The side door was usually left open until Patrick closed and locked it before going to bed. The Blazer was in its stall at the far end. Without pause, I opened the door and removed its cell phone and quickly dialed 911. *"Help!"* I said to the operator and gave her my location. Noise on the gravel outside startled me and I dropped the phone on the concrete floor. I crawled under the car and hid between the two front tires. The door opened and two pair of footsteps entered. A light flashed around the room as the strangers came closer.

Honk! Honk! A car horn sounded loudly from somewhere below; the men turned quickly and ran. I could hear sirens blaring in the distance but I stayed put. My head throbbed and my heart pounded. The next thing I heard was gunshots.

Chapter Twenty-Nine

A High Tower

*I*n silence, I kept my vigil in the dark waiting to see what would unfold next. Shivering on the cold concrete, I prayed Isabelle would be all right in her damp hiding place in the tower. The words of the Psalmist floated through my mind and gently calmed my fears;

> *The LORD is my rock, and my fortress,*
> *And my deliverer; my God,*
> *My strength, in whom I will trust;*
> *My buckler, and the horn of my salvation,*
> *And my high tower.*[10]

How apropos that Isabelle was hidden in just such a place.

Suddenly, the outside lights came on and sent radiant beams filtering into the darkened garage through the open door. The electricity was on once again.

"Rachel!" The voice echoed my name and calmed my trembling heart, but I knew his was filled with fear and panic.

"Christopher!" I yelled back to my husband while struggling to climb out from underneath the car. Limping to the open doorway I practically fell into his arms.

"Rachel!" He said, pulling me close. "Are you all right? Where is Isabelle?" he asked, looking around the empty garage.

"Safe!" I said, "In the tower passageway."

Together, we went into the house through the open back doors, now swarming with police and servants, everyone arriving home at nearly the same time. Christopher left me in the parlor, and he and Patrick went upstairs to the bedroom, and through the secret passageway to find Isabelle and Baby safely sitting in the tower niche where I had left them. Chris carried her down to her room, where Patricia was waiting, anxious to care for her elderly friend. Martha and Chloe were busy in the kitchen preparing warm beverages and food for all. Sophie came up from the inn eager to assist them.

Later that evening we were informed of the capture of the suspects. A long and wild chase down Pacific Coast Highway had ended when their car collided with another vehicle and rolled over. One of the suspects had been killed at the scene; no one else was seriously injured and, after being examined by paramedics, they were taken away to jail.

The following day, men from the police as well as the FBI arrived to continue the interviews of the evening before. We found out from them that the men who had broken into the estate the night before had been identified at police headquarters; one was the alleged hotel bomber they were searching for. I easily picked him out from photos they brought with them and, later on that day, I made a positive identification in a lineup. Thankfully, he was now safely behind bars. Frank Crosby was informed immediately of his capture, and was also greatly relieved.

Dr. Everett, a family friend, had come twice already to see us. Isabelle was fine but he recommended she remain in bed for a few days; I did indeed have a sprained ankle and a few minor cuts and bruises. The security guard was in the hospital suffering from a concussion from the severe blow he received to the head. Several stitches were needed to close the large wound to his skull but he would survive. Unfortunately, the two other guards working at the estate had been badly injured and were hospitalized; the likelihood of their recovery was unknown.

In the days that followed between Christmas and New Year's, we had multiple visits from the police and the FBI, as well as the security experts that had been hired to protect us. They worked together to figure out how the men had gained entrance to the property, the power station and the house without being detected. Regrettably, it wasn't that difficult.

The FBI made several deductions that appeared logical with information obtained from one of the suspects. Parking on the farm road, out of sight, and with a guard posted, the bomber and an accomplice hiked up the trail that led to the back of house. The man left to keep watch approached the security guard on duty at the road below and attacked him. Another waited for the guard making his rounds around the house and, after hitting him over the head, he was dragged into the bushes and left for dead. The third accomplice took out the patrol guard at the rear of the estate, before heading toward the outdoor power station. The building that housed the main electrical feed for the house along with the emergency generator was unlocked. He simply walked in and turned off the auto transfer switch, which effectively disabled the generator and then he shut down the main power supply. Immediately, the entire estate was in darkness. It was all much too easy.

The breach of security at the estate seriously dampened our holiday spirit and left us all feeling somewhat insecure and vulnerable. I personally had always viewed The Castle as an impregnable fortress; now its weakest links had been made evident and exploited. The lives of those dearest to us were left unguarded and in jeopardy, and we wondered if we would ever feel truly safe again.

Many events change our lives as irrevocably as this one changed ours. Nothing would ever be the same again and we knew it, accepted it and moved forward.

A significant portion of our property had to be fenced off—a substantial task in itself but there was no other good alternative. Rock pillars would be built and wrought iron fencing placed in between, all around the top of the estate. Cameras placed at strategic places throughout the grounds would be watched and maintained by guards in a post built at the foot of the mountain at the farm road entrance. It saddened me tremendously. Papa would be as devastated as I was to see what America had become.

Chloe remained with us through New Year's. Although we had been invited to attend several big Hollywood parties we were too traumatized to mix in large social gatherings and decided to remain close to home. All we wanted now was a little peace and quiet. Sitting in front of the fireplace huddled close together, we reflected upon the events of the previous year and shared our plans for the year ahead.

"I'm looking forward to going back to school!" Chloe blurted out, somewhat unexpectedly.

"Really?" her father asked, one eyebrow askew, as if to ask why.

"Something new on your agenda, Chloe?" I questioned.

Chloe laughed. "Not something! Someone!"

We both looked at her, surprised.

"Who?" Chris asked, intrigued.

"Well," she began, face glowing, "his name is Scott and at the moment our relationship is somewhat hard to define. We met almost a year ago through mutual friends at a coffeehouse close to campus where we go to study. He's a Barista there; he loves jazz and books and politics. When we study late he joins us and we just sit and chat about everything. He can be pert and saucy when he feels like it, is astute and a little pensive too."

"What's his course of study?" Chris asked, now fully engrossed in the conversation with his daughter. His ears perked up as soon as he realized that Chloe was definitely involved.

"Journalism…he writes for the school newspaper. His articles are so interesting and thought provoking…I guess that's what makes him so attractive. A lot of my male friends are a little superficial, unfortunately. But not Scott," she said, proudly.

Christopher grinned.

Continuing her narrative she said, "We met the day before I left school for vacation. I told him I was coming here for the holidays and asked what his plans were. He said he had to stay at school and work because he supports himself. He's been able to get a few grants because of his high GPA and he has loans too and he works hard, terribly hard." Chloe was filled with admiration for her young friend.

"He sounds nice," I said.

"Oh, he is, Rachel. He's extremely nice."

"And?" Christopher asked, wanting her to continue.

"And he gave me a gift," she said, pulling a small package out of her skirt pocket. Opening the box, she handed it to me to look at. It was a small golden locket.

"It's lovely!" I replied, with a smile.

"It's the dearest gift I've ever received," she whispered softly.

"Does he have a last name?" Christopher asked with a smile.

"It's Williams…his name is Scott Williams, Daddy!" Looking up into her father's eyes, she then added, "and I believe he's the man I'm going to marry!"

Chapter Thirty

Women of Virtue

A few weeks after the New Year began, Marie came up to the estate for a weekend of relaxation. Chris was staying in Los Angeles, attending a premiere to promote a new movie while I remained at home to fulfill a variety of commitments of my own.

Women of Virtue, an organization begun by one of my old friends, was holding one of their largest west coast conferences in nearby Santa Barbara. The organizers had been planning the annual event for the past year and early on they had invited me to be their guest speaker. Regardless of what was happening in my personal life, I felt the obligation to attend. My reasons for doing so went beyond just duty—perhaps they were even a little selfish because I wanted a normal life—or as normal a lifestyle as my situation would allow.

Marie and I usually looked forward to this event with great anticipation because it was designed to be an avenue of encouragement to ladies from every spectrum of society. We arrived at the hotel in Santa Barbara, where the dinner was being hosted, in the newly hired limousine that Christopher now insisted I use. The black sedan was sedate and fairly inconspicuous and it was equipped with a multitude of security features that eased my husband's concerns for my safety. In addition, two full-time bodyguards escorted me everywhere.

Our rooms were lovely and I enjoyed my view from the balcony that overlooked the pool surrounded by tropical plants and trees. The air was cold, crisp and clear as the day quickly disappeared and the sparkling lights of the heavenly bodies above lit up the nighttime sky little by little.

When Marie joined me in my suite she was wearing a dazzling royal blue cashmere sweater with a matching full-length skirt. An attractive double strand of pearls wrapped loosely around her neck highlighted the beauty of her fashion. My choice for the evening had been more traditional. I loved black velvet. The top was boatnecked and sleeveless and complimented the straight long skirt. The ensemble had a matching waist length jacket with silver buttons. Christopher had given me a lovely necklace for Christmas that I was wearing for the first time. A thin strand of white gold wire with three small diamonds spaced an inch apart shined elegantly against the sleekness of the black fabric whose softness gently caressed my skin. My hair was simply wrapped up in a tight twist with tiny ringlets hanging near each ear and down the back of my neck. A small pair of diamond stud earrings, silver sandals and matching purse completed my attire for the evening.

The banquet room was softly lit with translucent lights from above. Every table was romantically aglow with sparkling candlelight glistening from under tall crystal hurricane lamps. Silver confetti was scattered around the tabletops and every place setting was graced with a long stemmed white rose, the emblem of the organization.

Marie and I were seated at the speaker's table at the front of the room below the stage and podium. Our delightful dinner began with a crisp salad of fresh greens tossed in vinaigrette dressing. The main entrée was wine-braised goose served with mashed yams and broccoli flowerets. Hot compote of spicy cinnamon apples and chopped walnuts was served on the side with baskets of flaky croissants. Heavenly coconut custard pie was a perfect choice for dessert!

Abigail David, the current president and this evening's chairwoman, rose to the podium and then gracefully presented me to the ladies in attendance.

"Rachel Elliott has been well known throughout this community for her philanthropic works for many years," she began cheerfully. "We welcome her tonight, with delight and heartfelt thanks." The applause was overwhelming as I humbly rose and made my way to the podium.

"Good evening, ladies!" I began, joyfully. "As I look out into the sea of smiling faces before me, I must admit that I am extremely pleased to see such a disparity of age, color and of advantage. Tonight, it is *my honor* to be able to address you.

"The biblical story of the potter and the clay is a particular favorite of mine and I often meditate on its message because it reminds me, more so than ever as I age, that we really are nothing more than clay pots fashioned in different sizes, shapes and color. The real value of the vessel is not its makeup but rather what it is designed to contain. Ladies, we are earthen vessels designed by a Holy God to be filled with Holiness—we are intended to be vessels of virtue.

"Tonight, I would like to share with you the stories of three virtuous women whom I believe are models we can learn from. In the world's economy there are many who will tell us that virtue is old-fashioned. But in God's economy moral excellence is never out of date. Virtue is a quality of strength that comes from within that enables us to conform to a particular standard of moral excellence regardless of what others may believe or practice.

"The Old Testament Scriptures are filled with the histories of men and women, both the famous and infamous. Elijah, sometimes called the Prophet of Fire, was a man of distinction. Tonight, we look at only one aspect of his ministry and then only as it intersects relationally with a woman who lived in the city of Zarephath.

"King Ahab, a wicked and idolatrous king of Israel, had sorely provoked the Lord to anger. Elijah, God's prophet, told Ahab that there would be neither rain nor dew in Israel until he should proclaim it. Following the Lord's direction, he fled from the presence of the king and hid himself by the Cherith River, where he remained, fed by ravens, until the brook ran dry. Leaving this place he was directed by God to go to the city of Zarephath, to a widow there, who was on the brink of starvation.

"Elijah came upon the woman while she was collecting firewood, and he asked her to give him something to eat. She told him that her cupboards were empty and that all she had left was a little bit of flour and a small vial of oil, just enough to prepare a cake for herself and her son, which they would eat and then die.

"He assured her that she would not die, but that she must make first a cake for him to eat, and that God would provide for her and her son. In obedience to the prophet, she took her jar of flour and vial of oil and prepared him a cake. This woman of virtue exemplified great faith in God by providing for His prophet despite her own intense needs. God rewarded her obedience by providing for her and her son during the long and severe drought and famine. Her jar of flour never ran out and her oil never ceased to flow.

"Another great prophet followed closely on the heels of Elijah; it was his servant and protégé, Elisha. He too had an encounter with a woman of virtue. The wife of another prophet, she was also faced with a difficult situation.

"One day, this widow came to Elisha in need of his counsel. Her husband had died and left her poverty stricken and in debt. Her creditors were demanding the sale of her two sons into slavery to pay off her indebtedness. When Elisha asked her what she had in her home that could be sold, she replied that they owned nothing, and had only a small vial of oil.

"Elisha then gave her instructions to go to all her neighbors and borrow all the jars she could from them. She obeyed. Once she was home and alone with her sons, she used her small vial of oil and began pouring it into the empty vessels. Miraculously, each jar was filled and the oil continued to flow as long as there were waiting open and empty vessels. The woman then sold the oil and paid off her debts.

"This woman of virtue demonstrated her great hope of God's deliverance. Regardless of her circumstances, she listened to the prophet, obeyed his voice and was rewarded. Her dreams and visions for herself and her sons knew no bounds, as she demonstrated in the multitude of empty vessels she sought to fill.

"The last story I want to share with you this evening is of another woman of virtue, who sought after a greater Prophet than either Elijah or Elisha, and yet He was a Servant of all men.

"In Bethany, at the house of Simon the Leper, a woman came to see the Man of God, the Messiah, having supper there. She brought with her an alabaster jar of sweet-smelling spikenard. While the Man reclined at the table, she broke the wax seal and released the fragrant oil; its luscious perfume filled the air. She poured the costly ointment upon His head. Her sacrificial gift was a deep expression of the virtue of love; it won His approval and her lifelong commendation.

"Three women with three vessels expressing three virtues. The first woman emptied her vessel in faith, believing and trusting that God would provide and deliver. The second woman emptied her vessel into other empty vessels in hope, expecting with confidence that God would fulfill her dreams of a brighter future. The third woman broke her vessel in sacrificial love, regardless of the cost, and poured out all that she had. In doing so, she found the censure of men but gained the approval of God.

"These women were vessels of faith, hope and love. Today, we can learn to be like them. We can learn that obedience brings blessings; that while faith trusts, and hope expects, love must give its all. Each day brings us closer to eternity. There, faith becomes vision, hope takes on possession and love continues on forever and never fails. Therefore it is the greatest of all three virtues.

"Remember, to be vessels of virtue we need to be filled with the holiness of God—overflowing with the oil of His Holy Spirit. Only then are we able to pour into the empty vessels of mankind: those hungry for the bread of eternal life, those needing freedom from the slavery of sin and, most of all, those wanting to know the forgiveness and love of our Heavenly Father.

"As Paul the great Apostle to the Gentiles once wrote, "But God commendeth his love toward us, in that, while we were yet sinners, Christ died for us."[11]

I stepped down from the podium and returned to my seat next to Marie. The room was subdued as Abigail returned to the platform.

"I am overwhelmed!" she began with tear-filled eyes. "And I feel challenged to become a better vessel." The room filled with applause and my heart rejoiced at the sight of so many smiling women.

~ *Chapter Thirty-One* ~

News! News! News!

*I*n mid-February, Christopher and I returned to Beulah to celebrate our first wedding anniversary. It was warmer this year and there was little snow on the ground. Some of the children had been here the summer before, enjoying the cottage and visiting the Grand Canyon. Chris had purchased more acreage and had workmen building a variety of small cabins throughout the forested grounds. This way we could put up family and friends who wanted to come and rest in this peaceful woodland.

We heard often from Miss Flowers, now Mrs. Edward Fox, who had settled down happily to married life. Now living in Europe, she wrote that it was extremely cold there but she didn't mind. She had fortunately acquired a teaching job at the military base school.

Devon and Joseph had returned to their busy work schedule after Sasha and Petey returned home to their mother. Our infrequent conversations seemed to center on the children and the adjustments they all had to make with their departure. I felt their loss keenly, having already experienced the pain an empty nest brings. Life moved on slowly for them but they endeavored to soothe their pain by pouring themselves out for humanity in science and research at the Center for Disease Control in Atlanta.

Victoria called often to share about her life in England. We were happy to hear that Allen's mother, Audra, had improved so much that they were contemplating their return home even though they hadn't made any definite decisions.

Chris was more relaxed about Chloe's declaration of her feelings and intents toward Scott Williams than I would have believed. He did manage to squeeze in a brief trip to Palo Alto to meet the young man and all fears were allayed at his approval. I was looking forward to my opportunity to meet him and hoped that he would come soon for a visit with Chloe.

Sarah and John Edwards were busier than ever now that they had a new baby to care for along with J.J. Their second son was born in September and they named him Jude Justus, a unique but powerful name. He was a sweet little boy with a cherubic face that quite resembled his mother.

Miriam and Noah and Hannah were blooming as a family and she seemed more vibrant than ever. Tabitha's House was flourishing too and had filled to capacity all too quickly. The cookbook had come out just prior to the holidays and was successful and generating a small income for the shelter. Unfortunately, as with all charities, we always needed to be looking toward the future and new projects that would generate funds.

While most of the family appeared to be doing well, Charlotte's health had become a cause of concern. She looked pale and was much too thin. She insisted that she felt fine but she had scheduled an appointment to see the doctor just to be sure.

Christopher kept Wesley busy working on his correspondence and taking care of his business affairs. He had become a rather permanent fixture at the estate after we renovated rooms on the third floor for him.

I was sitting in my study leisurely reading a book while they were busy answering some letters when the telephone rang abruptly and startled me. I jumped up from my old comfy chair and walked to the desk. Routinely I picked up the receiver on my private line and was pleased to hear Charlotte's melodious voice ring out.

"Mom, I'm pregnant!" she exclaimed with a loud squeal.

"Pregnant! Oh, Charlotte, how wonderful! I can't believe it…I'm going to be a grandmother again. *Please* tell me you're not moving to London!" I said teasing.

Charlotte laughed lightheartedly. "Don't worry, Mom. I'm not going anywhere. As a matter of fact, I have to stay in bed for a while."

Alarm arose in my heart. "Charlotte, what's wrong?" I demanded fearfully.

"Nothing to worry about, Mom. I'm fine! Really. I've had some irregular bleeding. That's why I never suspected I was pregnant. The doctor thinks it might be a good idea for me to stay in bed for a while, so I'm going to have to take a leave of absence from school. I'm so happy, Mom!"

"Oh, Charlotte! I'm so happy for you. Hold on, I've got to call Christopher." I put the telephone receiver down and ran to find Chris who was now foraging in the kitchen for a snack. He picked up the extension there.

"Charlotte, congratulations!" he said enthusiastically. "When is the baby due?"

"Goodness," I murmured, softly, standing next to him, "I didn't even think to ask her that myself." Taking the phone away from my husband I repeated the question.

"Yes, when is the baby due, Char?"

"Not sure really, but we think around the end of July."

Christopher took the phone back and asked for Edgar and congratulated him on the prospect of becoming a father. They chatted for a while and I heard Chris promise to buy a box of cigars before handing the telephone back to me.

"Charlotte," I said once again, "you're going to need someone to help you at home. Would you like me to call Mary and see if she's available?"

"Oh, Mom, would you?"

"Of course I will. Now you stay off your feet and get plenty of rest. I'll come down in a few days to visit."

"Thanks, Mom! Edgar has been a wonderful help to me but my being on bed rest will eventually take its toll on him and my house. He's very busy right now with the school music competitions—it keeps him pretty distracted. Not to mention the fact that his cooking leaves a little to be desired," she laughed, "but don't tell him I said so."

"I won't, don't worry. I love you, Charlotte," I said a bit tearfully and she told me she loved me too and then she hung up.

"What's that rascal doing in me kitchen, Mum?" I heard Martha say as she entered her sanctuary from the hallway door. With hands placed sternly on her hips she gave my husband a scowl.

"Having a wee bite to eat, dearest!" He uttered smoothly while teasing his favorite Irish woman. "And I haven't made a mess." His handsome smile and winsome ways were too irresistible for even Martha who truly doted on him.

"Martha, Charlotte is pregnant!" I exclaimed.

Her attention diverted her scowl instantly turned to a smile. "Lord, bless her!" she proclaimed with spirit as she bounded across the room to give me a hug. "Our baby is having a baby, Mum. Ah, the Lord is surely good to us." I agreed.

"Martha, the doctor wants Charlotte to stay in bed for a while and she'll need someone to take of her and the house. Do you know if Mary is available to stay with her?"

"Don't ya worry now about a thing, Mum. As sure as I'm Irish I promise ya that my sweet sister will be on Charlotte's doorstep tomorrow!" Martha tenaciously headed for the telephone and in a matter of minutes she and Mary had worked out all the arrangements. After all, their Irish heritage depended on it.

Patricia was upstairs sitting with Isabelle in her room so Martha and I brought up a teacart filled with hot drinks and almond cookies to munch on as we shared the latest family news.

Two days later Martha and I, along with my entourage, drove down to see Charlotte, who was still pale but feeling somewhat better. Martha acknowledged that Mary's care was always exceptional but insisted on bringing some of her own homemade goodies for the three of them to enjoy. Everyone knew that her soups, breads and pastries were fabulous; she could make anything taste great. But I knew the real issue wasn't about food—that was just the way her love for people was manifested. Martha loved the girls; her life was intricately involved with theirs. After all, we had all grown up together.

We had barely returned from our visit when I received an excited telephone call from Devon.

"Hi, Grandma!" she yelled into the telephone, bubbling with joy.

"You've heard the news!" I said pleased. "Were you surprised?"

"Surprised? No, not really," she responded. "But how did you know?"

"Well, Charlotte told me of course."

"Charlotte told you? But we haven't even talked to her."

"Then how did you know that she's pregnant?" I asked, now completely confused.

"*Charlotte's pregnant?*" She asked and then burst out laughing.

"Why yes. I thought you knew…isn't that why you called?"

"Mom, I called to tell you that I am pregnant!"

"*Oh, Devon*, this is wonderful. I can't believe it…you're both pregnant. Congratulations!"

"Thanks, Mom. Wait a minute while I tell the news to Joseph. He'll be amazed as well." She quickly related the surprising news to Joseph and then returned to the conversation.

"Oh, Devon. I'm so sorry…I didn't realize when you called me Grandma…"

"Mom, don't worry. It's okay. Who knew?"

"When is the baby due?" I asked.

"Around August," she responded. "When is Charlotte due?"

"Probably the end of July but they're not sure…she's had some complications." I explained the problems Charlotte was having and Devon understood the seriousness much better than I.

"I wish you weren't so far away from us," I said, sad to think she would be going through her pregnancy alone. "How are you feeling? Are you going to continue to work?" I asked.

"I feel wonderful fortunately. And I'm not going to work much longer. Actually, I've already given my notice. A great many things are changing for us," she said. "I know I've been a little secretive lately," she began, "but I didn't want to say anything to anyone until I was sure about the future. Mom, Joseph and I are moving to Los Angeles!"

I was speechless.

"Mom, did you hear me?" she said.

"Oh, Devon, really?" I cried. "Are you really coming home?" Tears streamed down my face.

"Yes, Mom. I'm really coming home!" she answered softly. "Joseph's been offered a position at UCLA. It's a great opportunity for him and it means being closer to family. It's sooo strange. I didn't think I'd ever have children…I was so wrapped up in my work. But when Joseph's niece and nephew came to stay with us, everything changed. I never thought having children underfoot could be so wonderful until they left and when they did a piece of me left with them.

"But I guess I was afraid…because being a parent is such a heavy responsibility. Joseph always wanted children but I wasn't sure I did. And now that I'm pregnant I just can't believe how happy I am. And we knew almost immediately that we wanted the baby to grow up close to family. So, Joseph pursued a job opportunity at UCLA and they've made him an offer.

"Eventually, Victoria will move home to Northern California and Dad and Jess don't live far away from her. Charlotte is already close to home and now that she's pregnant too, the children will be able to grow up together. I guess I didn't realize how much I miss everyone.

"We won't arrive for a month or so. We've given notice at work and need a little time to pack. We were hoping we could stay with you until we can find a house. If that's okay?"

Words didn't come easy amidst the flow of tears.

"Devon, this home is your home, for as long as you want," I said, wiping my eyes with a tissue. Was it really possible? My children were coming home.

Chapter Thirty-Two

Sophie Anastasia

*T*he happy news of our rapidly growing family was shared with our closest friends as we awaited Devon and Joseph's arrival with great anticipation. I contacted the real estate agency that had sold the home that Paul and I once shared and asked them to begin looking for housing in the university area.

The second floor of the south wing was more or less kept open now with family and friends coming so frequently to visit with us. When the children arrived they made themselves at home in one of the lovely suites that faced the ocean. Devon was radiant with joyful expectation. Joseph traveled to and from the estate to the university as often as was necessary. During the week he took up residence at our apartment in Los Angeles, while working and screening property. Devon was excited when he called to say he had found a home he thought she would like.

The neighborhood was old and quiet and just a block away from Sunset Boulevard. A small three bedroom home built in the thirties it was perfect for their small family and would be close to the university hospital where Joseph would be working. They quickly made the purchase and patiently waited for escrow to close. Devon was enjoying the relaxing pleasures of being at home where she could be pampered by a host of matronly women. She enjoyed a restful week in the city visiting with Charlotte who was now doing much better. Devon returned home elated that they were able to share the wonders of their pregnancies—an experience she would have missed had she remained in Georgia.

Our conversations were focused on babies; we talked about baby furniture, room décor, potential male and female names while perusing baby magazines, stores and books. The prospect of having two new grandchildren prompted me to have two rooms in the south wing redecorated; one would be a nursery, the other an educational playroom.

Sophie, so close in age to my daughters, watched all from the sidelines regardless of my attempts to draw her in. Only an invisible wall of her own making kept her on the outside.

She and I met on business one sunny afternoon on the small outdoor patio located on the east side of the Victorian—an area reserved solely for the guests of the inn. The ground was covered with cobblestones and lovely greenery. There were small tables with umbrellas and chairs and a few recliners that faced the ocean for guests to lounge in. The morning sun kept the tiny refuge warm and inviting and in the afternoon everything was pleasantly shaded by the shadow of the house.

"You're doing a very good job, Sophie," I began. "Noah and I are both pleased with your work!" She smiled and said thank you.

"I've still got a great deal to learn but Miriam has been a wonderful teacher. She's a fabulous cook, too. Would you like to try a piece of cake that I baked yesterday?" Sophie asked eagerly.

"I'd love to!" I responded and she quickly dashed into the kitchen. Moments later she returned with a pot of hot coffee and two plates topped with generous slices of cake. I took a bite and savored the taste.

"Mmmm. Peanut butter?" I queried and she nodded. "Sophie, it's heavenly!"

"Thank you," she responded with joy. "I think so too." Whipped cream separated each of the four layers of cake, which was frosted with mocha butter cream icing. It must have been laden with calories but I ate every delicious bite nonetheless.

"It must be nice having your daughter home again," Sophie said casually. Was it an attempt to know and be known? I wasn't sure.

"Yes, it is!" I replied. "And I think she needs as well as deserves a rest before her baby is born; it also gives us an opportunity to spend some time together to strengthen our relationship."

"Have you and your daughters always been so close?" she asked shyly.

"Honestly...no, we haven't," I answered candidly. "Of course, I love each of them...very much. But the truth is that some relationships are just more complicated than others...regardless of affection. We're uniquely different people...and our personality and temperament affects how we relate to one another."

"I'll say!" she agreed strongly. "I have a *very* difficult time getting along with my mother! Every discussion we have seems to end in an argument!" I was surprised by the anger I heard in her voice. It was the first time Sophie allowed herself the freedom to express her emotions and once she did they poured forth like a waterfall. "I don't see much hope for us. I'm not sure either of us will ever change enough to have a good relationship. There are times when we barely communicate at all."

"Every relationship goes through stages, Sophie, especially those between parents and their children; nothing is hopeless where love abounds."

"Oh, Rachel, I do love my mother," she cried mournfully, "but we fight so much!" Her eyes were filled with tears and for the first time ever I saw Sophie lower the wall that kept the world out. "It seems that no matter what I do, no matter how well I perform, I never measure up to her standards. I've become such a perfectionist trying to please her...trying to win her love, I guess. And when I fail, I feel worthless. I'm frustrated and...sometimes I feel so bitter towards her...I don't know what to do." Her tears poured out and my heart ached for her.

"I'm so sorry, Sophie!" Soft words of genuine concern came forth from my heart as I reached out to ease her misery "It's very difficult when we feel we aren't loved or accepted for who we are by the people we desire most to please. And so often we don't mean to hurt one another…but sometimes we do."

"But why?" she cried tearfully and between sobs she verbalized the pain that filled her hurting heart. "Why doesn't she like me? I *know* she doesn't like me, Rachel!"

It was hard for me to respond. Silently I sat thinking of my brief relationship with my own mother. Quietly, in my mind I found the words to express the feelings in my heart.

"My parents died when I was ten so we never really had much time to argue or disagree. And even though we had little squabbles every now and then, there was never much friction between us. My mother was a really sweet-tempered person…everyone loved her; I was blessed in that respect."

"It must have been hard for you…growing up without them," she said, softly.

"Yes, it was. You know, Sophie, life is terribly unpredictable. The impact of a single event can alter the course of our history dramatically. In a moment of time my life was changed and irrevocably redefined. I don't think I've ever spent a day since without thinking about my own mortality. Life is a precious gift that we often take for granted."

"But what can I do, Rachel?" Her defenses were up. "My mother and I are so different that we clash constantly!" Her face mirrored the pained confusion she felt within. "We're both outspoken and opinionated…that's part of the problem." Quietly she continued, almost thinking aloud, "I think she wishes I were different; I know I wish she were."

"Being a parent isn't easy," I said thinking of the problems Devon and I had been through. "We're all different people, Sophie. Too often we grow up with unreasonable expectations of the people we love. Children see their parents through rose-colored glasses until they grow up and realize that they are human beings with imperfections. Parents have hopes and dreams for their children, which can be good and bad at the same time. Some of those dreams are realistic and some aren't. I've seen too many parents attempt to live vicariously through their kids and when they succeed or fail, they feel it as keenly as if it had been their own success or failure.

"In a perfect world, we would all learn to love and accept one another for who we are, distinctly different and wonderfully unique. We would all be a great deal happier if we could learn to accept one another."

"My mother will *never* accept me for who I am!" she sighed.

"I hope that's not true!" I said searching for words that would encourage my young friend. "And while I believe that nothing is impossible, I realize there are many things that we are called to do that are extremely difficult...growing up without a mother and father was difficult but I managed. Part of the woman I am today is the result of that great loss and even now when my life doesn't go as I hope or plan, I work to adapt."

Unconsciously, I reached down to loosen the strap on my new sandals. The leather fit too snugly across my foot and pinched a bit. I smiled.

"Sophie, my grandfather used to say that adapting in life is like finding your feet then learning where to put them to make the most progress." Her eyes easily expressed her misunderstanding.

"Find your feet, Sophie. Be yourself—the best you can be—and allow your mother the same freedom. You can't be someone you're not and neither can she. Love needs to be free and unconditional." Sophie just stared.

"Rachel, I do love my mother. Sometimes, I just wish she could be more…" she stopped abruptly then looked at me with startled eyes.

"You can't change anyone but you, Sophie."

"I know that but… what do I do when we don't agree on something that's important?" she asked, searching for direction.

"Love allows for disagreement. Love shouldn't enslave us—it should free us. My love for someone should grant him or her the freedom to disagree with me without the fear of losing my love. Anything else would be control or manipulation. If you want your mother to love you for who you are, you must do the same for her. Love her for who she is, as she is. Learn to accept her, warts and all." She laughed and then cried and then sighed a huge sigh. Was it relief? She wiped her eyes with a tissue; they seemed to sparkle. It's hope that makes the eyes sparkle I think.

"Where do I start?" she asked, sincerely.

"That's a good question. Why not start with forgiveness? Forgive your mother and forgive yourself. We hurt one another and we get hurt ourselves. No one is perfect—not parents, not spouses, not siblings, not children, and certainly not friends. My mother used to recite the proverb that says, 'Hatred stirreth up strifes: but love covereth all sins[12].' Perhaps that's one of the reasons she was so sweet-tempered. She chose to focus on the good in people. Sometimes that means simply wiping the slate clean and beginning again."

~ Chapter Thirty-Three ~

Alone but Never Lonely

*M*y conversation with Sophie stayed in my heart for days and I prayed that my words would be a help to her.

Growing up without a mother sometimes made it difficult for me to relate to the girls my own age, especially when they would come to me to complain about their own. So often I just listened quietly without comment to the tales of woe they shared about their pushy domineering mothers; it was difficult. More than anything, I wanted a mother, even a pushy domineering one. The more insensitive girls would say, "Rachel, you're so lucky!" I never thought so.

Of course, there were those other times when my friends would tell me they went shopping or out to lunch or some other "girlish" function with their mothers they deemed fun and adventurous. Then it was just the opposite. Then they all felt sorry for me.

My grandparents and I had occasional disagreements so I did experience some of the animosity that young people felt toward their elders, especially when they thought they were out of step with reality and the times. But honestly, my grandparents were such wonderful people; there was little I could complain about, even if I had wanted to.

Talking to Sophie had stirred up old memories of past feelings I had long ago dealt with and learned to leave behind. My childhood anger with God for the loss of my parents and only sibling was over. The memories of the brief but happy time we shared together I kept locked inside of my heart. I knew we would one day meet again!

Christopher went riding with John Anderson on Friday mornings whenever he was home and unoccupied and that was my time alone to catch up on my correspondence. Today, I was too restless to write letters. I walked over to Isabelle's room to see how she was and found her quietly sleeping with her Bible next to her on her bed. Devon was spending the week in Los Angeles with Joseph and they wouldn't return until later in the evening. Alone, I decided to take a trip back into the past so I climbed the stairs to the third floor where many of my childhood treasures were now kept. Before Chris and I married, I moved many of my personal favorite things to an empty unused room that faced the front of the estate and looked out at the ocean.

I kept the handmade quilt Grandmother and Isabelle has made for me and it covered a lovely old four-poster bed I had used as a young girl—a very special gift from Papa. When I walked into the room, it was like walking into the past...Riley's old wooden rocking horse was in one corner surrounded by his train set, treasures I would never part with. A lovely dresser, filled with awards and mementos of my school years, stood in one corner and my vanity complete with a silver brush, comb and mirror, was in another.

The windows were heavily draped and I pulled them open to let in the sun. The windows flung open easily and in poured the fresh sea air.

My favorite dolls lined a long wooden shelf. In the middle of the room was a round oak table with four chairs that Papa had carved for Grandmother when they were newlyweds. There were old family pictures everywhere. I walked around the room glancing at the photos on the wall. I smiled at the one of Papa and me together riding down at the old paddocks. I was mounted on Daisy, my little Welsh pony, his gift to me on my eleventh birthday.

An old steamer trunk filled with Mama's and Papa's letters and personal papers stood at the end of the bed. I opened it and took out several folders of brown paper wrapped in red ribbons—letters my mother had written to my father before they were married. I kissed them and put them back in the trunk. I found the old port-folio box I was looking for and laid it on the bed and sat down to open it. I reached inside and gently removed a small stack of papers, essays my mother had written while she was at school. There weren't many and I guess I knew most of them by heart. Grand-mother had saved some from her early years in school and some were found when they sorted through their belongings after they died. I was so happy my grandparents had kept them. They gave me a glimpse inside my mother's heart and I was able to see her in a way that would otherwise have been impossible.

My favorite was on top. Carefully, I held the old yellowed page written in my mother's small and elegant script now faded and blurred. A creative writing assignment for an English class, she wrote of her love of the ocean—something we both shared and delighted in.

The Ocean
By Rebecca Winthrope

The beach is busy today—so many people enjoying the sun and the surf. I often wonder if they experience the seashore as I do…in my soul. We are mysteriously linked, the ocean and me—perhaps because it is the place where my heart feels most at rest. When I think of the ocean, I think of home and a sense of gladness fills my being.

Come with me, on an enchanted journey. Our destina-tion is a place of serene tranquility. Where rest and content-ment may settle into the heart; no matter how troubled inside you may feel at the moment. Experience the ocean through my eyes.

I love the warmth of the gritty sand as it slips beneath my feet each time I take a step. Dancing in the briny waves as they churn in and out is exciting. You can feel the awesome power of the deep. I've tasted the salty water and breathed in the crisp fragrant air. The mist dampens my hair and leaves it hanging in long soft ringlets and when the wind blows it lifts and pushes it against my face. And the music...the glorious music of the noisy gulls circling overhead somehow blends in peacefully with the roar of the waves as they break majestically upon the shore. It inspires me!

The warm summer sun shines brightly upon the massive charging waters until little by little it moves through the sky and slowly disappears beyond the horizon leaving only a stream of brilliant orange color upon the now darkening waters. The blue quickly turns to purple and before long descends into blackness, only the frothy peaks of white foam bubbles remain visible in the darkness.

Occasional gems of light from the starry skies above glisten like diamonds on the immense pool of darkness and the cold of the deep creeps up into my soul as I stand and listen to the waves quietly beating in the night. I am alone but never lonely. The peace of God fills my heart and my soul longs to praise the One that gives so completely to feed my being with His Love.

The morning comes quickly as the first glimpse of sunlight pours onto the beach and diffuses the darkness of the night. The sand is reddish-brown once again, the waves endlessly churning are bright blue, and the gulls begin to circle overhead and are joined by a flock of sandpipers scampering on the shore. Seashells and seaweed and pieces of driftwood decorate the sand with natural beauty. A new day has arisen, and life begins again.

Here I stand, like a tiny grain of sand, small and insignificant and surrounded by the billions of others clustered about me, alone but never lonely. Why? God is with me. He created the world. He gave it to us as a gift. We plunged it into darkness with sin. But wait...a new day dawns, He has resurrected it and me.

My journey to the beach has ended; but my journey with God continues on.

My mother was only seventeen then. Her words touched me the first time I read them. They continue to touch me freshly each time I read them again and I gain something wonderful from the knowledge that I glean. This one short commentary of her thought life taught me a little about her and gave me a sense of belonging. It was comforting to know she felt as she did about the ocean…and God. It was a bond we shared…not hemmed in by time or space…one that goes on into eternity.

I closed up the old portfolio and returned it to its secure place in the old wooden trunk. I went to the big window and looked out at the ocean, the surf was high today and the waves were crashing on the shore dressed in all the splendor of their briny robes.

The door opened behind me and I turned to see my husband, dressed in riding apparel, come in through the open portal. We smiled at each other.

"Reminiscing?" he asked with a grin.

"Yes!" I responded soulfully as he wrapped his arms around my shoulders. We stood in front of the window for a few quiet moments and then peacefully departed into the present, leaving the treasures of the past behind once again.

Chapter Thirty-Four

The Danger of Compromise

Chris was home a great deal in the spring and when we weren't busily employed with fund-raising activities we spent as much time as possible supporting our new senator and dear friend, Frank Crosby. Even the young John Anderson had become more involved in politics; the bombing, which had taken Jennie's life and nearly taken my own, had clearly affected almost everyone we knew. I guess it's true that when things become personal, they take on greater urgency for all of us.

Anxious to introduce Frank to our community of friends, we decided to host a "Get Acquainted Gala," one evening in early May. Fortunately, the estate was spacious enough to hold hundreds of people. The grand ballroom was both regal and luxurious—a proud display of Grandfather's workmanship that we could now put to good use for events that were both entertaining and beneficial.

Devon and Joseph had finally taken possession of their new home and she was engrossed in decorating during the hours he was occupied settling into his new job. Daily they shared their excitement about their new home, Joseph's work and the measures being taken to prepare for the arrival of the new baby.

Charlotte, Devon and I spent many happy days together picking out nursery furniture and layettes. My decorator was called in to provide her assistance and advised them on what would be best for each home that would also suit their personal preferences. Once the girls had chosen a theme, color and style, the decorator was set free to make it all happen. The girls also made several purchases of new maternity clothing for the hot summer months ahead. How wonderful it was having them so close to home that I was able to share in all their excitement.

Charlotte's health had improved and she was finally taken off of bed rest. We were further delighted when we learned that she was expecting *twins*. The babies were all due to arrive during the summer, and the suggestions for possible names continued to flow forth from a variety of sources.

Chris commiserated with Chloe when she called to say that Scott was unable to accept our invitation to visit at the end of the term. He was offered a position as an intern with a local newspaper, which would begin as soon as finals were over. She accepted the sad news gracefully and he assured her he would come as soon as time allowed.

Working on the guest list for the gala was a difficult enterprise that involved a host of people. Frank and his assistants along with Chris, Wesley and our security firm scrutinized every name. The security measures being taken were intense but the diversity of the attendees was such that it was required.

Our Hollywood friends were a very eclectic group but they usually blended in easily with our political friends since most were fairly conservative. We invited many of the neighboring ranchers along with prominent business people from the community. There were leaders from local churches and synagogues as well as our family and personal friends. Chris, like Papa, thought it was wonderful to mix and match people from different stratums of society—diversity broadens one's horizons—or so they both said. I had to agree.

Dressing for any event was always a large part of the fun. Devon, Charlotte and I spent several days shopping for "the perfect gown." They wanted something long and loose fitting. Devon chose a lovely powder blue silk chiffon gown with quarter length sleeves and a round neckline. It was free flowing with gathering just under the bust line. Charlotte, always attracted to vintage fashions of the thirties and forties, found a unique rust colored gown of silk crepe inset with ivory lace. It had long flowing sleeves and a high collar at the neck.

Beaded gowns can be heavy but their beauty makes them worth the weight. I delighted in finding a dazzling hand-beaded lace dress in a golden apricot color. It was sleeveless with a square neckline and small train. It fit snugly—like a glove—sleek and comfortable. Diamond stud earrings were all the adornment the gown needed; anything more would detract.

The evening air was balmy, though perhaps a little warm for May. Security had arranged for the guests to park their cars down below in a private area near the restaurant and be shuttled by limousine to the mansion above. This way each guest's identity was checked prior to their ascending the mountain. Uniformed guards on foot and those traveling the perimeter by vehicle surrounded the grounds. News of the special event had spread and the highway was lined with a variety of newspaper reporters and their cameramen.

Christopher relaxed comfortably on the couch in our sitting room listening to some jazz recordings while I finished dressing. His tuxedo was the traditional "white tie and tails" made by his favorite European designer. His handsome face was tan and glowing; the steel gray eyes always shimmered with mischievous delight. His hair was a tad longer than he traditionally wore it and its jet-black color showed only the slightest touch of gray at the sides.

"I'm ready!" I announced while placing a small tube of lipstick in a tiny golden purse. I twirled for his approval.

"Lovely!" he said as he arose from his cushy spot on the couch and put his jacket on. Then, taking my hand, he lightly kissed my cheek and together we made our way downstairs walking in the direction of the open ballroom, which was festively decorated in red, white and blue. The tables were gaily topped with patriotic floral arrangements, each sporting a tiny American flag.

The noise in the room was clamorous and upon our arrival it went up several decibels. A throng of admirers immediately surrounded Christopher, and I left him to his fans in order to greet our other guests. The atmosphere around him was charged with electricity. I only smiled.

Some time later while mingling with my guests, Charlotte motioned me over to her. She was seated at a table by the fireplace sipping a glass of sparkling water.

"Mom," she whispered delicately, "don't you think Christopher needs to be rescued?" She laughed. "He's been inundated with women since he walked into the room."

"He's just too handsome and charming," I proclaimed. "Actually, he doesn't mind socializing with his public. I think he rather enjoys it." I looked around the beautiful ballroom until I found my husband and made eye contact. Silently, I made my way through the throng of people that filled the room until I reached the orchestra. I made my request and then moved toward Christopher. Gracefully I took hold of his hand and making our excuses he escorted me onto the dance floor. With thankful eyes he took me in his arms.

"Thank you, Holmes!" he said as we began to dance.

"You're welcome, Watson!" I replied. "Honestly, Darling, if you could manage to look a little less charming, I wouldn't have to rescue you so often!" He laughed as we danced gaily around the floor where we were soon joined by a host of others.

Frank Crosby graciously moved about the ballroom meeting his new constituents sharing his thoughts on a variety of topics. Dinner was lovely and dessert was delicious. Eagerly, we waited to hear from the evening's guest speakers. Aaron Cohen, who was a gifted Hollywood screenwriter, a Jewish Conservative and a special friend to Mr. Crosby, was on the platform first. Humbly he stood before our diverse audience.

"Ladies and gentlemen," he began quietly, "thank you for inviting me here tonight. I am honored to be in the company of so many fine men and women.

"I am seventy-five years old and have worked in Hollywood for more than fifty years. I understand the necessity of compromise, without which no two people let alone any two nations could peacefully coexist. The very complexities of our diversities make concessions necessary by the members of a civilized society to live harmoniously within their homes and among the nations that inhabit the globe. In this vein compromise is always good.

"And yet there is another type of compromise, one which is so common and prevalent today that many fail to recognize just how insidious it is. It is that compromise which asks the individual to give up or weaken the very principles they need to live by, to exist in society with ethics and integrity. It is just this type of compromise that is weakening the moral fiber of America, and if it is not stopped—it will ultimately bring about her downfall.

"I'd like to tell you the story of a man—a military leader of intense passion and great potential that was destined to become the champion of his people. He was a patriot: a strong, virile man endowed with the ability to deliver his countrymen from the oppression of their enemies.

"This man grew up in a good home with good parents who taught him godly values. His childhood training set him apart from infancy so that he might grow to fulfill his destiny…to become a pillar of his community. He served his country for twenty years; in battle, his military conquests were magnificent and successful. He was prepared to sacrifice all to overthrow the enemies of his people. His greatest act of faith and heroism cost him his life but immortalized his name in the hero's Hall of Faith.

"But," Aaron said, sharply, before he paused to slowly evaluate the intrigued faces of his captivated audience. With a slight smile, he began again with ardor, "BUT, his service, like that of so many other great men, was flawed by weakness. Because *Samson*, you see, was given to compromise. He was strong in body but weak in character—a man that gave in to his passions. Given to lust and revenge, the obsessions of this willful man proved him often foolish and self-indulgent. Unable or unwilling to curb his own natural desires, he allowed them to run free, unchecked…and in the end it brought his downfall.

"Samson was a passionate man. But passionate men must also be discriminating men…and the ability to rule others wisely begins first with good self-government. Passions uncontrolled soon run amok and we, like this great man of the past, may find ourselves ensnared in controversy and sin and taken captive. Vision can then become distorted and even tainted until we eventually end up losing our way, and possibly our reputation and position—and sometimes, ultimately even our lives. In the end, Samson made a difference, but he was capable of so much more.

"Personally, I am proud to support our new senator. Frank Crosby is a good man, a fine lawyer, and a person of integrity and character. He is a man, which I believe will *definitely* make a difference. Won't you welcome him to the platform?"

The applause that filled the room was deafening. Senator Crosby spoke succinctly for the next hour. Reform within the government was necessary, he agreed, but it began with the reform of men and women who, like himself, would agree to govern with integrity.

Chapter Thirty-Five

A New Generation

Devon's first ultrasound had revealed the fact that she and Joseph would be raising a daughter. Devon's pregnancy had been easy; she gained only twenty pounds and moved about with relative ease.

Poor Charlotte! The twins had caused her abdomen to grow rather large and she often complained about feeling like a beached whale. Getting in and out of bed or a chair became a major problem as the months went by. Her first ultrasound showed two tiny babies in her womb; one was definitely a boy. The second baby they found out much later was a little girl.

Chloe was home for the summer and gloried in being a part of a big family for the first time in her life. Isabelle had been teaching her to cross-stitch and was helping her create baby bibs for her new nieces and nephew. We traveled together to my daughters' homes to see how their nurseries were developing.

Charlotte and Edgar had decided on a Classic Winnie the Pooh theme, as it would be compatible with both sexes. The room was painted in yellow and blue with a Classic Pooh wall border placed in the middle between the two shades. Cherry-wood sleigh-style cribs were on opposite walls with matching dressers and changing tables in between. A big throw rug in the center of the room was home to two reclining rockers, one for Mom in soft yellow and the other for Dad in dark blue.

Devon and Joseph chose the Little Lamb design for their baby from the Lambs & Ivy Collection. The room was painted beige and white and decorated with the cute gingham accessories that were designed to coordinate with the collection. Their crib was a traditional oak with light finish. A tall dresser and changing tower were designed to go with it. They chose a glider rocker and ottoman and placed it in a corner near the bedroom window.

The girls had decided early on to have one large baby shower for both of them, which we scheduled for the end of June. We were surprised but thrilled when Victoria called from London to say she was flying over to attend. Michael would be coming with her, and Allen also, if his schedule permitted.

Anxiously, Christopher and I awaited their arrival at the airport. Allen's face was the first we saw. He had Michael in his arms. He was sound asleep with his Teddy Bear cuddled closely under him. Victoria followed them carrying his toddler bag. We were completely unprepared for the surprise that greeted us with her arrival. Victoria was expecting as well.

"I can't believe it!" I said, looking at my very pregnant daughter. "Why didn't you tell us?" I admonished as I gave her a hug.

"When I found out I was pregnant, I knew I wanted to come back to the United States. And yet, I wasn't sure how Allen would feel, and we didn't want to leave Audra. I kept the pregnancy a secret while I prayed for God's direction and the most amazing things began to happen." On the way home Victoria related the story of her answered prayers.

"Allen has made numerous friends at the university and many of them visit us regularly." Her voice had a slight English accent to it, picked up from two years living in London. "One is an older gentlemen, a professor named Preston Lawrence, I think I may have mentioned him to you on occasion. He's on the verge of retirement and he's been helping Allen with a variety of projects so he's been to the house often. He's a kind man, a widower, and a little lonely I think, so trips to our home have been a welcome diversion for him. At any rate, he seemed to enjoy our company and we his. Allen was extremely pleased that he was always attentive to Audra. He even took her to the theater and the ballet when she was well enough to go, but more than anything they seem to enjoy just sitting together conversing. You know her health has improved a great deal in two years.

"One evening about a month ago, Preston was at home visiting with Audra. He had been invited to dinner, which wasn't uncommon. The cook had prepared an elegant dinner and while we were eating Preston quite matter-of-factly announced that he and Audra planned to marry! It was incredible. He is absolutely devoted to her, and Allen and I couldn't be happier. They were married in a small intimate ceremony last week.

"Later that evening, while Allen and I were alone in our room, I told him I was pregnant. He kissed me gently and said, "Time to go home!" I wholeheartedly agreed.

"So, here we are. Allen was able to secure his former teaching position and begins this fall. We didn't tell anyone about the baby because we wanted it to be a surprise."

"Oh, it is!" I laughed. "Wait until your sisters find out that *you are pregnant too!*"

"Mom, keeping this secret has been sooo hard! Actually, I couldn't believe it myself when I realized we would all give birth around the same time this summer."

"Amazing!" I said still stunned by this latest development.

"Beyond belief!" she uttered. "God answered my prayers in a way I never expected and in doing so my faith has grown dramatically."

I only smiled. When the conversation returned to the subject of babies, Victoria gladly informed us that they already knew the baby was a boy.

The weekend of the babies' baby showers arrived with great haste and expectancy. The girls had busily worked together planning the event with our baby coordinator and their plans were easily adjusted to include Victoria. Three expectant mothers at one event certainly needed coordinating and my own staff was already busy with the food and decorations so I used a professional from Santa Barbara to handle the affair.

The ballroom was opened once again as it was the largest room at the estate, able to accommodate all our guests. It was divided in three and each one the girls had their own section with a table decorated in the color of their choice.

Charlotte picked yellow and green while Devon chose pink and Victoria opted for blue. Their guests were seated at tables decorated with the same color design. Porcelain cherubs topped each table and sported a banner with the expected baby's name embossed upon it. The ladies received matching nametags in the corresponding color, which made it easy to distinguish whose guests belonged to whom. It was really tremendous fun for all.

The girls and I all agreed a morning brunch would be fun so the kitchen staff, supervised by Martha, had a number of delicious entrees on the morning menu. Belgian waffles with strawberries and whipped cream appeared to be the most requested meal but the chocolate chip pancakes were running a close second. There were smoked sausages and bacon and vegetarian meats of all kinds. Eggs and omelets and O'Brien potatoes were fresh and hot, along with the homemade buttermilk biscuits. Several varieties of scones with raspberry or lemon curd and clotted cream were more of a dessert but enjoyed regardless. And of course there was an assortment of hot coffee and fragrant teas and a nice selection of juices.

The ballroom was imbued with perfume. The sweet familiar faces of friends and family filled our home and brightened it with the amiable rays of benevolent love.

Edgar's mother and father had flown down from Seattle and would stay until the babies were born. Joseph and Allen's families were unable to attend but sent lovely gifts. Jessica, my daughter's stepmother, had been invited and came with several female members of her family. She was always pleasant at family functions and never tried to take my place in my daughters' lives. I appreciated her astuteness and knew that my children had grown to respect her because of it. We had all learned the benefits of grace and forgiveness.

The coordinator had us play a number of games and the ladies who won were able to select a prize from among the beautifully wrapped packages on a table near the fireplace. As a special gift for their attendance, every guest received a small basket of treats, which were now available from *The Cottage Gift Catalog.*

The morning was wonderful but tiring, especially for Charlotte who was exceptionally large and needed a great deal of rest. When the last of our guests had departed, she went upstairs to her old room to lie down.

The men had all been out of the house that morning while it was inundated with women but we were all together that evening for dinner. As usual, the topic of conversation was centered on babies.

"Edgar and I had a difficult time deciding on a name for our little girl," Charlotte began, "but in the end we had to go with Elizabeth!" She announced the name with great emphasis.

"Don't tell me!" Allen began playfully tormenting his sister-in-law. "*Pride and Prejudice!* Elizabeth Bennet, your favorite Jane Austen heroine!"

"As a matter of fact, dear brother-in-law, Elizabeth Bennet is *one* of my favorite fictional characters. She's a woman of many strengths but she's also teachable."

"Elizabeth Jane is a wonderful name!" Christopher agreed. "Mr. Darcy highly approves of your choice," he said bowing to Charlotte. "And Elijah James for her twin brother is equally as good!" he continued and bowed toward Edgar. Everyone laughed.

"They are wonderful names!" I agreed, fully approving of both.

"Joseph and I wanted a strong biblical name for our daughter," Devon began, "that's why we chose Devorah."

"Oh, I think Devorah Anne is lovely!" Chloe interjected. "Using the Israeli spelling for Deborah makes it more unique, too!"

Victoria and Allen were listening intently to the conversation. Victoria looked at me and smiled and I smiled back. I already knew the reason they had decided to name their future son Riley Conan MacDonald; it was to honor my only brother.

∽ Chapter Thirty-Six ∽

It Only Takes One

Marie came to the estate for a week's vacation during the summer while her husband and boys were off camping and Christopher was away busily involved in one of his many projects. She was overjoyed that her business was prospering. Their success enabled them to hire some additional help so they could take an occasional break and relax to enjoy the fruits of their labor.

A day at the beach lapping up the sun's heavenly rays was like a trip to heaven for us. We drove to a secluded little spot in Morro Bay that Chris and I usually frequented. Security was still a major concern for me—a part of life I could not alter. My husband, always so wisely astute, especially when dealing with the women in his life, dealt with the problem at hand as concisely as any other. He had the security firm find and hire a female bodyguard who could live and work at the estate full time. This made shopping and other personal excursions seem much less intrusive. Her name was Prudence; she was intelligent, kind and *extremely* capable.

Marie and I spread our beach towels out under the hot summer sun and then slathered our bodies with sunscreen. Large brimmed sunhats and dark glasses shielded our faces from the destructive rays of the glowing sun now beating down upon us as we leisurely basked in its warmth.

"Gosh, this is wonderful, Rae. I miss getting out in the fresh air, it's always so exhilarating," she said and then glanced at Prudence who was watching us from a spot on the dunes near where we lying. The second guard who had traveled with us in a separate car was nowhere to be seen. But he was out there. "I guess you miss the freedom you used to have." She spoke so softly it was difficult to hear her voice. She turned in my direction. "I'm sorry, Rachel...gosh, I'm so sorry all this has happened to you!" Her compassionate eyes were filled with tears. She was my dearest friend and she felt my pain and truly understood.

"Don't feel badly for me, Marie," I said with a thankful smile. "I'm learning to live with it." Looking out at the vast ocean in front of me, I silently wondered if things would ever change. "I've lived with restrictions most of my life. People think money is a cure for everything; how little they understand that it gives freedom and imprisons one at the same time. Being a celebrity can be like that as well, a blessing and a curse."

"When I was a little girl growing up," she said retreating into the memories of her mind, "I used to dream of becoming a Royal Princess. How happy I thought I would be. Now that I'm an adult I can see how difficult it is being famous. Especially if it means losing your freedom."

I closed my eyes and listened to the sounds of the surf and the gulls flying nearby. "Freedom is much more than we often realize, Marie. I'm at peace with God...so inside...I'm always free!"

We didn't wait long to open the delightful picnic lunch that Martha had so lovingly prepared for us. Our lunch basket was a treasure trove of goodies. We began with cool cucumber cups stuffed with shellfish. Marie loved the tasty egg salad sandwiches on sourdough bread and I devoured the sliced melon and fresh raspberries. We both enjoyed the Irish shortbread cookies and iced coffee reserved for dessert. As usual the focus of our conversation ran the gamut of topics and eventually settled on our children. Marie's boys were growing up as all children do. She was both anxious and elated that her oldest son, Adam, would be starting college in the fall.

"Adam has decided to major in political science!" she responded to the question I asked about his educational preferences.

"No!" I replied with surprise. "I thought he wanted to be a forest ranger? Or was that an astronaut?" We laughed together. "They change their minds so frequently when they're growing up. Didn't he also want to be a deep sea diver?"

"No, that was Tim, who I actually think will go into marine biology. He shares your passion for the sea!"

"That's wonderful! Maybe Tim would like to spend part of his summer vacation next year here at the estate? He could check out Cal Poly San Luis Obispo and see what they have to offer."

"Great idea! I'll ask him…I'm sure he'd love it here."

"Just let me know! Getting back to Adam, what made him choose political science? I thought his interests were more academic?"

"Well, his interests have always been rather diversified. He's a good student, organized, something of an overachiever and fairly conservative…typical firstborn child. But a great many things have happened in the past year that I think have contributed to his political interests."

"Such as?" I queried, enjoying the discussion.

"Well, he's always enjoyed his history and government classes. He was very involved in the mock elections his high school ran during the presidential campaign. He participated in the Academic Decathlon this year and thoroughly loved being a member of the speech and debate team."

"Perhaps some of his teachers are influencing him as well. He does have a great deal of potential. And he's very charismatic!"

"Actually, I never heard him mention politics before the Columbine High School shootings," Marie confessed. "And the bombing at the hotel angered and horrified him immensely. His sense of fair play is very acute, you know. He thinks the world should be safe for everyone and that playgrounds shouldn't be battlefields."

"And I think most sane people would agree with him. Well, with the right attitude, he may be just the one who can and will make a difference."

"It only takes one! Right?"

"Right!" I exclaimed removing a plastic bottle of water from my tote bag. I took a deep drink to rehydrate my throat.

"*Youth! With eager zeal they swim into the ocean of life; many are swept away or engulfed in a sea of indifference! Most embrace the tide and simply go with the flow but a few…a brave few, steadily plod their course refusing to be set adrift by opposing winds until they reach their destination. In the end, only these will make a lasting difference.*"

"That's interesting!" Marie said, listening intently to my recitation. "Who wrote it?"

"My mother," I replied proudly.

"Indifference is epidemic today, Rachel. The struggle for daily survival is all encompassing to so many that they have neither the time nor the inclination to bother with anything that doesn't directly affect them."

"I'm aware of that. But making a difference isn't as difficult or as time consuming as most people may think; and attitude is everything because you never know what you can do until you try.

"Look at Mother Teresa—one small fragile woman. She didn't set out to change the world…she set out to care for the poor and dying one person at a time. Ultimately, her life and example impacted the world tremendously.

"The ocean is very still today," I said staring at the beautiful blue waves quietly breaking on the shore. "But when a storm is raging it's a scary place to be. Papa used to tell me a story he heard when he was a boy. It was about a group of inexperienced young men who decided to spend the day out on the ocean deep-sea fishing. The day was cloudy and rain seemed imminent but the men were determined regardless. Out on the ocean the waves grew and eventually the rain pelted the small vessel being tossed about like a tiny twig. One large wave crashed over the deck and swept two of the men into the swirling black water. Screaming for help their cries went unheard by the others who were now clinging desperately to the ship in fear of being swept overboard as well. Only one young man had the courage to grab a life preserver and without hesitation he jumped into the violent waters. He swam to the man who was closest and was able to rescue him; sadly the other man drowned. Both might have been saved if anyone else had been willing to leave the safety of the ship.

"The storms brewing on the ocean of life are immeasurable. Too many people are being swept into the swirling waters of death; too few are brave enough to try to effect a single rescue."

"So many people are gripped by fear of the unknown that they don't want to venture out from their places of comfort and security," Marie declared.

"You're right," I responded. "And it's sad because you'll never know if you can walk on water until you get out of the boat!"

Chapter Thirty-Seven

The Journey Continues

We celebrated greatly the births of our new grandchildren and eagerly welcomed each into our happily expanding family.

Charlotte delivered first on a warm day in July. The doctor had determined early on there was too much risk to have the babies delivered naturally so on the prescribed day, the twins came into the world. Elizabeth was first; she was a hearty four pounds eleven ounces with a crop of dark brown hair; Elijah was last and weighed five pounds and two ounces. His hair was lighter and his skin a little more ruddy than that of his older sister.

Devon's baby was born in August; it was easy and without complication. Devorah was a healthy seven pounds and nine ounces and her hair was platinum blonde—just like her mother's was when she was born.

Victoria's second son was also born without complications. At the end of September young Riley came into the world squealing with delight. Michael was in awe of his new younger sibling.

Isabelle was so excited to see the new generation of children come into the family and was now a proud great-grandmother to five. She had spent most of the summer in bed as her health had declined but she never uttered a word of complaint. She worked tirelessly crocheting each child a beautiful hat, sweater and blanket. They were wonderful keepsakes that the girls would hold dear even after the babies had outgrown their usefulness.

When autumn arrived and the children and grandchildren had all departed the household grew very quiet.

Isabelle and I shared almost every afternoon together in her room. Occasionally, when she felt well enough, we had tea on my bedroom balcony overlooking the ocean and we enjoyed every moment we shared.

Often I read to her different books and letters, and several times we both escaped into the past as we reread the essays my mother had left behind. She never tired of telling me about the childhood they shared, she and my mother. I never tired of listening. I had been greatly blessed…more so than I ever deserved.

October was warm. We had very little rain the year before and we were praying this year would be different. The warms winds blew furiously and frequently, which kept everything drier than normal.

Isabelle continued to suffer from poor health and frequent bouts of pneumonia. She had been in and out of the hospital several times and just couldn't endure being away from her beloved home. Finally, her doctors agreed to allow her to remain in bed in her own comfortable room where she found the most peace and contentment.

"Oh, Isabelle," I said, standing in front of one of her bedroom windows, "it's a beautiful day outside, warm and windy but crystal clear. And the sun feels luxuriously warm. Mmmm!" I uttered while stretching my arms out wide. "How about a cup of tea?"

Isabelle smiled lightly and nodded her head and I called the kitchen and asked them to send up a cart. I was sitting by her bedside reading from the Psalms when Patricia arrived. The fragrance of cinnamon filled the air and eagerly I poured two cups of the hot spicy brew. I lifted Isabelle's head slightly to help her take a sip. It was good and I could tell she enjoyed it.

I munched on a shortbread cookie while I continued to read Psalm 119, one of Isabelle's favorites.

"Have you ever thought what it might have been like for King David, when he was a young shepherd boy, out tending his father's flock in the open countryside?" she asked, in a voice just above a whisper. "I imagine it must have been difficult at times and even frightening for him. After all, he did encounter a lion and even a bear." I just listened as she talked.

"Rachel, did you know that when I was a young girl, I was afraid of the dark?"

"No, I didn't," I replied shaking my head. I never would have thought that possible. She seemed so strong and confident.

"Well, I was. I used to have terrible nightmares and wake up screaming. My mother would always come to my bedside to comfort me; she would hold me in her arms and sing songs to me or recite Scripture until I would fall back to sleep. She taught me to memorize Psalm 91. It helped me overcome my fear. Even now, certain verses bring me such comfort.

> He that dwelleth in the secret place of the most High shall abide under the shadow of the Almighty...There shall no evil befall thee, neither shall any plague come nigh thy dwelling...For he shall give his angels charge over thee, to keep thee in all thy ways.[13]

"All these many years that I have journeyed on this beautiful earth, God has watched over me. It took time but I overcame my fears and learned to trust Him completely. I have never been sorry or ashamed of my love for God. He has been patient with me and kind, extremely kind. Even now, He has graciously allowed me to see the birth of a new generation. Your children have been my children, Rachel. I have taken as much delight in them as I always did in you. You have been such a source of joy to me, my very special blessing from God. You know how much I love you."

Tears streamed down my eyes and my heart began to ache inside.

"Don't cry, dearest. My time to journey on has come; I am ready and you must let me go." She closed her eyes for a moment and when she opened them again her face was beaming with delight.

"Do you remember when your Papa died, Rachel?" she asked, but I couldn't reply. My face was buried in her chest and I cried silent tears of sorrow. "His face is so clear in my mind just now—his thoughts were always of God. He was a father to me also you know. He taught me from my childhood to reverence the laws of God. He lived them out every day in his life; nothing was more important to him. He said they were like a song that needed to be sung throughout the journey of our lives. I have never forgotten those words.

"My pilgrimage has reached its end, Rachel, but yours continues. Who knows how long it will last? There is much yet for you to do…do it well and with honor."

Isabelle placed her old gnarled hands lovingly upon my head and, in a moment, she was gone. Peacefully, I remained clasped in the arms of the woman who had been my mother for many years, a woman whose whole life had been one of service—a woman who had been consecrated to God. She was right; I also felt there was still much for me to do.

My pilgrimage continues and I pray that it will be an echo of my ancestors. God's principles have become the song that I will sing in this world wherever I go and they will remain with me for as long as my journey continues.

Psalm 119:54–57

*Thy statutes have been my songs in the
house of my pilgrimage.*

*I have remembered thy name, O LORD,
in the night, and have kept thy law.*

This I had, because I kept thy precepts.

*Thou art my portion, O LORD:
I have said that I would keep thy words.*

Notes

1. Ecclesiastes 3:1
2. Job 28:10
3. Isaiah 62:4,5
4. Ecclesiastes 1:9
5. Proverbs 9:10,11
6. John 11:25,26
7. 2 Corinthians 5:1-4
8. John 14:2,3
9. Declaration of Independence of the United States of America, July 4, 1776
10. Psalm 18:2
11. Romans 5:8
12. Proverbs 10:12
13. Psalm 91:1, 10-11

The Pilgrimage
Order Form

Postal orders: Peggie Scarrott
3658 Township Ave
Simi Valley, CA 93063

E-mail orders: miscarrott@juno.com

Please send *The Pilgrimage* to:

Name: _____

Address: _____

City: _____ State: _____

Zip: _____

Telephone: (_____) _____

Book Price: $15.00

Shipping: $3.00 for the first book and $1.00 for each additional book to cover shipping and handling within US, Canada, and Mexico. International orders add $6.00 for the first book and $2.00 for each additional book.

Or order from:
ACW Press
5501 N. 7th. Ave. #502
Phoenix, AZ 85013

(800) 931-BOOK

or contact your local bookstore